D0975891

Sleep Wakers
#1

SAM SAVES THE NIGHT

BY SHARI SIMPSON

DISNEY • HYPERION

Los Angeles   New York

For Mama Rose, who's waited a long time for a proper dedication.
You are my heart and my soul and my love.

All rights reserved. Published by Disney • Hyperion,
an imprint of Disney Book Group. No part of this book may be
reproduced or transmitted in any form or by any means, electronic
or mechanical, including photocopying, recording, or by any
information storage and retrieval system, without written
permission from the publisher. For information address
Disney • Hyperion, 125 West End Avenue,
New York, New York 10023.

First Edition, October 2019
10 9 8 7 6 5 4 3 2 1
FAC-020093-19228
Printed in the United States of America

This book is set in ITC Berkeley Oldstyle Pro/Monotype;
Bourbon, Canvas Script, Lipstick, Lulo Clean, Movatif/Fontspring
Designed by Whitney Manger-Fine

Library of Congress Cataloging-in-Publication Data
Names: Simpson, Shari, author.
Title: Sam saves the night / by Shari Simpson.
Description: First edition. • Los Angeles ; New York : Disney-Hyperion, 2019. •
Summary: Chronic sleepwalker Samantha "Sam" Fife, thirteen, discovers a whole
world of disembodied SleepWakers after undergoing an experimental treatment.
Identifiers: LCCN 2018011991 • ISBN 9781368007610 (hardcover)
Subjects: • CYAC: Sleepwalking—Fiction. • Insomnia—Fiction. • Soul—Fiction.
• Bullying—Fiction. • Human experimentation in medicine—Fiction. • Science
fiction.
Classification: LCC PZ7.1.S5654 Sam 2019 • DDC [Fic]—dc23
LC record available at https://lccn.loc.gov/2018011991

Reinforced binding

Visit www.DisneyBooks.com

It is the brain where lies the cause of insomnia and sleepwalking, of thoughts that will not come, forgotten duties, eccentricities.
Hippocrates, *On the Sacred Disease*, 400 BCE

Being a sleepwalker sucks.
Sam, 2019

one

"HEY, FREAK! WAKE UP!"

It's not unusual for an older brother to be a bit nasty to a little sister. But in this particular case, the rude wake-up call was due to the fact that the little sister was holding a chain saw. Which was running. And she was standing on the deck of a half-built tree house. In a forty-foot-tall northern red oak. In the middle of the night. In a strange neighborhood. All of which *was* unusual.

Through sleep-fogged eyes, Sam could see her mother shouting something, too, but Margie wasn't as loud or as ticked off as Jax. It probably would help if the saw was turned off, but Sam wasn't completely coherent yet, and besides, she had one bare foot on the deck and one slippered foot precariously poised on a tree limb and the only thing that seemed to be keeping her balanced and upright was the blade whizzing through a two-by-four. In the remaining 3.6 seconds she had before the board split and she plunged twenty feet to the ground—decapitating herself and probably her mother, brother, and the family pug, Weezy, to boot—Sam assessed her situation and came up with:

Jump.

Which she did. Backward. Dragging the chain saw cord. Hoping she had sleep-built enough tree house to catch her.

As Sam landed flat on her back on a remarkably well-constructed deck if she did say so herself, she heard Jax scream like a little girl, Weezy belch thunderously, which he always did when he was held too tightly, and the sound of the chain saw bouncing against, and taking angry bites out of, what she only could assume was the trunk of the red oak. *Which is the state tree of New Jersey,* her brain informed her needlessly.

And then . . . silence.

Gasping for breath, Sam looked down to see a pajama-ed and bewildered-looking man holding a detached extension cord. Jax, her mother, and Weezy lay sprawled on the ground, panting, heads still attached. Then a little boy, hair so blond he lit up the yard like a miniature walking moon, slammed through the screen door, looked up at the tree house, and yelped:

"*Awesome!*"

✳   ✳   ✳

Sam slumped in the backseat of her mother's decrepit Toyota as Margie talked to the police and the pajama-ed man (Moon Boy had been sent back to bed). She could only hear snippets over Weezy's car-shaking snores, but she knew exactly what her mother was saying. After ten years of Sam's sleepwalking, Margie could recite it like a memorized monologue.

"I'm so sorry, *so* sorry, Samantha's been a sleepwalker all her life, it's hereditary, you know, her father was a sleep-walker, too, he's passed now, so it's just me and I've tried everything, *everything*, but nothing seems to help, we find her in the *craziest* places, doing the *craziest* things, you just wouldn't believe it, you won't press charges, will you, I'm a single mother and she's not a *criminal*, just a sick little girl, *sick*, I tell you—"

Margie was now tugging maniacally at the hair over her right ear, and Sam burrowed closer to Weezy, both to ward off the chilly autumn night air and to drown out her mother's voice by way of a flat-faced dog's breathing problems. She could see Jax pacing outside the car, slowing occasionally to give her a foul look. Sam knew Jax didn't care that she was a *sick* little girl whom Margie had tried *everything* to help; all Jax cared about was that Margie had a bald spot on the right side of her head due to anxiety and that the medical term for that anxiety was "trichotillomania" and that every time Sam ended up somewhere dangerous on her nighttime wanderings, Margie became more of a "trichotillomaniac" (not a real word; a Jax accusation word).

All Jax cared about was that their dad, Don Fife, had sleep-wandered off a bridge ten years ago and every time Margie thought she was going to lose her daughter in some similarly über-violent way, her bald spot widened.

All Jax cared about was that he was closely related to a loser. He never used that actual word because it was forbidden in their home (or "homes," really, since they had moved six times in the last ten years), but Sam saw it in every one of Jax's side-eye stink eyes.

Sam gently tucked Weezy's lolling tongue back in his mouth; he looked mildly perturbed, as if he had purposely left it out to dry in some sort of pug master plan. Margie was now highlighting some of the *crazy* things Sam had done while sleepwalking:

- Sleep-baked brownies
- Sleep-crocheted

- Sleep-mowed the lawn
- Sleep-sorted recyclables in a bin outside the Short Hills mall
- Sleep-stole a wheelchair from a rich octogenarian in an upscale retirement village
- Sleep-vinyl-sided a neighbor's house
- Sleep-directed traffic on Dodie Drive in Parsippany

And now add to the list sleep-built a tree house. Well, sleep-half-built, anyway. Sam absently pulled a splinter from her finger, sending up a silent prayer that Moon Boy's dad had some construction skills. Otherwise, Margie and Jax and Weezy would be out here again tomorrow night, trying to wake Sam up as she sleep-roofed.

Jax opened the car door and flopped his lanky body down on the passenger seat. "Got you out of another one. She shoulda been a lawyer."

For the millionth time, she said it. "Sorry."

"Uh-huh."

He didn't forgive her, and Sam couldn't blame him. Jax was sixteen, athletic, super smart, and a hottie-biscotti (not her phrase, obviously, because *ew*, her *brother*, but one she'd overheard whispered about him in a bakery). He should have been the most popular kid in his school. Instead Jax Fife was a dreamboat sinking fast, helplessly anchored to a freak sister, semi-bald mother, and drowned dad.

It was way past mattering that it wasn't her fault. Once upon a time, Jax had been her champion, defending her to anyone who would listen, "It's not her fault. Somnambulism is due to an immaturity in a person's central nervous system." Adorable coming out of the mouth of an eight-year-old boy defending the five-year-old sister who had somehow broken into her preschool in the dead of night and was found sleep-sterilizing baby bottles.

Less adorable when the preteen brother is trying to explain why his nine-year-old sister snuck into her elementary school gym at midnight to sleep-inflate droopy basketballs.

Totally unadorable when the high school sophomore's girlfriend dumps him because his preteen sister crept into her house through the doggy door and was discovered sleep-sequining the words "Is Evil" after the name "Tiffany" on said girlfriend's cheerleader uniform.

After the bedazzling debacle, it no longer mattered to Jax that Sam's central nervous system was immature. All that mattered was, *When the heck are you going to grow out of this?* Most sleepwalkers did, usually by the age when bedwetting stopped, and nearly always by puberty. But here she was, thirteen years old, and still sleep-wrecking their lives.

"'Scuse me? Samantha?"

It was one of the policemen, and he had an expression

on his face that Sam recognized. It was the "I can fix this" look that she'd seen on the faces of various pediatricians, psychiatrists, psychologists, principals, parents, police, palm readers, and even one phrenologist who swore that fingering the bumps on her skull would unlock the mysteries of her sleeping mind. All that experiment did was unlock the mystery of who started the lice epidemic at her last school, adding to Sam's reputation of highly contagious freakdom.

"Yes, sir?"

"I'm Officer Stanhope and I was just over there bending your mom's ear about how my nephew used to walk in his sleep, too. Now, it wasn't as, uh, extreme as your situation—he was three years old and all he did was urinate every night in the laundry room—but my sister and her husband tried a bunch of things that maybe you and your family haven't thought of yet."

Jax snort-laugh-eyerolled. Officer Stanhope chuckled warmly and continued, "I know, I know, most of what I suggested to your mom you've tried already, but she didn't have much to say about this one, so I thought I'd run it past you. Have you tried putting a bell on your door to wake you up if you sleepwalk?"

Jax snort-laugh-eyeroll-blew a raspberry. Sam felt a little badly for Officer Stanhope. *Poor misguided dude.* She answered as gently as possible. "Yes, sir. Tried that."

"And?"

"I, uh . . . melted it."

"You *melted* it?"

Jax didn't even turn around. "She sleep-escaped out the window, sleep-biked into town, broke into a welding shop, stole a blowtorch, and melted the clapper to the inside of the bell."

Officer Stanhope opened his mouth. Nothing came out.

"And then she welded the bell into a menorah and we found her in a synagogue two towns over, sleep-decorating for Hanukkah."

A mosquito flew into Officer Stanhope's gaping maw. He swallowed it meekly and scooted away, cutting a wide berth around Margie and disappearing into the squad car. Jax muttered under his breath, "Officer Stanhope*less*."

"He was just trying to help."

"No one can help us."

For the million-and-oneth time, she said it: "Sorry."

"Uh-huh."

Margie slid into the driver's seat. The lights of the retreating police cars reflected off her bald patch for a moment before she turned to Sam with a tremulous smile. "Um, sweetie? I don't suppose you know if I owe anyone for lumber, do you?"

Sam buried her face in Weezy's neck, overwhelmed

with the financial burden of her nighttime persona; she was already overdrawn on her allowance until the year 2024. And for what? The most random collection of bills, fines, bail, stolen merchandise reimbursements, and ER visits not covered by insurance that one girl had ever tallied in the history of sleepwalking. To Sam, that was the most frustrating part; there seemed to be no rhyme or reason or design to her midnight adventures. *Jeez, even Lady Macbeth wanted to out her damn'd spot for a reason.* But what was the pattern in Sam's sleep-wanderings? Seemingly, there was none—just a long list of *crazy.*

Margie gritted her teeth, yanked a fistful of hair out of her head, and made a declaration. "Okay, that's it. That's it. We're going to do it."

"What? Put her into foster care?" Jax offered hopefully.

"We're going to take you for a sleep study, Samantha."

Sam's heart and Jax's body sagged. "Back to the quacks with the electrodes? What was the diagnosis last time, sis?"

She mumbled into Weezy's fur. "That I'm a noctambulist."

"Right. That she's a noctambulist. A sleepwalker. What a shocker, huh? Mind. Blown."

Margie tucked the handful of hair into her purse. "Well, this guy is supposed to be, um, *different.* It's why . . . why we moved here."

Now this was news. All their other moves were defensive,

moving away from places where they owed money or Sam's picture had been in the newspaper. But an offensive relocation? That was bold. Sam felt a little flutter in her chest; maybe this time would be—

"Different? How exactly?" There was not a trace of expectation in Jax's voice.

Margie gulped. "Um, well, you could say that Dr. Fletcher is considered to be a bit of a rebel. He was, um, asked to leave the AASM for—"

Sam gasped. "He got kicked out of the American Academy of Sleep Medicine?!" Yes, she did know every parasomnia acronym.

"Not kicked out! They just had a difference of opinion over his, um, methods."

Jax looked glum. "Great. We're goin' rogue."

"But supposedly he's had a lot of success with, um, extremely challenging cases." Margie attempted a little laugh, which sounded more like she was trying to dislodge a particularly stubborn hairball. "And that's certainly us, isn't it?"

Sam closed her eyes, imagining for a moment what it would feel like to no longer be an extremely challenging case. Then she stuck a mental pin in her hope balloon. No matter how tiring it was being a sleepwalker, hope was way more exhausting.

two

THE ALARM CLOCK MODE was set to "Gentle Bird Chirps," but the sound still nearly sliced her skull in two. How the heck could it be morning already? Sam groaned, tried to move, but felt like someone had filled her body with kitty litter. Her back ached from the jump/fall on the tree house deck and her inner thighs were in knots, making her wonder just how long she had been poised in Russian splits over the chain saw last night. Weezy's snores only served to mock her pain further. It was one of the great ironies of Sam's life, having a pet that slept like a rock approximately twenty-three hours out of every twenty-four-hour day.

There was no way she could summon the energy to pick

out clothes for school. Knowing full well that it was social suicide, she grabbed the jeans and T-shirt that lay discarded on the floor from . . . two days ago? Yesterday? Didn't matter. Jaida would remember.

Sam's evil-super-archnemesis-enemy, Jaida Coakley, and her band of middle school minions had been tormenting Sam since her first day at Wallace Junior High—and for much more minor sins than wearing the same clothes two days in a row. But today's fashesty (fashion travesty) would still give Jaida all the ammunition a bully could dream of.

You're welcome in advance, O Evil One, Sam thought wearily as she pulled the T-shirt over her throbbing head. The great irony was that Jaida was not all that fashile (fashion facile) herself; her outfits fairly screamed *color-blind!*, her pants were frequently too short, and she wore an ancient sequined fanny pack with everything. But in some sort of "Emperor's New Clothes"–ish conspiracy, Jaida's entourage never seemed to notice, instead reserving all their mockery for Sam's missteps.

At the breakfast table, Margie was wearing a baseball cap sideways over her bald patch, looking like a sad suburban hip-hop wannabe. But her smile was bright and, for once, unforced. "Guess what, hon? I called Dr. Fletcher's office to leave a message and would you believe, he answered?! At seven o'clock in the morning!"

A disembodied voice came from the hallway. "Big deal. He's a sleep doctor, isn't he?" Jax slouched in, rubbing his eyes. "He better be at the office all night, or he'll lose his license. Oh, wait. He already did."

Margie ignored this. "And he's going to see you today after school, and do your in-lab sleep study tonight! Isn't that incredible?"

"Tonight?" Sam said uneasily. "Why so fast?"

"Probably because you're his only patient." Jax reached into the fruit bowl on the counter and came up with a banana so gruesomely overripe it was fit for neither man nor beast nor bread. He tossed it back. "The rest are wandering the highways at night, moaning, electrodes dangling from their flesh."

Margie tried to flash him a stern look, which was deflected by the bill of her sideways cap. "No. Because it's good timing, being a Friday and all. And of course, because I told him how serious our situation is. He seems very nice, Samantha, and very interested in your case."

Yeah, the Case of the Head Case, was what Sam thought. What she said, however, was, "Okay. Fine. Whatever. You're on lunch shift today? So you'll pick me up after school?" And when Margie's face fell at Sam's lack of enthusiasm, she added, "Sorry, Mom. I'm sure he'll be great!"—because every head case knew two things: how to apologize, and how to fake a gung ho response for the benefit of the non-head cases who suffered alongside them.

* * *

"Miss Fife! Are you in the land of the living?"

Sam started awake, because no, she hadn't been, and that just was not going to fly with Mr. Bain, who was old-school pre-algebra and pretty darn sensitive about students falling asleep on him. She shook her head to clear the midday-nap cobwebs and that's when she felt it.

There was something stuck to her face.

To be honest, it wasn't all that unusual for Sam to wake up in class with homework, tests, or even pencils glued to her cheek by means of crusted drool, but this felt different. And judging from the look of angry surprise Bain was wearing and the giggles permeating the room, loudest from Jaida's corner, it was not going to be a pleasant discovery.

Sam put her hand to her face and felt something small and stiff bridging her nose. The volume of the giggles increased in direct proportion to the decrease of her spirit.

It was a Breathe Right strip. A small bandage that problem sleepers placed over their nasal area to control snoring. How did Sam know this? Because she'd tried them, of course. She'd tried every sleep-related product on the market. As her eyes filled with tears, she wondered if tomorrow she'd be wearing a "Wake Me When It's Summer" eye mask, courtesy of Jaida and her demonic disciples.

"All right, who's responsible for—" Bain's would-be tirade was interrupted by a delicate tap on the door. And in she walked.

Madalynn Sucret. There was a collective intake of breath and the seventh grade became one with an enraptured exhale. The golden ringlets, each in spiraled perfection; eyes so blue and wide you almost expected an airplane to do a flyby through the pupils; and the smile. The smile! Gleaming, glowing, with a blinding sparkle when sunlight hit her teeth. Madalynn's smile was the stuff of legend, in large part because no one had ever seen it slip from her stunning face: a perfect, and permanent, fixture.

"I'm so sorry to interrupt your class, Mr. Bain." You could have dipped lobster in her voice, it was that buttery and melty. "I hope you can forgive me." A couple of girls in the back of the class teared up; could Madalynn Sucret *be* more thoughtful and humble?

"Mmmmflerbbbagggh," burbled Mr. Bain. Madalynn had the same effect on teachers as she did on students. Oh, and principals. And guidance counselors. And janitors. And lunch ladies. Even Angry Agnes, who dished out death stares with her corn dogs, became positively gooey around Madalynn Sucret.

"Principal Nussbaum asked me to visit all the classes to remind everyone about the anti-bullying pep rally on Tuesday. Remember, 'We stand against bullying and that's no lie, we're all united at Wallace Junior High!'"

The seventh grade broke into spontaneous applause. The two girls who had teared up just went ahead and wept. Sam, who had managed to yank off her Breathe Right strip and was in her own hypnotic trance of hero worship/post-Band-Aid-removal pain, tore her eyes away from Madalynn to sneak a glance at Jaida. Expecting a sneer, she was startled at the expression on her personal bully's face. Was it . . . awe? Admiration? Could the meanest girl in school be actually acquiescing to someone whose trademark was sweetness? Distracted momentarily by Madalynn throwing kisses to the adoring crowd, Sam turned back around and that's when it hit her.

Even though she couldn't imagine why anyone would look at Wallace's own Angel of Mercy and Beauty in such a way, the emotion she had seen cross Jaida's mug, however fleetingly, was obvious and one with which Sam was familiar:

Fear.

✳ ✳ ✳

"Over here, honey!" Sam felt badly for cringing, but *seriously, Mom? Sooo* not okay to pick up your daughter from middle school hefting a chunky pug under your arm and wearing pajamas and a lace-front hairpiece from the Raquel Welch Celebrity wig collection. Sam hightailed it to the Toyota.

Please let Jaida have some kind of after-school club, please let her not be coming out of the building right now—

"Whoa! Looks like fashtastrophes run in the family!"

—so she can tell the whole school that my mother is a "fashion catastrophe."

If Sam weren't so mortified, she would have been impressed at how Jaida managed to always be in just the wrong place at just the wrong time. Her posse snickered, fist-bumped, and made raucous snoring noises as Sam broke into an outright run toward her oblivious mother.

"I hope you don't mind, honey, but Dr. Fletcher said to come prepared since we probably won't be going home in between your intake and the sleep study, so I brought your pajamas, too—"

Before Margie could hold up the raggedy nightgown in front of Wallace's entire student body, Sam deftly maneuvered mother, dog, and sleepwear into the car and auto-locked the doors. There were so many things she wanted to say at that moment, from *Were you* ever *a kid?* to *Please, please, trim the front of your hairpiece. The wig cap is sticking out, like, three inches,* but she kept it to, "Mom, why did you bring Weezy? We're going to a doctor's office, for crying out loud."

Margie started the car and pulled out into traffic. "Dr. Fletcher said to bring him. He wants your sleep environment to be completely familiar and comfortable."

Sam sighed, patting Weezy, who was already curled up in a tight croissant and snoring at a heavy-metal-concert decibel. "Familiar, maybe. I don't know about comfortable."

"I also have your body pillow and your eye mask. Oh, honey, I don't know why, but I just have such a good feeling about tonight! Don't you?"

"Did Dad ever go to a sleep specialist?' The question was so startling to both of them that Sam clapped a hand over her mouth and Margie nearly veered into a parked Zipcar. They never talked about Don Fife. They never even talked about the fact that they never talked about Don Fife. It was just a given that Don Fife was a forbidden topic and usually Sam went along with this unspoken agreement to preserve her mother's scalp. But today was different, somehow; maybe because Sam was so many layers of tired, she couldn't seem to control her thoughts, or because last night she sleep-operated a power tool that could have cost her a couple of arms and legs. All Sam knew was that her sleepwalking was getting increasingly limb-threatening, and she needed answers.

Margie's hand strayed off the steering wheel, headed for her real hair underneath the fake. Her voice trembled slightly as she said, "Um . . . maybe we could talk about that with Dr. Fletcher? Not right away, of course, but maybe . . . eventually . . ."

Sam's heart started to pound. Not wanting to mess with this fragile moment of progress, she gently guided her mother's hand back to the business of driving, shrugging casually.

"Okay. Whatevs. Just wondering."

Which is the understatement of all time. Yep, just wondering about her dead dad and if he ever tried to prevent being dead so that she could prevent being dead, too. *So, yeah, whatevs.*

"We're here!" Margie nearly shrieked this news and Sam jumped. *Here?* She looked around in disbelief. They were pulling into the Guttenberg strip mall, less than a mile from her school. Two run-down nail salons, a 7-Eleven, and a Fred's Super Dollar were the only oases in a desert of empty buildings, and the Fred's sported a *Going Out of Business!* banner. "I know, it doesn't seem like there should be a clinic here"—Margie gave that wedged-hairball laugh again—"but sometimes good things come in odd packages, right?"

Sam's heart was now pounding for an entirely different reason. "Goin' rogue" was one thing. "Goin' slumber party in a sleazy strip mall" was something else entirely. Margie pulled up in front of a bleak storefront with a handwritten sign, *River Sleep Clinic*. The door opened to a man whose appearance caused the words "mad scientist" to flit through Sam's mind. He was six and a half feet tall and on the south side of 150 pounds, with unruly gray hair and huge eyes coupled with tiny pupils. There was so much white eyeball showing, in fact, that it gave him a look of perpetual astonishment.

"By St. Dymphna, it's good to meet you, Sam!" he shouted from the doorway.

This was Dr. Baptiste Fletcher.

Her supposed sleep savior.

three

DR. FLETCHER and his assistant were both staring at Sam, but Joanne didn't freak her out as much. The middle-aged woman's crisp uniform and shiny stethoscope made Sam feel like this might actually be a legit medical establishment and not a place where her liver would be extracted and sold while she slept. Also, Joanne's stare wasn't quite as, uh, *piercing* as the doctor's.

Almost as if he could read Sam's mind, Dr. Fletcher said, "Would you prefer if Jo started your intake? Most of my patients feel more comfortable with smaller sclerae." *Sclerae?* She glanced at her mother, but Margie looked as blank as

Sam felt. "By St. Dymphna, I'm sorry!" Dr. Fletcher smacked his forehead. "I have to stop using medical terminology! My gaze tends to be off-putting to some people due to the abundance of sclera—er, eyeball white."

Sam felt a little guilty. It wasn't Dr. Fletcher's fault that he had creepy peepers, and she knew what it was like to be judged for something you just couldn't help. "No, it's all right. You can both ask me questions, I guess."

Joanne and Dr. Fletcher exchanged a meaningful look. "See?" he whispered to her, beaming.

"Insubstantial," Joanne whispered back.

"Empathy is an indicator!" he whispered, rather passionately this time.

"But not conclusive!" she hissed.

"Fine! Fine!" Dr. Fletcher whisper-pouted, then turned back to Sam with a bright, "So! Do you have any questions to start out, Sam?"

Um, yeah, dude, what the heck was all that about?! What she said, however, was, "Who's St. Dymphna?"

Dr. Fletcher looked gobsmacked, for real and not just because of his startled eyeballs. "Why, the patron saint of sleepwalkers, of course!"

"Oh. I didn't know we had our own saint," Sam mumbled, feeling like a dope.

"Me either," piped up Margie, obviously trying to de-weird

the entire conversation. "Guess we should have been praying to her all along!"

Of course, this, along with her wedged-hairball laugh, managed to make the whole thing about a thousand times weirder. Joanne shot Margie a stern look, and Margie shrank down a bit, fingering her bald patch.

"I have a feeling," Dr. Fletcher said, shaking his head, "that you've been fed a lot of nonsense about your condition, Samantha. Have you ever been told that sleepwalking is the result of an immaturity in one's central nervous system? Malarkey!"

Sam's mouth fell open. Margie's eyes widened to the point of showing some extra sclera herself. "But . . . what?" Sam said faintly. "I thought that was, like, proven science or something."

"Proven science is highly overrated," sniffed Joanne.

"True!" Dr. Fletcher blared. "There is a staggering lack of humility in the scientific community. We all think we know so much. We know nothing! Zilch! Zero! Bupkus! What do we know, Jo?"

"Zip," Joanne said flatly.

"Zip!" Dr. Fletcher echoed.

Okay, totally not inspiring a lot of confidence here. Sam shot her mother a nervous look. To her surprise, Margie was nodding fervently. *Great.*

"And you've probably been told that your sleepwalking shouldn't affect your daytime behavior, yes?"

Sam gulped.

"*Flummery!*" Dr. Fletcher grabbed a piece of paper covered in scrawled notes and waved it wildly. "Everything your mother told me about the daytime you—the poor grades, detentions, moodiness, listlessness, and hopelessness—what do you think all that is? It's called *exhaustion*, Samantha. The kind of exhaustion that would make anyone wacko! The kind of exhaustion that would turn Gandhi into a machete-wielding despot!"

Sam's spinning brain spat out one coherent thought, *Google "despot" when I get home*, and then whirled into sputtering white noise. "But—I—they—all the doctors, they—I always thought—"

Dr. Fletcher put a bony hand on her shoulder. "Deep breath."

She took one.

"Good. Get some oxygen to your brain, because I have one last sleepwalking myth to debunk and it may make your gray matter explode."

Sam took a huge breath and held it, reserving as much air as possible for the mind blast.

"The medical 'geniuses' say that sleepwalking has nothing to do with subconscious desires." Dr. Fletcher paused for dramatic effect, then stuck his sclerae right in Sam's face and blurted, *"TWADDLE!"*

Unintentionally inappropriate-sounding expletive aside, Sam was lost. What on planet Earth was this dude talking about? It took Margie to put it together. "Are you saying"— her voice trembled a bit—"that the things Sam does when she's sleepwalking actually *mean* something? That deep down, she wants to, or needs to, do them?"

Dr. Fletcher breathed it out softly. "Darn tootin' she does." He then leaned back and fanned himself furiously with the page of notes, as if speaking truth made a person very sweaty. Joanne silently poured him a glass of water, which a dazed Margie picked up and drank instead.

Sam felt a little faint, both from this momentous news, and from the fact that she was still holding her breath. She finally exhaled, a huge rush of air accompanied by a rush of an unfamiliar emotion: relief. Was she finally going to get some answers about the long list of *crazy*? She opened her mouth to start her barrage of questions.

"Well, that's enough questions for now!" Dr. Fletcher hopped up and grabbed the receiver of an ancient, honest-to-God rotary telephone. "Let's order some dinner! Do you like Indian? I have Bollywood Grill on speed dial!" He stuck a skinny digit in the finger wheel of the phone and started turning it rapidly, giggling at his own joke.

*　*　*

As Joanne attached the sticky electrode pads to her head and chest, Sam fought mightily against burping up the chicken vindaloo she had unwisely chosen for her meal. Normally she would have picked the blandest dish possible, as numerous doctors had warned her (with data and graphic PowerPoint presentations) about the connection between spicy food and sleepwalking episodes, but since Dr. Fletcher was actually *hoping* for some midnight action, Sam had thrown caution to the wind. *And speaking of wind,* she thought, *there's gonna be some breakin' tonight.* Her stomach rumbled a rim shot.

"As you know, while you sleep, these sensors are going to be recording your brain activity, eye movements, heart rate and rhythm, and blood pressure. Comfy?"

Sam nodded, reaching down to unwind the snoring Weezy from a wire attached to her foot. "Um . . . so what happens to all the stuff if . . . when . . . I walk? Won't it just all, like, rip off?"

"Oh, you leave those worries to the professionals, dear." Joanne smiled coolly. "We have our methods."

Well, that's pretty dang scary, was what Sam thought. What she said, however, was, "Oh. Yeah. Sorry. You've probably done this a thousand times."

"Yes! But every time is just as new and exciting!" Dr.

Fletcher bounded into the room with puppyish exuberance. "Are you ready, Samantha?"

"I guess."

"Excellent." Dr. Fletcher waved to Margie, who was watching from the computer control room. She waved back and immediately resumed yanking out all her right-side hair by the roots.

Sam lay back on the exam bed, and that's when something strange happened. Well, you know, stranger than all the previous strange stuff. Dr. Fletcher and Joanne leaned over her, and their faces went all tender and sympathetic.

"When you wake up," Dr. Fletcher said softly, "everything will be different, Sam. I promise."

She felt a little confused because, *Isn't this just the test part?* How could monitoring her sleep patterns make any difference at all? But if it were possible to read a person's sclerae, Sam would have bet on Dr. Fletcher's. Because everything in the whites of his eyeballs made her a solemn vow.

four

IT SEEMED LIKE ONLY a moment ago that she had drifted into the night on the sound cloud of Weezy's labored breathing, but now sunlight was streaming into the clinic and Joanne was sucking down a Double Big Gulp of 7-Eleven coffee. Sam blinked a few times. Weird. She felt some kind of internal hum, a strange sensation of unforced awakeness. No alarm clock, no Jax yelling that she had five minutes to get her sorry butt out of bed, no Margie staring at her mournfully from the doorway. Just, like, awake. From, like, sleep.

Sam examined herself; except for one errant electrode that was now glued to Weezy's corkscrew tail, everything seemed to be just as it had been last night. Could it be possible? Had she really stayed in bed the whole eight hours like a normal human being who heeded the National Sleep Foundation's recommendations?

"Good morning, sleepyhead!" Dr. Fletcher crowed from the control room, then loped into the test area, narrowly missing banging his head on the door lintel.

Sam had to smile. "No one's ever called me that before."

"Well, it's a brand-new day, Samantha, *and* a brand-new world. As every new day should be." He started detaching the electrodes. "Which reminds me, I want to say thank you for rearranging my files last night. Jo always tells me that I should put all my info on*lie*—"

"On*line*, not on*lie*. Although your word is probably closer to reality," Joanne interjected, peeling the electrode off Weezy's tail.

"—but I do everything the old-fashioned way, including having a very messy file cabinet, like any mad professor worth his salt. So—"

"Wait, wait . . . what?" Sam felt her heart sink right into her bare feet. "Did I . . . sleep-file?"

Dr. Fletcher and Joanne exchanged a look that could only be labeled as Mysterious. "What do you remember about last night?" he asked gently.

She thought hard. "I . . . think I had a dream. I don't

know. I'm not sure I've ever had a real dream before. There were times I thought I was dreaming, but then it always turned out to be true. Like, I know normal people will dream things like they're in school with no pants, but they always wake up, you know, with their clothes on. Whenever I woke up . . ."

"You were actually doing the thing you thought you were dreaming about," Dr. Fletcher finished her sentence.

Sam nodded. "But last night . . . now I do remember something. Like, moving some papers around and stuff. So that wasn't a dream?" She fought against the thickness in her voice, the sudden suppressed tears. "I really sleep-organized? Why didn't you wake me up?"

Mysterious Look #2 passed between doctor and assistant.

"We should tell her—" began Dr. Fletcher in a loud whisper.

"Absolutely not," Joanne loud-whispered back.

"But it might help her tonight!" he shout-murmured.

"Or it might cloud everything!" she yell-murmured.

Then he muttered in so loud a mutter, it actually had to be considered full voice, "I just think—"

"No! Let the darkness do its work!" Joanne super-mega-muttered.

Well, that was bizzawkweird.

But Dr. Fletcher tried to pretend everything was chill.

"I'll be able to tell you more once I assess your data," he said. Then, with a dirty look at Joanne, "Or I guess you'll just figure it out for yourself."

"But—"

"But the main thing is, how do you feel?" He brought his face so close to hers she was temporarily sclera-blinded. "Tired? Or full of vim and vinegar?"

"Um . . . somewhere in between, I guess."

"Good! And it will only get better, just like I promised." He clapped his hands down on his thighs for emphasis; it made a rather harsh bony sound. "So get dressed and we'll get you outta here! Jo, I hate to do it, but we'll have to wake up Samantha's mother. Poor woman probably hasn't slept that well in years."

Joanne turned to go.

"Wait," the doctor said. "Now that I'm thinking about it, don't wake her up. We'll send Samantha home in a taxi."

Joanne looked at Sam. "You have your house keys, dear?"

"Uh . . . yeah. You mean you're really just gonna let her keep sleeping? In your office?"

Dr. Fletcher seemed hurt. "Well, of course. What kind of parasomnia expert would I be if I didn't care deeply about people's rest?"

"Oh. Sorry, I didn't mean to offend you," Sam said, but Dr. Fletcher waved away her apology and slumped back into the control room, his head hanging. Confused, Sam turned to Joanne, but she was bustling about efficiently, collecting Sam's things.

"Joanne? What did I do?"

"Oh, don't mind him, dear." She handed Sam her jeans and turned around, talking over her shoulder. "The doctor is just very committed to his work. Ten years of never leaving an office would make any man dotty—I mean, a little overly sensitive."

Sam paused with her pants halfway up her legs. "He hasn't left the clinic for *ten years*?"

"Well, I did say he was very committed to his work, didn't I? Of course, there's also the aquaphobia, but . . . Oh, I'm talking too much. Got everything?"

Aquaphobia? Sam wasn't sure why a fear of water would make a man a prisoner in a strip-mall sleep clinic, but she didn't have time to question. Dr. Fletcher stuck his head back into the test area—

"Taxi'll be here in two minutes!"

—and Sam found herself being bustled about, packed up, patted, hugged, and ushered into a cab with Weezy in her arms and a "Follow-Up to Sleep Study" sheet of instructions tucked under her chin. The driver screeched away from the clinic, making nauseating and completely unnecessary figure eights through the parking lot, but Sam barely even noticed. Because even though the taxi window was filthy, it wasn't filthy enough to obscure a sudden blinding flash of gleaming teeth and golden hair.

No way. There was just no way the owner of those pearly whites and bouncing ringlets was getting a fifteen-dollar mani-pedi or eating *anything* that could be found at a 7-Eleven, so why the heck was Madalynn Sucret walking through the Guttenberg strip mall on a Saturday morning at the butt crack of dawn?

✳ ✳ ✳

By the time she crawled into her bed that night, Sam had pretty much convinced herself she'd imagined Madalynn, the same way brain-baked travelers saw mirages in the desert. Crazy as that theory was, it made more sense than the actual eighth-grade goddess descending upon Fred's Super Dollar closeout sale. Besides, Sam had other things on her mind. Like the back-to-back mega-lectures she'd received from her brother and mother for leaving the clinic with only a comatose pug as chaperone. And why her new doctor wouldn't tell her if she'd actually sleep-organized his medical files. And what Joanne could have meant when she said,

"Let the darkness do its work," which sounded like a line from one of the survival horror video games Jax played endlessly.

And why am I trusting some dude who hasn't seen sunlight in ten years?

Groaning, Sam flipped on her side and pulled Weezy into a spooning position, trying to distract herself by whispering the word "brachycephalic" to the tempo of the pug's raucous breathing. She remembered when Margie taught her that word and that it meant the sweet little ball of fur her mother had brought home from the shelter was going to snore like an eighty-year-old man with a deviated septum. Jax had been outraged; Margie had gone to search for a dog who could protect Sam on her sleepwalking sojourns, like a German shepherd or pit bull. Instead, Margie had fallen for googly eyes and a face that looked as if it had been struck with a cast-iron skillet. When Jax had pressed her to explain her bizarre choice, Margie could only come up with, "He's an oddball, just like . . . us."

Like me, you mean, Sam remembered thinking. *You said "us," but you meant me.*

She pulled Weezy closer; he protested by way of a prolonged and noisy fart. Sam's eyes filled with tears, but not from the smell. Would the darkness do its work tonight? Would anything be different, like Dr. Aquaphobe had promised? Would she even be able to fall asleep, fearing the worst because she hoped for the best?

But she did, eventually.

Fall asleep.

And did, eventually.

Wake up.

In the middle of the night.

Standing at the door to her bedroom.

And for a brief moment, she rejoiced.

Because this *was* different. She had woken up by herself from her sleepwalking. She hadn't done anything dangerous. She hadn't even left her room. She could go back to bed and back to sleep without Jax yelling or her mother scalping herself, and without operating any power tools. So Sam turned around to do just that, to go back to bed and back to sleep without any yelling or scalping or sawing.

Except there was one problem.

There was already someone in her bed.

Her.

Her own body.

Sam's body, sound asleep, arms tucked around a snoring, skillet-faced dog.

Standing Sam looked at Sleeping Sam and did what any Sensible Sam would do.

She became Screaming Sam.

five

A DREAM. A NIGHTMARE. Sam was pretty certain she'd never had either, so how would she know? She was screaming, she could hear herself screaming, but it sure didn't seem to be doing a whole heck of a lot to wake her up. She suddenly recalled Dr. Fletcher's words, *"You were actually doing the thing you thought you were dreaming about,"* and this made her scream even louder.

Her caterwauling, however, fell on the deaf ears of the night. She was still standing by the door to her room staring at what appeared to be her body spooning Weezy and snoozing peacefully. She tried frantically to reason with herself: *If this is a nightmare, I'll wake up eventually and have a hilarious story to tell.* This calmed her slightly, the idea of being able to share a funny dream story like normal people who, you know, actually dream. *Dudes, you are so not gonna believe the nightmare I had last night,* she imagined herself saying and laughing so hard it made everyone else laugh. *I was floating outside my body and . . . and . . .*

And . . . that was as far as she could get. Because, first of all, she wasn't floating, she was just kinda hanging out. And secondly, unless she made up a bunch of stuff like *and then all my teeth fell out!* or *and then I realized I was totally naked!* this didn't really seem to fit the descriptions of nightmares she'd heard about. *Oh, and don't forget that you don't have any friends to tell a funny dream story to,* she reminded herself.

On that depressing thought, Sam knew that she was alone, as usual, and was going to have to just *deal.*

So, she stepped forward.

It felt like a regular step, a human body in motion, so she took another, and another, approaching the bed. She leaned so far over that she could not only feel Sleeping Sam's breath on her cheek, but also observe that Standing Sam's bare feet were actually hovering about an inch off the floor.

Her head and stomach started spinning in opposite directions, and she was suddenly convinced she was going to fall, fall through her own body, through the mattress, and the floor and the ground, and right into the center of the earth.

She stood up quickly and nearly flipped over backward, trying to gain traction on the air cushion under her feet; the room whirled, and that's when Weezy began barking.

At her. Standing Sam.

He was looking right at her with his saucer eyes, and barking like a pug possessed. Sam instinctively put out her hand to shush him, stroke him to silence as she'd always done on the very few occasions that he was awake long enough to bark, except this time her hand went right through him. Right through his little, round head, her skin like a mist, insubstantial and unsuitable for petting.

Sam felt another scream building in her chest, but before it could break out, the door opened and Margie dashed in.

"Shhh, quiet, Weezy, quiet!" She rushed right past Sam, the misty, insubstantial Sam, and leaned over the solid, sleeping Sam. "You're going to wake Samantha, silly dog!"

She scooped him up in her arms and dashed out again, but not before Weezy managed to look back, right at Standing Sam, and howl a soul-shattering howl, as if he'd seen a ghost.

Well, that's that. I'm dead.

She didn't feel dead; it just seemed like the simplest explanation. Or then again, maybe she wasn't fully dead, since that thing under the covers was breathing. Maybe she was having an . . . *oh, what was the acronym again?* An NDE, a near-death experience, like that story about the little kid who died in an accident, but then revived and said he'd been chilling with the angels.

But there were no angels in her bedroom. No bright light, no feelings of peace and serenity, no dead relatives in white robes beckoning to her. She was hovering slightly, but not floating up near the ceiling. So . . . she probably wasn't dead, or even near dead. And as far as she could tell, she wasn't having a nightmare, a dream, or a hallucination. She was just . . . herself. Except in two places.

Sam stared at the Sam lump under the covers. *Holy crow, is that what I really look like?* It wasn't like looking in a mirror, when she knew how to smile and turn to just the right angle to make herself look her best. It wasn't like a photograph or even a selfie, not that Sam ever really took those because, um, *why bother?* This was real seeing, the way other people must see her, soft and vulnerable and unfamiliar. And freckly. And asymmetrical. Seriously, why had she never noticed that the two sides of her face didn't match at all? Like she needed any more reasons to hate her life.

Sam forced herself to look away from the unbalanced weirdo under the covers and took an inventory of the room. Everything was in its usual disastrously chaotic place, and she marveled, not for the first time, that all her past sleep-walking "projects" never once included tidying her own space. Her eyes landed on a sheet of paper on the messy desk: It was the "Follow-Up to Sleep Study" sheet of instructions.

Her heart (or the center of her mist body, at least) started to pound. Why had she not read this yet?! Distracted by the Madalynn strangeness, sure, and then exhausted from the Jax tongue-lashing about leaving Margie sleeping at the office of someone who was probably the New Jersey Slasher, but *still*. Sam walked/levitated slowly toward the paper, praying fervently it said something like *1. When you wake up outside of your own body, don't freak.* Not that she could have followed such a directive, since as soon as she tried to turn the paper toward her and her hand slid right through the desk, she was again very, very close to freaking out in a very big way.

Sam drew a gasping breath and craned her neck over to read the paper sort of sideways:

What to Expect After Your Sleep Study

Oh yes, please fill me in, thought Sam in her most sarcastic inner voice.

Once the sensors are removed after a polysomnogram (PSG), multiple sleep latency test, or maintenance of wakefulness test, you can go home.

Where you will have an out-of-body experience and your pug will think you are an evil spirit, Sam thought, her irritation growing.

You will not receive a diagnosis right away. Your sleep specialist will need time to determine if your disorder is a public or personal safety concern.

Seriously?! This was obviously just a form letter, since it had been determined long ago that Sam's "disorder" was not only a public safety concern, but a certified public menace. She wasn't sure why the impersonal nature of the instructions was making her so angry, but if it weren't for her unusable cloud hands, she would have torn the paper to bits and fed it to Dr. Fletcher in his Bollywood Grill takeout. *Maybe I can spit on it. But would I have real saliva or would it be like invisible un-wet vapor?* She leaned over to deposit whatever would come out of her mouth on the offending paper, and that's when she saw it. At the end of the typed list of instructions, a handwritten scrawl:

One more thing, Samantha: Be careful. The night has a way of revealing things. People show who they really are in the darkness.

Before she could even begin to fathom what that could mean, Sam heard a voice.

"Hey! Newbie!"

Her misty body seized up in fear. There was a boy outside her window, and he was looking right at her. And he was super cute, with huge dimples and a shock of chocolaty hair. Unfortunately, this did not make him any less terrifying. She dropped to the floor and military-crawled/floated to the wall underneath the windowsill.

"Oh, shoot. Sorry to scare you. I always forget that new Wakers are kinda nervous."

Why is there a super-cute ghost boy outside my window and what the heck are "new acres"? Sam curled into a fetal position, simply unable to process any more horrors.

"Did you faint or something? Listen, if you just stick your head out, I can explain everything."

As tempting as an explanation of this insanity might be, at the present moment Sam was more in the mood for mind-numbing silence. She would have put her hands over her ears, except they would probably go right through her skull into her brain. The thought made her whimper.

"Well . . . okay. Don't worry about it. I'll come back tomorrow night and introduce you around. Later."

Sam heard no steps walking away, but then again, do

disembodied hot guys' feet make noise? *And introduce me? To who, exactly?*

She just wasn't up for finding out the answer to either of those questions, so she tightened her pretend body even more. And as she tried to disappear into her own mist, Sam could only come up with one thing: If the darkness really did reveal who a person was, Ghost Boy appeared to be a helpful (and gorgeous) new acre, and she, Samantha Fife, was a coward with a warped face and, apparently, a split soul.

six

THE NEXT MORNING, Sam woke up, jumped up, and shrieked "Evil twin!" all at the same time. Her heart drumming, she laser-focused downward. From the looks of the pale legs tangled in the sheets, it appeared that she was in her bed again, but her eyes flew over to see if there was a second Sam haunting the space beneath the windowsill.

Empty.

Apparently, Sleeping Sam and Standing Sam had reunited. *And both of us are confuddled,* she thought. *Just call me the Combo Sam of Confuddlement.*

"Good morning?" Margie stood in the doorway, holding a tray of breakfast, except it was really just a plate of food, silverware, and a shaky glass of orange juice balanced on a coffee-table book since trays were too much to pack when you were moving houses every six months. "How are you feeling, honey? I made you some waffles?"

Two out of three of those questions really should have been statements, but Sam couldn't fault her mother's tentativeness when she was feeling so unsteady herself.

"Thanks, Mom. I'm hungry."

Which was true, surprisingly. Her confuddlefication had seemingly not affected her appetite.

Maybe because I'm eating for two now.

Sam grunted. Her inner voice was really starting to piss her off.

"You didn't walk last night." Finally, a statement from Margie.

Sam swallowed hard, focusing her concentration on syrup application. There just was no way she could come up with a response that wouldn't have Margie dialing up yet another person of the psychiatric persuasion.

"I'm not trying to jump the gun or anything, but, I'm just saying . . . you didn't sleepwalk. That's all I'm saying."

"Okay." Sam was now adding tiny drips of syrup to each waffle pocket.

"Just an observation. Just putting it out there."

Sam nodded, using her knife to rejigger the flow. She fought off the desire to encourage her mother with an *"I know! Right?"* since it would have to be followed by a *"But I did possibly sleep-levitate."*

Margie responded with a half nod/head tilt, clearly showing that she wanted to do more than just put the information out there but couldn't with someone so obviously consumed with perfect syrup distribution.

"Well . . . we can talk more later. Enjoy!" And she was gone.

Five seconds later, Jax walked in and examined her plate. "Substandard syrup dispersal." He grabbed the waffle, jammed it in his mouth, and strolled out.

Sam sighed. *Yeah, we can talk later. Way later. Like, after I interrogate Dr. PsychoStare about what he did to make me a double me.*

* * *

Not that it would be easy to judge a look of surprise on the face of someone with perpetually astonished eyeballs, but Dr. Fletcher was clearly expecting her. At least it seemed so by the way he yanked her inside the clinic door.

"We have to hurry," he said by way of a greeting, "Joanne

went to get us maple sausage melts and the breakfast guy at Seven-Eleven is super speedy. She doesn't like it when I explain too much."

"Explain too *much*? How about explain at all?" Sam nearly shouted. "What the heck did you do to me?!"

"Language, young lady." Fletcher peeked nervously through the window. "It's just going to take a little getting used to. After a week or so, you'll fit right in."

"What? Fit in with who?"

"Why, the SleepWakers, of course. Didn't you meet any of them?"

"I—uh . . ."

Hot ghost boy. What had he said? *"New acres are kinda nervous."* No, not *new acres. New . . . wakers. Sleep . . . Wakers.* Whatever the hot ghost boy was, the doc here knew all about it.

"What . . . did . . . you . . . do . . . to . . . me?"

"I detached your soul. Well, your consciousness, really. From your body." Dr. Fletcher delivered this solemnly, but then as if he just couldn't help himself, his face broke into a huge grin. "Isn't that *cool*?"

Sam sat down. She'd always thought it was dumb when people in movies and books couldn't stay standing because they were so overwhelmed with freak-out, but here she was, her legs collapsing, her butt hitting the chair with a dull, fleshy thud.

Dr. Fletcher motored on in delight, not even noticing the heinie smackage.

"For the longest time, I didn't even know it was happening myself! I'd do a sleep study on someone—a sleepwalker, always a sleepwalker, it doesn't seem to work with the other parasomnias—and they'd come back with some outlandish tale about floating out of their body, and I'd be all, 'Oh, twaddle, you're obviously having a night terror,' or 'Sounds like REM sleep behavior disorder. Tell me, did you punch anyone?' But pretty soon they were coming back with stories about floating out the window and meeting *other* people out on the street who were *also* saying that they had jumped out of *their* bodies and they were all *my* patients! How epic is that?"

Sam had spent the entire duration of this monologue trying not to drift any lower than the chair she was already in, but fighting the faint had been challenging. Even now, all she could manage was, "How . . . ?"

Fletcher shrugged casually. "How does it happen? Oh, I don't know."

This incredible statement had the effect of a bracing slap. Sam's lolling head shot up. "You don't know?! You're sucking souls out of bodies and you don't know how it works?!"

Seemingly unfazed by her outrage, Fletcher held up a set of electrodes, staring at them reverently. "All we've figured out so far is that the electrodes we put on our patients to monitor their vitals seem to perform a different function in certain sleepwalkers, the ones who've had extreme episodes like yourself. For those walkers, if I set the system at a particular frequency, instead of *receiving* information, the electrodes appear to *inject* some sort of electrical impulse that stimulates the prefrontal lobe . . . well, this is getting super dull and technical, so all you need to know is some kind of jolt happens and the essence of the person just flings right out of their flesh, like popping a cosmic pimple."

"That is *not* all I need to know! And, seriously? *Gross.*"

"It's a stunning visual, though, right? Okay, so what else do you need to—" Dr. Fletcher stopped short, his face falling into a skin puddle.

Sam smelled Joanne before she saw her. The maple sausage melts were particularly whiffy.

"Oh, hey, Jo," Fletcher said weakly, gesturing to Sam. "Look who's here."

Joanne regarded them so coldly, the steaming beverage in her hand was in danger of becoming an iced coffee. "How much did you tell her?"

"Hardly anything!"

"Not enough!"

Sam and Dr. Fletcher spoke simultaneously, gave each other dirty looks, and double-blurted again,

"Just the basics!"

"Basically nothing!"

"Good." Joanne briskly handed Dr. Fletcher a wrapped sandwich, the paper so greasy it nearly slipped out of his hands.

"No! No, not good!" Sam was aghast. She stood for emphasis. "Let's be crystal about this, okay? Last night I walked out of my skin! I was invisible to my mother! My dog thinks I'm Satan! There was a ghost outside my window who says he's coming back tonight to introduce me to the *other* ghosts! And"—Sam pointed angrily at Dr. Fletcher, who already had a mouthful of maple sausage—"I have a doctor who's inhaling a breakfast melt instead of explaining why!"

Joanne's granite face softened just a squidge. "Samantha. I know this may be hard to believe, but it is the truth, nonetheless. We are *helping* you."

"And you're going to help *us*," interjected Dr. Fletcher, holding up a greasy finger.

Joanne's face hardened back into rock and she bit out, "Too soon!"

Fletcher groused back, "Better sooner than later!"

Joanne grabbed Fletcher's hand and popped his greasy

digit into his mouth. He sucked on it, pouting a bit, and Joanne turned back to the stunned Sam.

"We can't tell you everything," she said, her voice now gentle, "not yet. But one thing is certain: Your body will now be getting the rest it needs while your soul accomplishes its purpose."

"What does that *mean*? I don't understand!" Sam's voice quavered, despite her best efforts to appear maximally straight-up livid.

"It means you have been given a great gift. The gift of two lives, a daytime one and a nighttime one. Two *functional* lives, instead of one desperate, exhausted life."

With this remarkable statement, a vibrating silence took over the room, broken only by the crackle of sandwich paper as Dr. Fletcher dropped his melt in awe. Sam sat back down very slowly, digesting Joanne's words. And as often happens when something is digested, her gut eased. It was utterly true—she *had* been living a life of desperation and exhaustion. Wasn't it painfully obvious from all her sleepwalking insanities that her inside self had a different agenda than her outside? Sam had never thought about identifying it as her "soul," but whoever it was building tree houses and decorating synagogues was still *her*. And maybe, just maybe, it was a her she needed to understand.

But, still . . . *All I ever wanted was to be normal.* Why the heck was her stupid soul fighting that?

"So! We good, Samantha?" This breezy question came from Dr. Fletcher, belying the plaintive look in his sclerae.

Sam sighed mightily. "I don't know. I still have so many questions. . . ."

"Of course you do. Some you'll figure out in the darkness and some we'll be able to answer—in time." Fletcher smiled reassuringly and crammed the remainder of the melt into his mouth.

"In time," Joanne repeated soothingly, handing him a napkin.

"Just one last thing . . ." Sam swallowed. "If my soul, or consciousness, or whatever we're calling this thing, is tooling around town at night, won't it—I—it . . . get lost?" The thought made her goose-bumpy. "What if it just floats up into the sky, or falls into, like, some thirteenth dimension and can't get back to my body?"

"Oh, no, that's not possible," said Dr. Fletcher. "Because of the silver cord."

"The silver cord?"

"The invisible rope that connects soul to body. It can be stretched as far as you need it." Delivered by Joanne in a firm voice, as if to end this line of questioning.

"And you won't die unless it's severed," added Dr. Fletcher helpfully.

Sam's mouth dropped open.

Joanne abandoned her professional demeanor, rolling her eyes, and even her neck, at Fletcher. "Really? *Really?* You're gonna go there?"

"Can that happen?" squeaked Sam. "What would sever it? Are we talking a lawn mower rolling over it or something worse? Like some crazy evil spirit with, like, astral scissors? What the *what*, people?!"

"Oh, no, no, no, by St. Dymphna, no," Dr. Fletcher backtracked quickly. "It would take something big— cataclysmic!—to sever the silver cord, Samantha, no worries, no worries!"

"Yeah? 'Cause you saying 'no worries' doesn't make me any less worried!"

"Everyone calm down," Joanne broke in, returning to her role as sleep clinic corraler. "There will be no silver-cord severing on our watch. Samantha, this is not something you need to be concerned with. Dr. Fletcher has been detaching souls for nearly ten years, and we've not lost one yet."

"Ten years?" This somewhat diverted Sam's attention away from the prospect of her own death. "Whoa. How many of these . . . SleepWakers . . . are out there?"

Peace restored, Joanne and Dr. Fletcher exchanged

a proud look. "Well, of course, they're not *all* mine," he demurred humbly. "But I'd have to say—"

"Wait, what? What do you mean, they're not all yours?"

Joanne put a friendly and forceful arm around Sam's shoulders, propelling her to her feet and toward the exit. "Another story for another day."

Fletcher followed, adding with a wink of his overworked eyelid, "Wait till you see, though. I hear it's *epic*."

❋ ❋ ❋

Sam was so distracted on the way home, she couldn't help thinking that it wouldn't take a cataclysmic silver-cord severing to kill her; she was obviously going to ride her bike into a tree way before that. After narrowly missing a fire hydrant and coming *this close* to getting hit by a jogging stroller, she even stopped and slapped herself in the face.

"Pay! Attention! Idiot!"

And, of course, there she was—wrong-place-wrong-time Jaida with her bootlicking lackeys outside the Taiwanese bubble tea shop.

"Aw, Sam, you don't have to do that yourself! We'd be glad to smack you upside the head," trilled Jaida. Her parasites laughed uproariously, their bullying glee obviously fueled by the sugary caffeine in their giant plastic cups.

Jaida didn't have a drink; apparently, she was just running on *mean*.

"Wow, we are a true fashualty today!"

Fashualty? Oh, fashion casualty. Sam suddenly noticed that she'd biked over to the clinic in her pajama pants. Which, of course, made her want to slap herself again.

Jaida's flunkies minced over and surrounded her bike. Sam didn't know all of their names—she wasn't even certain they all *had* names other than "Jaida's fan"—but it was obvious they knew *her* name: *Target*.

"So, we were talking about you and we had a couple of ideas about why you snore through all our classes," Jaida said with a faux-thoughtful look on her face.

Sam's stomach lurched. This is how it always happened; she and Jax and Margie would move to a new town where no one knew about her sleepwalking, but before long someone would figure it out, either from her bizarre daytime behavior or by simply googling her name and finding all the newspaper articles. And then would start the long downward spiral of people gossiping about her, being afraid of her, requesting a special police committee to monitor her, and then, finally, driving her out of town with pitchforks and torches. Okay, maybe not quite that medieval, but almost.

"Amy says you're so stupid that you sleep to hide the fact that you can't answer any of the questions," mused Jaida.

A girl peeked out from under her designer sunglasses and giggled.

Amy, I presume, thought Sam.

"Gina says you're just a loser, and losers snooze," continued Jaida. Sam didn't need anyone to tell her which girl was Gina; she had been calling Sam a snoozing loser from her first day at school. But just in case Sam had forgotten, Gina treated her to a long, loud snore sound accompanied by the L-shaped hand gesture on her forehead.

"But *I* think you have narcolepsy." Jaida got right up in Sam's face for this, her voice low and deceptively gentle. "You a narcoleptic, Sam? Hmmm?"

Suddenly frozen with fear, Sam stared back at her accuser. *Too close.* This was too close to the truth.

"What's narcolepsy?" a piping voice asked. Jaida flashed a death look at the tiny, dark-haired girl, who promptly spilled her bubble tea in alarm. She had a flower name, Sam remembered. Was it Daisy? Jaida then resumed her menacing facial position two inches from Sam's nose.

"It's a brain disease that makes you fall asleep in the daytime, like, even when you're walking," said Jaida.

"Brain disease! Sammy's, like, sick in the brain!" chortled Gina. The gaggle of giggly girls erupted, elbowing each other.

"So, tell us which one it is," Jaida continued in that

smooth voice. "Stupid, loser, or narco? Just tell us the truth and we'll be on our way."

For a moment, just a moment, Sam considered fighting back. For just a moment, she thought about *actually* telling the truth, actually asking, *What did I ever do to make you hate me this much?* But that moment passed into knowing that a truthful question would only earn her double the hatred, with a side helping of scorn. So . . .

"Loser," Sam croaked. "Just your average loser."

The girls shrieked with laughter, but Jaida stared at her for a long moment. Then her lips parted in a slow, knowing smile. "I don't believe you."

Sam's eyes burned with hot tears. *Cue the pitchforks and torches.*

And then, just as quickly as it had started, it was over. Without warning or explanation, Jaida turned on her heel and walked away, followed shortly by her confused tea-sucking posse. Sam realized that she was clutching the handles of her bike so tightly that her knuckles were drained of color. She let go and rubbed her sleeve across her eyes, hiding her face in the crook of her elbow until her breathing returned to normal.

It wasn't until she put her trembling hands back on the handlebars and slung her leg over the seat that Sam saw what had probably spooked her trolls.

Madalynn Sucret was standing in the doorway of the Kwik Kustom Signs and Banners Shop across the street, oh so casually running her hands over a sign that said *Bullies* in a red circle with a big slash through the word. She toted the sign over to a waiting convertible with two impossibly gorgeous, near-albino-blond parents and climbed in. As they drove away, all three smiled, the sunlight glinting off their blindingly white teeth.

It was an unseasonably warm day, so Sam wasn't sure why she suddenly shivered.

seven

THE FIRST THINGS SAM SAW when she opened her eyes were streetlights.

Uh-oh.

She was standing at her window and it was most definitely dark out there. Most definitely, night. Which meant—

She turned slowly, bracing herself. *Yep.* There was a Sam body in the bed, curled around a pug that was snoring at a decibel level comparable to a Boeing 747 takeoff.

It was official. She was a detached soul. An essence escaped. A consciousness done broke free. *I'm a SleepWaker.*

"Hey, Newbie! You're up!" Gorgeous Ghost Boy was right

on cue. Sam turned back to find the grinning teenager out-side. "Come on out!"

You are so stinkin' cute. The thought came unbidden and it was super annoying. Seriously, how shallow was she? Her soul had left her body and was about to embark on possibly the adventure of a lifetime, and all she could think about was some dude's dimples and light brown skin?

"Uh . . . how do I do that? I can't open the window. My hands don't, you know, *work*." Sam held up her useless appendages.

"Yeah, I know, you don't know how to be solid yet. S'okay, just walk through it."

"Walk through the *glass*?"

"Come on, Newbie, we don't have all night. Just trust me."

Sam's misty heart skipped a couple of beats. *Only a cata-clysmic event can sever the silver cord,* she tried to reassure herself. *Like being chopped into a million pieces from jumping through a window for some cute-ical on my lawn.* But then she remembered that last night she had stuck her hands right through a barking dog. So maybe . . . ? *Ooookay, here goes.*

It was the most peculiar feeling ever, like all the molecules in her pretend soul body shifted just enough to accommo-date the window's molecules. Like walking through a grater and she was the cheddar, except she somehow reassembled into a solid cheesy block on the other side. And suddenly, there she was, outside the house and standing next to her amused fellow SleepWaker.

"Weird, huh?" Ghost Boy laughed.

"I . . . I *felt* it. Like, *through* me," Sam whispered in awe.

"Yeah. That's good, actually. It means it'll be easier to teach you how to be solid."

"What does that mean, 'solid'? I'm assuming it's not like 'do me a solid, bro,' right?" *Whoa.* She definitely sounded more sassback than she meant to. Especially since this was the longest conversation she'd ever had with a person of the male species who wasn't a medical professional or a disgusted brother.

"Simmer down, Newbie. We'll get there. I'm Byron, by the way. At your SleepWaker service." This, with a little bow that was somehow both genuine and mocking.

"Sam. Samantha, I mean. Being that I'm a girl." *Oh, come on, dorkus.* She might be nothing except an essence, but apparently even an essence could turn red in the face.

He flashed his ridiculously deep dimples. Seriously, you could hot tub in those things. "Okay, Samantha. You ready?"

Sam shivered. Even though she had obviously been outside in the middle of the night about a kajillion times, she'd always been, you know, asleep. And only awake when someone was yelling at her or arresting her. She'd never been out in the *quiet* of night. The silence was a presence, promising awesome and terrible things. The darkened houses whispered stories, the trees were witnesses, the parked cars potential monsters.

"Depends on what I need to be ready for," she mumbled.

"You're gonna meet a few of the tribes," Byron said. He turned and walked (floated? hovered?) off. Sam forced her misty legs to move after him, even though the feeling of the air in between her bare feet and the ground gave her immediate motion sickness.

Can a soul puke? She forced her focus up, level to Byron's retreating back, willing her nauseated cloud body to follow.

"Tribes?"

"Yep. We'll start with the ones in this sector. Don't think you're ready to hyper-cross," he tossed over his shoulder.

"Uh . . . yeah . . . 'hyper-cross' definitely does not sound like something I'm ready for," Sam's voice wobbled. "Since I'm having trouble with just . . . non-hyper-crossing . . ." As if to prove this point, the upper half of her soul body got ahead of her lower half and she started to tip forward, her legs helplessly spinning through the atmosphere. "Byron . . . !"

He turned around. "Whoa! Okay, use your arms. It's a little like swimming, so, uh, I guess, backstroke . . . ?"

She flailed her arms backward in wild, klutzy circles

and her soul body righted itself. Byron's lips twitched. "Well, that wasn't pretty, but don't worry. You'll get the hang of it."

"Uh-huh. Sure," Sam said drily. "Just an FYI, I almost drowned in swim class. They switched me to ballroom dancing. Think I can cha-cha my way through this?"

He grinned and set off again. Sam gingerly moved forward, just trying to stay vertical. "So . . . what are the 'tribes'?"

"The different groups of Wakers. In this sector, there's the Achieves, the OCDeeds, the Juve—"

"Slow down! The Achieves?! The OCwhos?! What are these, like, code names?"

"Sorta, yeah. I don't know how much Fletch told you—"

"Fletch? You mean, Dr. Fletcher?" Sam would have paused for this line of questioning, but she was managing the forward float-walk better and didn't want to lose her momentum. "Did he detach your soul, too?!"

"Yep. Fletch did a lot of the Wakers in this sector. I can't believe he didn't brag to you about it." They were cutting across a lawn, and Byron walked through a tree. Right through it. *And that seems normal now.* But she still cut around the trunk, not quite ready to be absorbing bark into her essence. "Did he give you his line about the darkness revealing everything?" Byron said as he reappeared on the other side.

That did sound familiar. "Oh yeah. It was on my sleep study follow-up. Something about people showing who they really are in the dark. What does that mean?"

"Well, I guess the best way to explain it is, your night-time self is the opposite of your daytime one."

Sam processed this for a moment, then, "Oh, so my SleepWaker self is gonna be normal?" The bitterness in her voice surprised even her.

Byron gave her a once-over; he seemed to be trying to figure out how, or if, to respond. "Anyway . . . that's what the tribes are. You just kinda go with your people, once you know who they are. And who *you* are."

They were crossing the street, a large park in front of them. As they walked through the pools of light from the streetlamps, Sam noticed that she and Byron cast no shadows. *Just like vampires. Teen vampires wandering the night looking for their people. I'd write a YA book if someone hadn't already done that.* Sullenly, she mumbled, "Why do I need to *go* with anybody? I do better by myself. *You're* not with a tribe."

"That's different. I'm a Roamer." Before Sam could question this curious title, Byron continued, "And to answer your question, even if it takes a while to find your tribe, you do because it's safer. Especially for a girl—"

"Especially for a *girl*?" Now *that* really frosted her dough-nut. "What is this, 1950s sleepwalking? Maybe I should wear an apron over my jammies and join a tribe that cooks and cleans for the strong male souls!"

Byron sighed. "You didn't let me finish my sentence." He stopped abruptly and faced her. Sam also stopped, backstroking a bit, as it would not be cool to mist through another person's soul body, no matter how delish that person was. "I was going to say, especially for a girl like *you*."

This left Sam feeling all confuddled again. First of all, Mr. Roamer was still identifying her as a girl, which, she was pretty sure was, like, SleepWaker sexism or something. Secondly, *duh*, she *was* a girl, but why would that be a safety matter if she didn't even have a real body to protect? Thirdly, dude was looking at her with such a weird expression of understanding and compassion it was making her heart— or whatever that thing was in the center of her pretend chest—do flip-flops. Fourthly—

But there was no fourthly. Because Sam had just seen them—the other Wakers—and her eyes widened in awe.

"What?" Byron looked over his shoulder. "Oh, right. Meet your first tribe, Sam. The Juvenold."

Running, jumping, sliding, climbing. Teenagers pushing each other on swings. Tweenagers sitting on top of the monkey bars. All pajama-clad, all barefoot, all shouting and laughing. Sam moved closer, this time hardly noticing herself gliding through space. There were gangly teens piled on each end of a seesaw with green frog seats and preteens shooting out of the end of a rainbow tube slide. How could there be so many? How could there be this many souls freed from sleepwalking bodies? *I'm not the only one. I'm not alone.* She'd never had a thought like that in her life.

Her eyes fell on a girl standing on the rubber seat of a swing and pumping her legs like mad, going higher and higher on each pass. Sam gasped. *Alyssa Del Rio?!* Alyssa was in the eighth grade at Wallace! But it was only the bright blue hair whipping in the wind that clued Sam in; other than that, Alyssa was unrecognizable. By day, she was an all-black-wearing, eye-rolly girl who sported a prodigious face full of makeup and bragged about all the high school seniors she was dating, notorious for her response of "*What . . . Evvvv . . . Errrr . . .*" to any question posed by her long-suffering teachers.

But that was not the Alyssa that Sam was observing in the middle of the night; the Alyssa rocking the swing was barefaced, smiling ear to ear, and singing "100 Bottles of Milk on the Wall" at the top of her lungs. Sam wasn't sure what was more mind-blowing: that there was another sleepwalker at Wallace, or that *this* was who that sleepwalker turned into in the darkness.

"They're something, huh?"

Sam started. She had almost forgotten Byron was there.

"So . . . according to Fletch's theory, this is who they really are, inside?" Sam said slowly. "Like, they were sleep-walking because their souls actually wanted to ride on frog seesaws?"

"Well, if you're gonna bottom-line it, yeah," mused Byron.

"But wait, there's one thing I don't get. How come they can hold on to the swings and sit up on the bars without sliding right through?" Sam lifted her mist fingers. "It's not like we're, you know, real people with workable hands or anything."

Byron appeared to be mildly offended by this. "Uh, we *are* real people. You just have to practice being solid."

"Right, right, 'solid.' And how does *that* work?"

He looked at her without a shred of irony. "You have to believe."

This was too much. "And if I clap my hands, the fairies won't die, either?"

Byron kept his steady gaze. "I'm serious. You have to believe in the weight and possibilities of your own soul."

Sam smirked and looked away. "Oh, well, then, I'm in big trouble."

"HEY! HEY, YOU! I KNOW YOU!" Alyssa had slowed her mad swinging. She leapt from her wobbly perch and dashed over to Byron and Sam. "I know you from school, right? You're in seventh?" Her grin was so big and infectious that Sam couldn't help smiling herself.

"Yeah. Hi, Alyssa. I'm Sam."

"Sam!" Alyssa made a move to give her a hug, but Byron intervened.

"Whoa! Hang on, Juvie, Sam doesn't know how to be solid yet. Don't freak her out on her first night by falling through her."

Sam mouthed a "thank you" to him.

"Your first night?! Awesome! Come and play with us!" Alyssa jumped up and down, spun like a hyperactive toddler, and fell on her butt. Laughing uproariously, she bounced back onto her feet and looked at Sam with fervid anticipation.

"Um . . ." Sam was laughing now, too, although possibly with an edge of hysteria. "I don't think I'm a . . . Juvie. . . ."

"You don't have to be," Byron interjected. "You can try out all the tribes until you find where you belong." He directed his next sentence at Alyssa, who was now scraping her blue hair into a ponytail fountain springing from the top of her head. "But since Sam is still a bit, uh, *hazy*, maybe another night."

"Sure! Cool! *Whatever!*" Alyssa's catchphrase took a perky twist that Sam wished her teachers could hear. "And listen, Sam, I probably won't talk to you at school, but don't take it personally, 'kay?"

"I won't," Sam promised. "I get it."

"Neato!" Alyssa crowed, then proceeded to skip back to the playground, colliding with another Juvenold. They both toppled to the ground, screaming with laughter. "This is Minnie!" Alyssa shrieked, pointing at the slender girl who was doubled over, guffawing. "I call her . . . Minnie Mouse!" This sent both of them back into paroxysms of glee.

"Wow." Sam shook her head in disbelief.

"Right?"

"You have no idea who that person is in the daytime."

Byron grinned. "Oh, I think I can guess. Ready to move on?"

"Lead the way, Roamer," Sam said wryly. As they walk-hovered away, she looked back at the Juvenold tribe, tumbling and playing. They all seemed so . . . what? *Pure.* It was a word she'd never thought before, much less used in real life, but it fit.

"They're all kids," she pointed out. "Where's the adults? Do they have their own tribe?"

"I asked Fletch the same thing. Apparently, it's really hard to spring grown people. Fletch says their souls are too attached to their bodies. He did manage it with one, but then the guy tried to sue him, so that was that."

Almost as if on cue, the shape of a man appeared before

them and Sam squealed. Head down and shoulders hunched, he walked slowly into their path.

"It's okay, he can't see us," Byron said offhandedly. Sure enough, the man crossed in front of them and continued on his plodding way. "He's a Later."

"A *what*?"

"A Later. A person who's out late in his physical body." Byron laughed at her skeptical expression. "Hey, listen, I didn't make up all the tags. Some of them are a little on the nose."

The guy's slouchy back and lumbering gait as he walked past the Juvenold made her rather sad, for some reason. It didn't seem right that their joyousness was invisible to him. "So how can you tell who's a SleepWaker and who's a human?"

" 'Later,' *please*. It might be a stupid name, but we're *all* humans, so that one doesn't work. You just have to look for the cord. Wakers have the cord, Laters don't."

"The cord? You mean, like, the silver cord? You can *see* that?!" Sam immediately looked but didn't observe any kind of shiny rope attached to Byron's soul body. She did notice, however, a whole lotta muscles defining his snug T-shirt; pretty cool that someone's consciousness could be so ripped. *Okay, get a grip, girl.*

If Byron noticed her dreamy gaze, he was nice enough not

to embarrass her. "There," he said, pointing. "Do you see?"

Sam gasped. How could she have missed it? A delicate, spiderweb-thin trail of light fluttered behind her, stretching into seeming infinity. She knew it wasn't real infinity, the cord only reaching back to her physical body, but it struck her as having the pulse and color of life itself.

"That's . . . unbelievable."

Byron nodded. "Sometimes it's a little hard to spot at first, but once you do, you'll never miss it again," he said softly. He briskly started moving up the sidewalk. "So don't worry about the Laters—you'll know them. And since they can't see you unless you want them to—"

"Yeah, how is that?"

"It's pretty much the same as being solid. You have to decide if they'll see you or not. To be honest, though, I don't know why any Waker would *want* to be seen. Unless, of course, you're a Prank and you like messing with people's minds."

This made Sam wince, but she tried to be light about it. "I'm guessing a Prank is, hmmm, let's see, someone whose secret desire is to play pranks?"

"Told you some of the tags were a little obvious."

"Gee, ya think?" Her tone was suddenly acid, and Byron looked at her quizzically. "Sorry. I just . . . I know some people who play mean tricks during the daytime and don't bother to hide it." It gave her a soul-ache to think about Jaida and her evil clowns.

"Well . . ." Byron said gently, "maybe if they were SleepWakers, they'd be nice to you at night. Opposites, right?"

She smiled at him gratefully, and they glided along in companionable silence.

"I'm going to take you to meet the Achieves, and that should be enough for tonight. Don't want your consciousness to explode," Byron teased. He started moving faster, and Sam managed to keep pace. It was getting a little easier, this motion of her essence through space. The breeze around her even seemed to agree with her progress, helping the flow with smoothly imperceptible gusts.

"Byron, were all those Wakers in the park Fletch's patients?"

"Doubt it. I don't know all of them, but probably some are from the other docs."

"Other doctors?" Even though Dr. Fletcher had sort of half mentioned this, Sam was still shocked. "How many people are making a career of springing kids' essences out of their bodies?"

"Well . . ." Suddenly his face darkened. "Right now, there's five." Then he added quickly, "That we know of."

"Really? Five?! Where are they all? Do they know each other? Did they learn how to do it together, or did one of them teach the other ones?" All her questions came out in a rush.

"Hang on, we're coming into a Later zone," Byron cut her off. "Even though they can't see us, you don't want 'em walking through you—it feels nasty." They were nearing an intersection with a gas station and a bar. Blaring music poured forth as a group of people stumbled out. They were talking to each other in unnecessarily loud voices, and laughing, although their laughter was as different from the Juvenold's in the playground as night from day.

One couple lurched toward Byron and Sam, the obviously drunken man fumbling for his car keys in his date's purse. The woman giggled, "Wait, wait," tucked a lock of her curly hair behind her ear, and dug around in the bag herself. She pulled out the keys and was rewarded with a patronizing pat on the head and a sloppy kiss, eliciting an audible *"ewww"* from Sam.

The curly-haired woman paused for a moment, looking around with a curious expression. Byron shot Sam a warning glance, and she froze, completely confused. *Did she hear me?* The woman shrugged it off and followed her boyfriend to his car.

When the car door closed, Sam hissed to Byron, "I thought you said they couldn't see us unless we wanted them to!"

"They can't," he said slowly. "But once in a while . . . sometimes there's a Waker who can be . . . I don't know, I guess, perceived? Not sure if she saw you, or heard you, as much as she . . . *felt* you."

Sam was mildly horrified. "That's not good, dude! I don't want to be felt!"

He gave her a reassuring smile, although it seemed a bit forced. "Don't freak out. You'll be able to control that, too. Probably." He turned on his heel and cruised off.

"*Probably?*" Sam yelped. But before she could follow, she had to deal with the incredibly uncomfortable feeling of a car passing through her soul body. The curly-haired woman in the passenger seat looked back with the same curious expression. Sam shuddered. *That* was *nasty. Note to self: Don't let people drive through you.*

She took off, follow-floating Byron down a hill. They reached a two-lane highway that seemed pretty deserted, for which Sam was grateful. "Hey, Byron? Where are we? This doesn't look familiar anymore."

"We're going to Fairleigh Dickinson. That's where the Achieves meet."

"Fairleigh—the college? Isn't that in Madison?" Sam questioned.

"Yep."

"But that's like fifteen miles away!"

"Not anymore." Byron pointed to a sign about a block ahead. Sam squinted to read *Madison Train Station*.

"How . . . ?!"

Byron smiled mischievously. "We may have . . . sped up a bit. Not hyper-crossing, not yet, just a little . . . uh, jacked-up crossing."

Sam shook her head, dazed. "I didn't *feel* like I was zooming or anything. Were we going, like, car fast or airplane fast?"

Byron shrugged. "It's soul speed. I kind of describe it as the speed of imagination, except you can't go to pretend places or another planet or, like, heaven or anything. You gotta stay on Earth."

"Oh. Good. Staying on Earth is good," Sam said faintly. "But if it's like the speed of imagination, why can't we just, I don't know, *think* it and we're there?"

"You're still not getting the soul thing. A soul isn't just your mind or your thoughts or even your—what did you call it before?—your essence. It's a real thing, in the real world. It has weight and—"

"Possibilities, yeah, yeah, I remember," Sam said rather grumpily.

"Anyway, you don't have to stress it tonight, 'cause we're staying in Fletch's sector. He's got Jersey." Byron tossed this off as casually as if he were making a vacation recommendation. "We can do another state tomorrow."

Despite her nerves, her mist heart performed a jumping jack of excitement. "Like . . . Pennsylvania? Can we go that far?"

Byron just grinned. "You'll see . . ." he drawled. The jumping jack turned into a full-fledged thrill-burpee.

Within moments, they were outside a large brick building. This time Byron didn't even stop to encourage her; he just disappeared right into the wall. Sam sighed; apparently having a window and a car pass through her soul wasn't enough for one night. She followed, noticing that the sensation of brick moving through her essence was decidedly different than either glass or metal. *Great,* she thought, *my physics teacher would be so proud.*

Sam found herself in some type of common room, filled with SleepWakers. There was so much going on, it took her a few minutes to process what she was seeing. There were Wakers practicing violin concertos while repeating phrases in Mandarin from Rosetta Stone software while extending their legs on a ballet barre; a group avidly comparing passages from the Bible, Qur'an, Torah, Tao Te Ching, and Upanishads while performing the most pretzel-y yoga positions Sam had ever seen; there was even one lone Waker hanging upside down from an acrobat's bar while performing some sort of science experiment with his dangling hands. He noticed Sam staring and smiled at her, saying proudly, "Algae biofuel lab." Sam smiled back weakly.

"So?" Byron appeared beside her. "What do you think of the Achieves?"

"Well . . . they're definitely . . . achieving," was all Sam could manage.

He laughed.

"Okay, but what I don't get is . . . if this is the stuff their souls want to do, why can't they just do it in their real lives? You know, in the daytime?" Sam questioned.

Byron picked up a vial of algae biofuel and examined it. "You're a sleepwalker. Why don't you tell me what *your* daytime life has been like?"

Sam stared at the cloudy liquid, trying to clear her foggy mind. "I guess . . . I'm exhausted all the time. . . ."

"What else?"

". . . Kinda depressed . . ."

"Uh-huh."

"And"—this was painful to say out loud—"everyone thinks I'm a freak anyway, so why bother?"

"Bingo. You want to achieve anything, you gotta believe in yourself, obviously. But you also have to have somebody, *anybody*, that believes in you, too. That's not easy to come by for some people."

Faces popped into her mind: Jax, always so frustrated and sarcastic; her mother, ripping the hair out of her own head in hopelessness; every exasperated teacher or doctor she'd ever had.

Jeez, even Weezy looks at me like I'm weird, and he's a dog with severe breathing problems and a face like a furry dinner plate.

"I get it," she said quietly.

But Byron wasn't listening now. He was staring at the Achieves, a little worry wrinkle creasing his forehead.

"Byron?"

"Seventeen," he responded absently.

"Huh?"

"Supposed to be seventeen of 'em." Byron shook his head. "Hang on a sec," he said, trotting/floating over to the upside-down Waker. They spoke in whispers as Sam tried to count the Achieves. It was no easy task, as the yoga crew had moved on to some insanely knotted group pose, and there were legs and arms sprouting out like weeds, but . . . *Sixteen.* As far as she could tell, by attempting to count only heads and ignore limbs, there were sixteen Achieves in the room. And for some reason, that number seemed to be making both Byron and the algae biofuel kid agitated.

"Is there a problem?" she questioned as Byron hovered back to her.

"Nope!" he said, sounding far more confident than he looked. "No problem at all. It's just that it's gonna be dawn soon. Wherever you are when your body wakes up, the silver cord will yank your soul back in. But that takes some getting used to. If you're far away, it feels pretty sucky. That might be too much for your first night, so let's get a little closer to home, 'kay?"

He delivered this rather important piece of info rapidly, then zoomed out through the brick wall. Sam followed him onto the lawn, her mind spinning like a Ferris wheel run by a caffeinated carny.

Was someone missing? Who? Why?

There was just too much to process. She'd only seen two of the tribes, and already there were so many souls, so many lives, so many stories. How could she grasp all of this? *And where do I belong? Anywhere?*

"Aw, *man*." Her brain flagellation was interrupted by Byron's groan. "They found us."

This sounded rather ominous. "What? *Who* found us?"

Byron looked positively glum. "Probably just my opinion, but only the most annoying tribe in the whole SleepWaker world."

That's when Sam heard what sounded like about a hundred people clinking their water glasses with spoons, and a rather impressive four-part harmony.

Oh, Waker, you are new
So this is what we sing to you . . .

She turned slowly to see a group of SleepWakers moving toward them. Wearing tap shoes.

True! True! Oh so true!
You'll find yourself to be true blue!

"Samantha, meet"—Byron sighed—"the Broadways."

And then they were around her, a bunch of big, burly teenaged boys and some smallish girls wearing glasses, all singing lustily, doing jazz hands, and stretching their floaty feet down to the ground for optimal tap-to-sidewalk contact.

Welcome to the life of night
Where what was lurking just out of sight
Comes bursting forth into plain view
The truth of you, oh so true blue!

A hulking redheaded boy launched into a tap solo as Sam leaned into Byron and whispered, "Explain, please."

"You don't have to whisper. They're in their own little world," Byron said in a normal, if somewhat agitated, voice. "From what I've been able to get out of them—which isn't much, since they *refuse to talk*—their souls just want to burst into song. Like in Broadway musicals. I've tried to reason with them, told them even in musicals the characters speak in sentences sometimes and the songs are saved for, you know, moments when words aren't enough—"

"You sure know a lot about musicals," Sam murmured, biting her lip so as not to laugh.

"—but no, they don't care, they're just gonna sing everything! Because, in their daytime lives, this instinct is stifled. That's Chadney." Byron pointed to the red-haired giant who was in the middle of a triple time step. "He's a senior at my school and he's, like, this football god, but of course he won't even look in my direction in the daytime. I think all of the guy Broadways are sports stars, and the girl ones are brainiacs. Their words, not mine. *Sung*, of course."

Sam couldn't hold it in anymore; she burst out laughing. Byron gave her a peeved look, just as Chadney finished his solo with four backward wings. Sam applauded.

"Please don't encourage him," Byron said grimly.

"Come on, you gotta admit that was pretty awesome. Especially for a guy who's built like a flesh mountain," Sam said, gesturing to the massively muscled redhead.

"Well, it's easier to do when you're floating, don'tcha think?" He flipped his hand dismissively at Chadney, who was now starting to beatbox. Byron groaned. "Aaaaand the worst genre of all. Hip-hop musical. Thanks a lot, *Hamilton*."

It's night and the tribes rock
It's night and the tribes flock
But don't look behind ya, there's sumpin to mind ya,
The tribe with the night lock
Take stock
Don't shock
The tribe with the night lock
The midnight teems, ain't all it seems,
Ima be carefuling of the MeanDreams—

The what? She heard Byron curse softly.

"Wait, what was that? What are MeanDreams?" she asked.

But before Byron could answer, she felt a slight tug, like someone was pulling her hair, except all over her entire body. And then with a stomach-churning, brain-rattling yank, Byron, the Broadways, and the lawn of Fairleigh Dickinson became a backward sonic-boom blur, and Soul Sam landed back in her body with the force of a space shuttle reentering the earth's atmosphere. She groaned.

The Roamer was right. Sucky.

eight

THE GOOD NEWS WAS that once Sam's mega-harsh reentry into her bod was complete, a new feeling came over her: She felt *light*. Like someone had snuck in and cleaned out the litter box of her extremities. *What is going on?*

Joanne's words came back to her: *Your body will now be getting the rest it needs while your soul accomplishes its purpose.*

She turned to Weezy, who had somehow managed to take up overnight residence in the middle of her pillow, and said, "Wanna go for a walk before I leave for school?" He opened his headlamp eyes and gave a snort of surprise. "I know, I'm shocked, too." She snuggled him, breathing in his warm-Fritos-and-moist-feet scent and whispered, "Just between you and me, I'm hoping for a lot of surprises today."

✸   ✸   ✸

And Sam wasn't disappointed. At breakfast, Margie was outright humming as she tied her sassy head wrap, and Jax tossed off, "Two whole nights of sleep. We might not have to give you up for adoption after all."

At school, she not only managed to stay awake for pre-algebra (aka, second-period "nasal strip–fest"), but was still awake in social studies (fifth period, which was usually when she slid under her desk). By the time sixth-period language arts rolled around, the entire class was laying bets as to when Sam was going to drop, but instead she actually answered a question ("Dangling participle!"). It was official: Samantha Fife might just possibly be maybe kind of normal, maybe. She could see the potential of a new assessment on her classmates' faces, and it was utterly thrilling.

Of course, some people preferred to stick to their old views.

"So, Sam," Jaida purred from her locker, which, abiding by Murphy's Law of Middle School Bullying, was situated directly across from Sam's locker. "Did your shrink find a new drug for your brain disease? Or did your mom buy you coffee today instead of spending her money on synthetic wigs?" Amy and Gina dissolved into rhapsodic giggles.

Sam felt her insides begin to do their usual lava slide, all the good stuff of the day turning molten. She tried to focus on opening her locker to just get her stuff and disappear, but there was one problem.

There were no numbers on the lock. Someone had painted over them with black paint, so there was no way to do the combination. Sam just stared, uncomprehending, as Amy and Gina doubled over laughing and Jaida turned away with a satisfied smirk, snapping her weird retro fanny pack around her waist.

But, being a day of surprises, there was another one in store.

Madalynn Sucret passed through the hallway just at that moment. Sam looked up from the lock of darkness, and Madalynn winked.

That couldn't have been for me. Not possible. A speck of dust must have had a death wish and flown into Madalynn's transcendent eyeball. Nevertheless, Sam found herself wandering away from her attackers and following the winker down the hallway, as if the flutter of those eyelashes had cast a magic stalker spell. Madalynn disappeared into the auditorium, and Sam paused at the door, on which a sheet of paper bellowed:

Set Crew Needed for Fall Musical!

Okay, so maybe it was the headiness of her physical self having slept for two nights straight, or the sudden memory of her well-built half tree house, but a thought crawled into Sam's nearly coherent brain: *If my soul wanted to use power tools, maybe my body will, too.* And as if that thought had given her hand permission, she was suddenly signing her name on the sheet. Sam looked around to see if anyone was going to yell at her for desecrating school property, but the hallway was empty.

Piano music trickled out of the auditorium, and Sam couldn't resist peeking through the door. She saw Madalynn, wearing a little nurse's cap and singing in an angelic soprano—

> *The soldiers all call me a scamp,*
> *but I prefer "Lady with the Lamp"!*

—while a chorus of students in casts and bandages danced around her.

Whaaat exactly am I seeing right now? Sam gave a perplexed look back at the sign-up sheet for the actual title of the fall production:

FLO! THE MUSICAL
THE LIFE OF FLORENCE NIGHTINGALE

Oookay. "The Broadways would be thrilled," she mumbled to herself.

* * *

That night, Sam's soul woke up while still in Sam's body. It was the strangest sense of "otherness" she had ever experienced; she could hear her body breathing from inside her own head, and her heartbeat felt like a Siamese twin. *I'm like an alien inside a host.* Somehow this thought made her grin, and then she couldn't help herself. Rising up from the bed, literally splitting from her own self, Sam gave it her best horror film intonation, *"She's aliiivvvveee . . . !"*

Byron's applause was a little unnerving, to say the least.

"Dude! What the heck?!" Sam yelped, jumping the rest of the way out of her body.

"Sorry! I swear I wasn't watching you sleep or anything," Byron laughed, putting up his hands in surrender. "I just popped in when I heard your Dr. Frankenstein voice."

"Uh-huh," Sam said, with just the littlest bit of side-eye.

"Scout's honor. But I gotta say," Byron continued, "it's a miracle I could even hear you over the buzz saw."

They looked at Weezy, who had his flat, vibrating face pressed against Bed Sam's skull.

"I know. How can I sleep through that?" Sam shook her soul head.

"I guess it's a testament to Fletch's mad skills. His patients are gonna get their rest no matter what, even if Pugsy has adenoids," mused Byron.

"Weezy."

"Huh?"

"His name is Weezy," Sam said.

Byron nodded, grinning. "I get it. 'Weezy.'"

Sam rolled her eyes. "You *think* you get it. But that's not why my mom named him that."

Byron cocked his head to one side. "What other reason could you have for naming a wheezing dog 'Weezy'?"

"Uh, because my mother is a big fan of sitcoms from, like, the last century and her favorite character was Louise on this show called *The Jeffersons*. Nickname, Weezy."

"Huh. Wow." Byron was trying valiantly to grasp this. "That's so . . ."

"Random?" Sam said wryly.

"Yep."

"If you knew my family, trust me, this would not be the most random thing." Sam sighed. "It's all downhill from there."

"You can tell me more while we hyper-cross." Byron was brisk again, moving toward the window.

Sam swallowed nervously. "You think I'm ready? I don't even know how to be solid yet."

"You don't need to be solid for this."

She stubbornly stood her inch-off-the-ground. "Well, it would help if you could actually grab on to me if I went spinning off into space, don'tcha think?"

"No one is going to be spinning anywhere. Just stay close, keep moving, and ignore the blur." He walked through the window.

The blur?

"No way am I going fast enough for stuff to blur, dude!" she yelled after him. This got no response from Byron, but Weezy woke up and started howling that awful pug-sees-Beelzebub howl again. Sam had no choice but to escape as quickly as possible, somehow managing to pass through not only window glass, but frilly curtains, part of the fiberglass wall, and some cheap siding in the process.

Outside a light rain was falling. Sam stood for a moment, trying to fathom the sensation of water passing through her essence, water that didn't feel wet. *Yeah, but what does "wet" feel like?* It was as if she needed a whole new vocabulary for the Waker world. Or maybe even a new language. Byron was watching her closely, almost as if he knew what she was thinking and was waiting for some profound statement to spring forth from her lips. Instead—

"I got nothin'," Sam offered.

He nodded.

"So. I guess now we hyper-cross?" She delivered this with a wince.

"Don't worry, Newbie, it's all good."

"Uh-huh. Sure."

They moved out, Sam forcing herself to look straight ahead. She imagined that the "blur" of their soul speed would be like star trails she had seen in photographs and science fiction movies, and she just wasn't ready to visually acknowledge such a phenomenon. But even with her eyes fixed, it felt like she had just stepped onto some sort of moving walkway at an astral airport; her steps did not equal the velocity at which she was traveling. Trees started to streak past her peripheral vision in long ribbons of green, and the wind became a continual unceasing shriek. Within seconds, everything swam by in a giant swathe of color and motion. A sudden, ripply burst of light—was it another Later Zone? Or an entire city in one brilliant flash? Sam barely had time to consider all the elements of electricity and hints of human-ity she had just bypassed in a breath, when she realized that they were on water.

Literally. *On* water, but boatless. So, yeah, *walking* on water.

This deserved a shout-out. *"Byron?!"*

He winked and yelled over the din of splash and gale, "Sailor Sam!"

Sam tried to laugh, but the strangulated bark flew back in her face.

"Don't freak, it'll end soon. Lake Michigan isn't that wide," Byron hollered.

Lake—?! She didn't even finish that thunderstruck thought before they were over land again and then, "We're here!" and it all came to a screeching soundless stop. The whole world vibrated around her for a moment, then stilled.

Sam swallowed, gagging slightly, and waited for her soul stomach to catch up and redeposit itself into her being. She finally dared to turn her head. They were standing on a dark corner in front of a tiny restaurant called the Taco Stop; the entire rest of the street was taken up by a long, low building that would have looked like a warehouse if it hadn't been for the mirrored full-length windows down the length of the structure.

Summoning her weak knowledge of the Midwest, Sam whispered, "Wisconsin?"

"Illinois, actually." Byron pointed up at a sign on the building. "The Numbs love this place."

GALLOPING GHOST ARCADE

The "Arcade" portion of the sign was jumbotron big, but just in case anyone was still confused as to the nature of the establishment, underneath it said:

Games! Games! Games! Games!

Sam took a deep breath, still recovering from her thirty-second stroll halfway across the country. "Okay, I'm just spitballin' here, but the Numbs? They like to . . . what, numb out and play video games?"

"Aaaand she's back!" Byron grinned and disappeared into the building. Sam followed quickly; after what she'd just experienced, walking through a mirrored wall didn't seem like such a big deal anymore.

But nothing could have prepared her for the assault on the senses that was Galloping Ghost Arcade. There were literally hundreds of pinball machines and video games, and it seemed like nearly every unit had a Waker yanking levers, slamming buttons, jiggling joysticks, shooting guns, and spinning steering wheels; the flashing lights were blinding and the bings, beeps, and boooonnnngssss deafening. It was a sensory overload of the highest order.

"Biggest arcade in the United States!" Byron shouted in her ear.

"Well, yeah!" Sam shouted back. "But how the heck are they—? Why haven't the police come?"

"Oh, they have, but—" A Numb started a game of *Mortal Kombat 4* right next to them, and Byron motioned Sam over to a slightly less eardrum-bursting area near a bank of *Frogger* machines. "But that's where the Pranks come in. The one time the cops showed up, they didn't get what was going on 'cause the Numbs are invisible to them, of course, so all they saw was the video games playing themselves. Freaky enough, right? But *then* the Pranks joined in and started knocking off their caps and grabbing their Tasers, levitating their guns, and they flipped out for real. Now the patrol in this area just steers clear, unless they have a rookie they want to haze a little. It all works out."

Despite her personal distaste for practical jokes, Sam had to laugh. She looked around at the SleepWakers and couldn't resist the joy on their faces. "So, I'm guessing that during the day the Numbs are . . . what? Not allowed to have screen time?"

Byron called to a Waker who was playing *Frogger* with one hand and shooting walking dead bodies on *Zombie Raid* with the other. "Hey, Olivia! Got a newbie here! She wants to know what you do all day!"

"Study!" Olivia shouted as she managed to run up insane numbers on both games. "I'm a Mensan!"

"Member of Mensa," Byron supplied helpfully. "The high-IQ society."

"My parents want me to be a neurosurgeon!" Olivia continued, typing her initials into the high-score field on *Frogger* while pumping her gun for a *Zombie* reload. "But neurosurgeons have really expensive malpractice insurance costs, so I have to make sure I'll never make a mistake! I study for about seven hours after school every day!"

"How can a person never make a mistake?" Sam tried to shout-whisper this to Byron, but Olivia still overheard and turned around with a smile.

"I know, right? What kind of psycho pressure is that? No wonder I was walking in my sleep! Thank God for Dr. Mahdhav! Right, Kyra?" Olivia leaned over and tried to fist-bump a heavyset Waker in red flannel pajamas, who was playing a *Nightmare in the Dark* game as if her life depended on it. Olivia was left hanging.

"How are you doing, Kyra? You adjusting okay?" Byron somehow managed to sound caring even when yelling over zombie deaths.

"Fine." Kyra didn't take her eyes off her game.

Sam shout-whispered to Byron, "Is Dr. Mahdhav one of the other Waker docs?"

He nodded. "This is his sector. He's kind of a man-child, so it fits that he has the Numbs and the Pranks."

"You said there were five doctors. Where are the other three?"

"There's Dr. Hopkins—she's in North Dakota; Thomas has Manhattan; and Knavish is in—"

"Byron! Brah!" A scrawny teenaged boy approached, sporting the humble beginnings of a soul patch and hitching up pajama pants that were about three inches too short for him. "Whatcha doing in Mahd's quad? Slummin'?"

"Hey, Noa. Just helping out a new Waker," Byron said. "This is Sam."

"S'up, Sam?" Noa gave her a little salute. "You meet Kyra yet? She's a newbie, too, only been detached a couple of days."

"Uh, yeah, sort of," Sam said.

"How's she doing?" Byron sounded concerned, casting a glance over at Kyra, whose nose was about two inches from the *Nightmare* screen.

Noa shrugged. "Still won't talk much, but Olivia did get a nugget of info out of her. Seems her little bro has Asperger's and *Nightmare in the Dark* is his favorite game."

Byron nodded, thoughtful. Sam wasn't sure what was on his mind, but then again, she wasn't hip yet to the inner workings of the SleepWaker world.

"Hey, Sam, you wanna do some *'Roids*?" Noa drawled.

She must have looked startled because Byron jumped in, "He means *Asteroids*, not performance-enhancing drugs."

"Oh. Oh! Right." Sam breathed a sigh of relief. "Thanks, but I, uh . . . I'm still kind of useless." She held up her mist hands.

"Naw, don't say 'useless.'" Noa looked at her earnestly. "You're just an embryo, waitin' to hatch into a swan."

"Why don't you try, Sam?" Byron leaned in and said this in her ear, which would have given her chills if she weren't so distracted by Noa's mangled metaphor. "This is a good place to practice. No pressure, right, Noa?"

"Brah! Righteous! The daytime is mad pressure, but not here!" Noa crowed, gesturing grandly to the huge room humming with flashing colored lights and bright mechanical sounds. "Freedom! Freedom! Let your soul be a joy cannon!"

The cheesiness of this proclamation aside, Sam felt a little thrill ripple through her. *Maybe this is my tribe,* she thought.

Maybe this is where it all starts to make sense. Noa loped over to the *Asteroids Deluxe* game, and she found herself following. As he pressed "Player One" and started to shoot rocky planets and flying saucers, Sam stared at her hands. *You have weight. You have possibilities. You can press a button and cause things to exist or be destroyed. You can play a stinkin' video game, for Pete's sake.*

"Aw, man, killer satellite took me out," moaned Noa. "Your turn, Sam. Hope you win!"

Her heart started to hammer. *I don't need to win, I just want to exist.* She moved her hand toward the "Player Two" button. *I just want to be solid.*

And then her pointer finger slid right through the button and her whole hand disappeared into the control panel.

＊　＊　＊

"Sam! Sam!" Byron yelled after her as she doggedly stride-hovered forward. Maybe she couldn't achieve hyper-cross speed, but she could at least leave the Galloping Ghost behind. "You don't even know where you're going!"

Awww, crud. She stopped so abruptly that Byron blew right through her soul body to the other side. He turned around sheepishly. "Sorry."

Sam shrugged. What did it matter? She was immaterial,

nonexistent; everything could pass through her without even noticing she was there.

"Don't take it so hard," Byron said. "You'll get it eventually. Being solid takes practice." He was using his "concerned" voice again. Only this time she wasn't buying it.

"Oh yeah?" she countered. "How long did it take you?"

He shifted uncomfortably. "That doesn't matter—"

"How long did it take Kyra? She's only been around a few days, and she's as solid as a rock!" Byron seemingly had no answer for this; he just looked down at the sidewalk. Sam snorted a bitter laugh. "Uh-huh. Listen, why don't you Roam off and haunt someone else? I'll just start my own tribe, the Double Losers. Losers by day, *and* by night. We'll meet up in Times Square and let cars and Laters blaze through us until one of 'em manages to *snip snip* the silver cord and puts us out of our misery—"

"Stop." At first Sam thought that Byron was reacting to her rant, but then she saw his face. "Come here right now." His voice was so commanding and serious that she obeyed immediately. They quickly slipped through the wall of the Taco Stop and hid behind a sign advertising a Friday night burrito special.

"What's going on?"

Byron peered through the window. "They're not usually in this sector. Something must be up."

"Who?" Sam still felt irritable. "Is it the Broadways again? They come back to sing about my loserness?"

"Shhh!" Byron hissed and she shhhed reluctantly. He continued in a whisper, "No. It's . . . the MeanDreams."

Before "The *whaaa?*" could come out of her mouth, Sam remembered the Broadways the night before: *Ima be carefuling of the MeanDreams.* What she'd thought was just rapping grammar was obviously something more. She shivered slightly and peeked out the window past Byron.

A large group of kids in pajamas were gliding past them. At first Sam wasn't sure why this particular tribe was so automatically creepy, but then it dawned on her; they were silent. All the other Wakers she had seen so far seemed to have been released from their bodies into noise and thrill; the MeanDreams appeared to have been unshackled into grim and eerie quietness.

"What are they?" Sam breathed.

"They're the reason everyone needs a tribe to be safe," Byron muttered grimly.

The MeanDreams stopped dead in front of Galloping Ghost.

"Uh-oh," Byron said under his breath.

Sam gulped nervously. "What? Is it us? Did they hear us?"

"No. I think they've got somebody else." He craned his

neck, trying to see, but the group was in a tight knot now, their backs forming an impenetrable wall.

"They've *got* somebody? What does *that* mean?" This came out in an audible squeal that made her sound impossibly girly, but *seriously?* What the heck were they dealing with here?

"SHHHHH!" Byron hissed. "I don't know for sure! It's only a rumor at this point, just a suspicion. I haven't caught them in the act yet, and I never will if you don't shut it!"

Her entire misty body was vibrating now, and her whisper was just as wobbly. "In the act of *what*, exactly?"

Byron's mouth was set in a hard line. "Soul-napping. I think they're taking Wakers against their will."

With that hugely awful statement, all the playful joy and supposed freedom of the night was obliterated. *Against their will?* Even in the SleepWaker world, there were bullies? If it could happen even in the darkness, that meant there was no real freedom anywhere.

To this realization, Sam had a hugely awful reaction, although not the one she, or anyone else, would have anticipated. Because, the next thing she knew, she was out on the sidewalk, having leapt through the wall of the Taco Stop.

"HEY!"

Like gates opening up onto the driveway of hell, the

MeanDreams split down the middle and swung apart to see who would dare challenge them.

Sam gasped.

In the center of the group was Kyra, plucking anxiously at her red flannel pajamas with trembling hands. And right next to her was the most beautiful disembodied bully one could imagine in one's darkest imaginings: a stunning girl in a silky turquoise nightgown, the glow of her fair hair and blue eyes lighting up the night.

There was only one brightness missing.

Because, for once, Madalynn Sucret was most definitely *not* smiling.

nine

"MISS FIFE, are you in the land of the living?" Bain's (obviously) favorite saying cut through her fog. Sam sat up straight in her chair, shaking off the tornado of thoughts that had sucked her into the muffled eye of its storm.

"Yes, sir. I am."

"Glad to hear it. You've been doing better the last two days. Don't crush my dreams."

"I'll do my best not to, sir."

The class tittered, with a slight edge of surprise. Was Samantha Fife joking around with a teacher? Bain thankfully let it go, but Sam couldn't. Memories and images kept drawing her into the mental whirlwind. Had she *really* seen Madalynn Sucret and a super-scary tribe called the MeanDreams attempting to soul-nap the newbie Kyra? The same Madalynn Sucret who, in approximately eleven minutes, was donning her cheerleading uniform to lead a stomp and shake in Wallace's "Just Say No to Bullying" pep rally? And what had happened to Kyra? Had Byron been able to help her? For the twentieth time, Sam mentally cursed her bladder. If her physical body hadn't woken up to go to the bathroom, her silver cord wouldn't have yanked her back at such a crucial moment and she'd have more answers.

Or you'd have been soul-napped yourself.

Well, yeah, that was the other un-fun possibility. What on planet Earth had possessed her to jump out and confront a tribe that Byron had just pegged as probable Waker-stealers? Even now the memory was so overwhelming, her brain kept insisting that she'd imagined the whole thing. *Madalynn Sucret?* She knew the theory that a SleepWaker soul was supposed to be the opposite of the daytime self, but there was simply no way that the angel playing Flo Nightingale in the school musical was a nighttime bully. There had to be another explanation. There just had to be another detached soul out there with blond curlicues, oceanic eyes, and lips from a plastic surgeon's "After" photos file.

"Miss *Fife*." Bain's tone had upgraded from mild exasperation to plain old *are you kidding me?*

"Yes, sir, sorry. What was the question?" Sam grabbed her algebra book.

"The question was, are you going to continue to daydream in my classroom or are you going to the auditorium for the assembly?"

Sam looked around her; the room was empty. As she gathered up her things, she was tempted to say, "*Daydream? More like day*nightmare."

But she didn't.

✳ ✳ ✳

By the time Sam had reached her lock-less locker after the assembly (thank you, ornery janitor with a bolt cutter), she was convinced. There was no way that the shimmery girl who just led the entire school in a tear-choked plea to the universe on behalf of the downtrodden and disenfranchised was the same person slithering through the darkness like a pissed-off poltergeist.

No. Way. Sam slammed her locker closed to punctuate.

And like the sun breaking through the clouds, there she was in the flesh—Madalynn Sucret. "Hello, Sam," the girl purred.

Sam squawked in shock. Her first thought—*Locker Lurker!*—quickly gave way, however, to a starstruck *Madalynn Sucret knows my name?*

"I saw that you signed up for set crew for my musical. You want to head over together?" Madalynn radiated such warmth that Sam only mildly registered the "my" part of "my musical."

"Did you write it?" Sam said dreamily, basking in the Madalynn campfire.

"You are so sweet," laughed Madalynn, slinging an arm around Sam's shoulder. "No, I'm not that smart," she continued with a wink that clearly said, *Yes, I am totally that smart.* "I think it's awesome that you're talented enough to build sets, especially since you're so pretty you should be *onstage*."

They were moving down the crowded hallway by this point, Madalynn's arm still around Sam, and students' mouths were dropping open in succession, like the wave at a sporting event. Sam would have been amused, but she barely noticed. It was as if her ears were radio-tuned to the Madalynn Channel—*sweettalentedpretty*—and everything else was white noise.

Until Jaida, of course.

She was coming out of the girls' bathroom—alone, for once. And Sam was walking with Madalynn Sucret, who was basically the equivalent of a platoon of popular middle school girls. So when Jaida stopped dead and stared at them, she suddenly appeared to Sam as a solitary figure that seemed a whole lot easier to topple.

"Now . . ." Madalynn's whisper broke the spell. Sam turned back to that incandescent smile. Seriously, it was like the girl brushed her teeth with plutonium. "About last night . . ."

Last night? Her heart started to thrum. They entered the auditorium, and Sam found herself seated crisscross applesauce on the floor in a dark corner with her brand-new bestie. "Whaaa . . . what do you mean?"

"Oh, come on," Madalynn crooned. "SleepWaker sisters can talk about anything, can't they?"

Sam felt her face flush at the same time her hands went icy cold. "I—you—that *was* you?"

"Well, of course. Listen, I'm not sure what the Spy told you, but I'd like to clear up a few things." Madalynn said this in a conspiratorial whisper.

Now Sam's entire body became an ice sculpture. *The Spy?* Madalynn could only mean—

"You know Byron is Joanne's son, right? He's assigned to every new Waker to spy for Fletcher," Madalynn continued. Then, as she noticed Sam's expression, her eyes widened. "You *didn't* know, did you? Oh, sweetie, I'm so sorry! I thought *everyone* was onto Byron. We call him 'By the Spy.'"

Sam was reeling, but desperately tried to get a toehold. "S'okay, I . . . kinda suspected," she lied, forcing a laugh. "He's way too hot to be anything but the bad guy, right?"

Now Madalynn's gaze narrowed. "Exactly. Figures he would be a Roamer. They're so selfish."

I don't want to know any more. Don't tell me any more. But Sam couldn't stop herself. "What are they, anyway? He never said."

"Who, the Roamers? Well, during the day, they're super-overscheduled perfectionists, so at night they just roam. Alone, not connected to anyone else, no leader. Selfish, right?" Madalynn's voice was cold, dismissive.

Something about this tickled Sam's thinker. Flashes of Byron helping her, encouraging her, watching out for her. *Was all of that fake?* If a Roamer couldn't help but be solitary and uncaring, how could he even summon the energy to be a spy? Didn't that mess up the whole theory about SleepWakers being their essential selves in the darkness?

She was roused out of her miserable mind flagellation by the sensation of hands on her head; Madalynn was massaging Sam's temples tenderly. *Wow. This is really . . . awkward.* But it was working. All of her wounded, confused thoughts started to drain out as Madalynn murmured consolingly, "Don't fret, Sleep Sis. Forget him."

Forget . . . just forget . . .

Wait a minute. She remembered something.

Sam pulled back from the hypnotic handling. "I saw you. With Kyra. What . . . what were you doing?"

Madalynn sighed sadly. "Oh, Kyra. Poor thing. Did you know her little brother has Asperger's?"

Sam nodded carefully.

"Well, my friend Bree—she's in our tribe—has a sister with special needs, too. We were trying to help Kyra figure out how to deal. Particularly with her parents, who just don't understand Kyra's side of things. Because that's what Dreams do."

"Dreams?"

"You probably heard us called something else, right?" Madalynn continued breezily. "Just another thing to thank the Spy for. He makes up all the tribe tags."

"I didn't make up all the tags." Sam felt sick. Had Byron lied to her about everything? Had he lied to her about the (Mean)Dreams? Who was telling the truth? Her head felt like it was going to explode.

Sam's brain bomb was going to have to wait, however, because just at that moment, Mr. Todorov, Wallace's excessively committed drama teacher, called from the stage, "Madalynn, dear, are you ready? We're doing the 'Queen Victoria awarding you with the Royal Red Cross' ballet."

Madalynn didn't miss a beat. "I'm just discussing the

construction of the Windsor Castle throne with the head of our set crew, Mr. Todorov. Have you met Sam Fife?"

"Oh my *Godspell*, it's a pleasure to meet you, Sam!" Todorov crowed.

"I'm the head of the set crew?!" Sam whispered to Madalynn in dismay.

"You *are* the set crew, so that automatically makes you the head, right?" Madalynn stood up and held out a hand. Sam took it slowly and rose to her feet, where she was enveloped in a Wonderstruck eau de parfum–ed hug. "No worries, Sleep Sis, you got this!"

Maybe it was Madalynn's confidence combined with the rubbed-off scent de Taylor Swift, or maybe just residual rage toward her former nighttime friend, "By the Spy," but suddenly Sam felt charged up. *I do got this.* And she didn't even care if her grammar was cringe-worthy enough for one of the Broadways' worst rap ballads.

✳ ✳ ✳

Two hours and one "how to build a throne" googling later, Sam stood back to admire her work. She still had to cover the seat in red velvet and gild the arms, but the structure was strong and the architecture solid; it looked . . . well, she was just going to go ahead and think it: *Majestic.* She heard a gasp behind her.

"Oh, Sam! It's gorgeous!" Madalynn cried. Sam turned to see the entire cast gathered behind her. "I just hope Queeny will let me sit in it," she added, smiling slyly at a skinny little girl who squeaked assent while trying valiantly to balance Queen Victoria's crown on her less-than-regal head.

Madalynn led everyone in a round of applause, including Mr. Todorov, who wiped tears from his eyes and shouted, "More *Beautiful* than the musical based on Carole King's life!"

"Oh . . . wow. Thanks," Sam said shyly, her face blazing. *Is this really happening?* She'd never had even one person look at her admiringly, much less a whole group.

Much less the enchantress of the eighth grade, she thought as Madalynn swept her into an arm link.

"Now . . . about tonight . . ." Madalynn whispered as she led Sam away.

"Tonight?" Sam murmured. Maybe Madalynn was going to invite her to dinner at her house. *I bet you have cloth napkins. Cloth napkins are so classy.* Jax always just threw a roll of paper towels on the table and Margie let Weezy lick any mess off her fingers—

"The Dreams are going to be in Fletch's sector. I want you to come meet us."

The entire SleepWaker world came rushing back to Sam in a freezing-cold tsunami of reality. She stumbled on the backstage stairs and would have fallen if Madalynn hadn't kept her arm locked in an iron BFF embrace.

"I know you're looking for your Sleep peeps, and I've got a good feeling about this. It's so obvious you've never been part of a group before, and I think it's because no one else has recognized your true potential. And that's so wrong. You need to belong." Madalynn moved her arm around Sam's waist. As Sam leaned gratefully into the support, it came to her in a flash: When was the last time anyone had touched her, other than for medical reasons? No wonder she went to sleep every night hanging on to poor Weezy for dear life. Madalynn continued with quite a remarkable statement: "I think *we're* what your soul has been searching for."

All at once, Sam was tired, weary beyond measure. Sure, her physical body was getting rest, but her emotions felt like they'd just completed an Ironman triathlon. And here was someone holding her up and promising her a tribe.

I do want to belong. Somewhere.

"Where do you want me to meet you?"

ten

NOT THAT SAM BELIEVED IN SIGNS, but when her soul woke up hiding behind her off-season clothes in the very back of the closet, it did not bode well for the night's activities. And apparently, even one's consciousness could have an attack of claustrophobia; she frantically tried to escape the suffocating darkness by pushing aside her winter coat, but only succeeded in falling through the polyester filling and fake fur trim, then passing through her long underwear and snow pants, then through all her in-season clothes, and finally, right through the closet door. The cheap plywood must have slowed her down slightly, because she managed to avoid a face-plant outside the closet and stood wobbling and waving like a pussy willow in a stiff wind.

Sam looked around nervously; no Byron morphing into her bedroom, thank goodness. She had to get out to her "appointment" without running into him, but how that might happen she just didn't know. Could he sense when her soul detached? Is that why he always showed up right on time? Or was he just floating around outside waiting for her? Both possibilities made her insides icky.

As she crept around the bed, she noticed that Sleeping Sam had a stranglehold on Weezy's fat neck. *Pathetic much? Exactly why I need to find my tribe.* The thought gave her new purpose and she march-hovered toward the window and looked out boldly. She didn't see any soul hottie spying on her house, but she had to be sure. Taking a breath, she pushed her face through, just as far as her ears. Having a pane of glass slicing her head in half was a bizarre experience, to say the least; like some low-rent version of a magician's assistant being sawed apart in a box. She peeked carefully to the right, then to the left, then down—

"Hey there." Byron was sitting underneath the window, at one with a shrub.

"Arrrrggghhh!" Sam jumped, her head sliding back into the house. She angrily jammed her face back through the glass. "Don't *do* that!"

Byron hopped up, unfazed. "Well, you told me not to just show up in your bedroom, didn't you?"

"Why did you show up at all? You're like a sleep-stalker!" Sam forced her whole body out and stood on the lawn, her mist arms crossed angrily.

"Whoa. Did somebody detach on the wrong side of the bed?" Byron put his hands up in mock surrender. "What happened after you got silver-cord-snapped last night? Couldn't fall asleep again?"

"No, I couldn't. *Obviously.* Otherwise, I would have come back."

"Well, I'm kinda glad you didn't. Pretty crazy, you know, jumping out at the MeanDreams like that." Byron shook his head.

You mean the "Dreams," By the Spy? Of course, she didn't say that out loud. "Listen . . . I want to be by myself tonight." She couldn't look him in the eye.

"Uh . . . really? I'm not sure you're ready for that." Byron was suddenly cautious and tentative. "How about I tag along one more time? You know, just until you got the hang of . . . everything."

"What, like being solid? Don't hold your breath," Sam snapped. "I'll be fine. I just want to be alone."

Byron became very still. "Something happened. What happened?"

"Nothing! Nothing happened. I just . . . don't like being spied on, okay?" She forced it out, looking at his face, suddenly, fervently hoping he would be blank, lost, like, *"What the heck are you talking about, Sam?"*

But Byron's trapped expression confirmed everything Madalynn had said about him, and her heart sank. He stammered, "Wait . . . what? Spied? Who—?"

"Forget it. Thanks for the laughs, dude. See ya." Sam turned and started off, angry at herself for hoping.

Byron wasn't about to give up, however. "No!" He zoomed next to her and kept pace, misting through rosebushes, streetlamps, and a Mini Cooper without so much as a pause. "You can't be alone yet! You're not ready!"

Enraged, Sam whirled around, catching Byron halfway through a public mailbox on the corner. "Joanne is your mom! You've been lying to me this whole time!"

"I did not lie!" He extracted himself, accidentally knocking a bunch of letters through the mail slot onto the ground, which only made Sam madder. *He gets to be solid even when he's not trying!* "Did you ever ask me if I was her son? No. So, I didn't lie."

"Technicality!" Sam shouted.

"Who told you, anyway? That's the important thing here." For the first time, Byron reached out and grabbed her.

Well, tried to, anyway; he settled for his hands floating in the general vicinity of her shoulders. "I'm serious, Sam. Was it that Juvenold Alyssa? I know she's at your school."

"In case you forgot, Alyssa made it clear that she would pretend I didn't exist during the day. Just like everyone else does." Sam meant that to sound defiant, but unfortunately her voice quavered. She steeled herself. "Everyone except Madalynn. Which is why I'm going to meet up with the Dreams and see if they're my tribe."

It didn't exactly have the effect she was hoping for. Byron didn't gasp. He didn't faint. He didn't wail "Oh nooo!" He just looked at her harder. And then said, softly, "They're not."

They stayed that way, staring at each other, for what seemed like an eternity, but it was SleepWaker time, so probably more like ten seconds. "How do you know?" Sam finally asked.

"Because I know who you were as a sleepwalker. I know the things you did. Like decorating synagogues and building tree houses for strangers. You are not a MeanDream. You are . . . something else entirely." His face got nearer and nearer to hers as he spoke. "I don't even know if there *is* a tribe out there that's yours. Not yet, anyway." Their noses were now so close that an ill-timed sneeze could be lethal.

"Byron . . . ?" She could barely breathe.

"Yes?" From the sound of it, neither could he.

"Byron . . ." She sucked in as much air as she could manage.

"Sam . . ."

"DID YOU READ MY CHART?!" Sam shouted so loud it literally blew Byron's hair back. "SERIOUSLY, DUDE, HAVE YOU EVER HEARD OF DOCTOR-PATIENT CONFIDENTIALITY?"

"I think you busted my eardrum." Byron shook his head dazedly, opening his jaw and closing it to reset his entire auditory system. "Is that possible if you don't have a body?"

"YOU . . . YOU *SPY*! YOU . . . PERSONAL-MEDICAL-RECORDS-READING . . . UH . . . SNEAKY JERK!" She was beside herself, pummeling him right through his mist body.

"Sam, come on! Listen to me!" He tried to catch her hands, but they were too fast and too insubstantial.

Suddenly there was the sound of fingers snapping in rhythm all around them.

"No! NO!" Byron yelled. "Not a good time, guys!"

The Broadways swooped in, dancing a vaguely *In the Heights*–ish snapping-and-leaping ballet. The ginormous red-headed Chadney sang lead in a rousing baritone.

Byron and Sam sittin' in a tree
F-I-G-H-T-I-N-G!
First comes attraction, then sensation
then a classic lack of communication
While the silver cord glistens
the lovers don't listen
The world falls apart while they're busy dissin'
There's evil afoot, which they'll never overthrow
'Cause they got too much baggage in their portmanteau!

Sam took a brief break from her rage. "What the heck is a portmanteau?"

Byron sighed. "Not a clue."

As the Broadways grapevine-circled Byron, Sam wheeled around and took off, her misty legs pounding through space, her pumping arms gliding through lawn decorations, the protruding branches of untrimmed bushes, and the prominent sideview mirror of a Subaru Outback. All she wanted was to put as much distance as she could between her and the Spy. *Who's not even following you, BTW.*

"Who cares?" Sam growled at her persistent inner voice. *And whose soul breath smelled like spearmint.* "Shut *up*, brain!" she yelled, pushing her Waker body harder. How the heck were you supposed to reach hyper-cross? 'Cause right now, she was at best doing the pace of Jax's Darkstar, and skateboard speed was just not cutting it.

She gritted it out, moving down a street lined with closed shops, and avoiding a potential Later Zone by taking a turn across a construction site. The levels of a half-finished parking garage stared at her with a multitude of dark, empty eyes. An orange sign warned her to watch for falling objects, which seemed like a bad joke since an entire building could fall on her un-solid body without causing damage. Sam paused for a moment, looking back to make sure Byron still wasn't following her. Which he wasn't. Which she was totally glad about. Totally. And after she craned her neck and stared in every direction for a while, he *still* wasn't following her and she was *still* totally glad about it. Totally. *Oh, just move, idiot!*

On the other side of the construction, Sam paused again, uneasy. *Is this right?* She briefly wished for some kind of Waker GPS system, because the streets were unfamiliar and not particularly inviting; a boarded-up diner scrawled with graffiti was the unwelcoming wagon and the rest of the landscape was littered with overgrown lawns, vacant lots, and houses seemingly on the verge of collapse. There had to be some mistake; why would the Dreams want to meet here?

"Hey, Sleep Sis," crooned a familiar voice. "You made it."

Sam turned slowly. Madalynn hovered at the front of a

large group of SleepWakers in various types of pajamas. Even though Sam was jittery and not nearly as relieved as she'd hoped to see her new bestie, she couldn't help but notice just how drop-dead gorgeous Madalynn was, even in the middle of the night. She wore a flowy blush-pink dressing gown and a satin sleep mask with embroidered eyelashes, pushed up sassily on her forehead to hold back her perfect flaxen curls. Seriously, how does someone look that good rolling out of bed, even if it's just your essence that rolled out? Life was so unfair.

"Hey, Madalynn." Sam tried to sound casual, as if meeting up with a bunch of detached consciousnesses in a run-down neighborhood in the dead of night was a normal occurrence. "Yeah, I made it!" She gave a thumbs-up and then silently cursed herself for being a geek in her soul as well as in her body. When the heck was she going to achieve her opposite self—you know, the cool one?

"Wonderful. Let me introduce you. This is Zac and Bree, my two right arms." Madalynn giggled at her joke as she gestured to the rather enormous SleepWakers flanking her on either side. Zac had a most peculiar shape; he looked like a human bullet, one continuous curved line from his shaved head to his sloping shoulders, wide body, and enormous feet. Bree was nearly as tall and just, well . . . *beige*. Her hair, face, and lips were beige, and she wore a faded, pale nightgown. She reminded Sam of a crayon color she'd had as a kid called "Saw Dust."

"Hi, Zac. Bree." She gave a little wave and a smile.

"So you think you're Dreams material, huh? We'll see." Bree looked Sam up and down with sallow eyes, then smiled back, showing pointed and, yes, beige, teeth.

"Oh . . . uh—" Sam didn't know how to respond to this aggressive personality that seemed in such contrast to Bree's remarkable colorlessness.

"Bree is very protective of our tribe. Loyal, you know?" Madalynn scrunched her nose adorably. "Isn't loyalty just the best thing *ever*?"

Zac, meanwhile, had begun administering rather strenuous noogies to various members of the group while braying, "Dutch rub! Get yer Dutch rub!" Sam thought she heard some groans of protest, but not according to Madalynn.

"I love how much fun they all have together!" Madalynn twittered, then threw her arms out wide. "Sam, meet your new tribe, the Dreams!"

"Nice to meet you guys!" Sam said. Her words were met with complete silence from the tribe. "Um . . . do they talk?"

"When it's deemed necessary," Madalynn stated evenly. Then, seeing Sam's startled face, she burst out laughing. "JK! We're just messing with you, Sam. You know, playing off that 'Mean' Dreams thing." She tossed this off to the group: "Right, guys?"

As if Madalynn had flipped a switch, the Dreams chanted together, "Messing with you, Sam!" then uttered one barking laugh in complete unison, and went dead silent again. *What the—?*

"Amazing, right?" Madalynn beamed. "They have such a strong bond, it's almost like they're one person."

"Yeah, they're so, uh . . . in sync. . . ." Sam peered into the group, and for reals, it was hard to tell one Waker from another; they just sort of blended. Except for Bree and Zac, of course. And one rather familiar-looking girl in red flannel pajamas.

"Kyra?!" Sam exclaimed.

The (former?) Numb was on the periphery of the tribe, slightly removed from the glut of bodies. She looked up at the sound of her name.

"It's me, Sam. I met you last night at Galloping Ghost, remember?" Sam moved closer. Bree and Zac also took a step forward, then stopped.

"Nightmare in the Dark," said Kyra, and smiled.

"Yeah, right, your game." Sam nodded. *She looks fine. Which kinda sucks.* Not that she wished Kyra ill, but it meant that Madalynn had been telling the truth, and Byron—

Almost as if she'd read Sam's mind, Kyra said, "I'm better here." Another smile, bigger this time. "This is better than a game. This is real. Thank you, Dreams."

"You're more than welcome, sweetie!" Madalynn gushed.

Zac lunged at Kyra and noogied her vehemently; her face disappeared into the crook of his beefy arm.

"Zac, dear. Un-noogie her, please," Madalynn purred. "Kyra's not used to your affectionate gestures yet." Zac obediently released Kyra, then turned and gave one of the other protesting Dreams an atomic wedgie.

"Zac." Now Madalynn had a bit more edge in her voice. "Soul hands to yourself, honey. Remember what we talked about." Zac looked crestfallen but nodded his bullet head.

"Such a sweet boy, really," Madalynn stage-whispered to Sam. "During the day, he's not allowed to have tactile contact with anyone, legally speaking, so he can get a bit carried away at night. Anyhoo! Let's get a move on, shall we?" She smoothly took charge, gliding forward. Sam wanted to talk to Kyra more, but she also didn't want to lose track of Madalynn as they burrowed deeper into the scaryhood, so she followed.

"Hey, uh, where are we going? I thought I was just meeting the tribe tonight," Sam questioned, casting a glance back at the group trailing them. Bree's dreary nightgown rippled behind her like wings; she resembled a bleached Batgirl.

"This is *how* you meet the tribe, Sam." Madalynn just kept moving, gracefully but with an underlying sense of urgency and purpose. "By understanding what the Dreams are about."

Are they about mowing dead lawns and stealing flat tires off rusty bikes? If not, Sam couldn't conceive of why they were here. Behind her, she heard Zac grunt, "Hey, you want a hertz doughnut?" then the sound of someone being punched, and a chortled *"Hurts, don't it?!"*

A few dismal blocks later, Madalynn stopped abruptly and Sam had to backpedal a bit. They were in front of a dark, ramshackle house in need of a serious paint job. A delighted smile spread across Madalynn's face as she pointed to one of the dirty windows. "Here we are! Take a peek, darlin'."

Despite Madalynn's perky tone, or maybe because of it, Sam was suddenly gripped with terror. The last time she remembered feeling such pee-inducing dread was when Jax took her to Hangman's House of Horrors on one of his torturous Halloween outings. But surely a noose-wielding zombie was not going to pop out of *this* window, because hey, this was her tribe, right? And your tribe might haze you a bit just to see what kinda stuff you're made of, but they don't make you wet yourself and then string you up from a sagging awning, right? *Right. Right.*

It was a bedroom, as far as she could tell in the dimness,

sparsely furnished and drab. Sam could see the lumpy bottom half of a bed, but the top half was hidden behind a smudge of God-knows-what on the filthy window. She shimmied sideways and floated up on her tiptoes. A figure was under the blanket and turned away from view, but even so, a pang of familiarity coursed through Sam's soul body. In the split second before the girl flipped over in her sleep and confirmed her identity, Sam already knew.

Jaida. Sound asleep, with an unfamiliar soft slackness to her face, but there was no mistaking her. Sam was peering into the lair of the enemy.

"Surprise . . ." Madalynn cooed behind her.

eleven

SAM STUMBLED BACKWARD, nearly invading Madalynn's personal soul space by accidental osmosis.

"Why are we here?" It came out angrier than she'd intended, but suddenly this felt like a colossal practical joke, like Sam was on some celestial hidden-camera show and all the SleepWakers were hanging out in front of a cosmic screen somewhere, having a good laugh together at her expense.

Madalynn spoke evenly, softly. "We're here because this is what the Dreams do. We make things right. We make them even. We use the darkness to avenge the wrongdoing of the light."

"Whoa. Deep," Zac grunted.

"Yes, it is deep, Zac," Madalynn agreed. "Now go stand over there." She pointed and Zac lumbered away obediently.

"Wait . . . so your tribe is about revenge?" Sam was trying to process, but everything about this night was overwhelming her brain.

Madalynn's voice was a warm bath brimming with emotional Epsom salts. "Oh, Sam. Not *re*-venge. *A*-venge. A common mistake. All the Dreams want is to see justice done. We don't want to hurt anyone . . ." She took just the slightest intermission, just a hiccup really, before continuing, ". . . without cause." She let out a heavy sigh and then, conveying all the angsty responsibility of being a highly attractive judge and jury, added, "Unlike Jaida, who went after you from, like, day one, for absolutely no reason."

Absolutely no reason.

As she had done so many times before, Sam pressed "play" on her mental highlight reel of encounters with Jaida, forcing her mind to reconstruct the scenes with as little revisionist history as possible, trying to find the source of Jaida's hatred. And as always, she came up with nothing.

Absolutely no reason.

Sam couldn't even remember the first time they'd met, or interacted, or looked slantways in each other's general direction, that's how *blah* day one must have been. But every day since was the same mental movie: Jaida taunting her, Jaida pranking her, Jaida sitting in the cafeteria, not eating, just staring at Sam to intimidate her. Jaida swooping in like a preteen vulture while Sam tried to play dead, constantly forgetting that death was the most tempting smell of all.

"It's just so unfair, isn't it?" Madalynn circled Sam in a smooth loop, tossing out her diamond-sharp questions as she glided along. "Don't you want her to feel like you did? Like you still do? Don't you want her to know what it's like to be attacked for absolutely no reason? Wouldn't that open her eyes? Wouldn't that actually *help* her?"

Now Sam was breathing hard, tingles rippling through her soul body. *Help her.* This was it. *Justice.* This was the answer. *Make it even.* Finally. *This is my tribe.*

"What do I need to do?"

Her reward was the most luminous smile she'd ever seen on Madalynn's face, and that was saying something. "Well, that's what we're about to tell you, Sam. And that's why we're called the Dreams. Because we make them come true."

Despite herself, Sam winced. That statement was painfully cornball, but she wasn't about to let it throw her off track. She had a mission now.

"So. Jaida and her . . ." Madalynn took that smidgen of a

pause again. ". . . friends . . . have a secret meeting place at school, where I'm assuming they go to plan their little cruelties. And I happen to know where it is."

"How?" Sam whispered, impressed.

Madalynn gave her a "really?" look. *Oh, right.* This was the Queen Goddess of Wallace Junior High. Some adoring maintenance worker had probably filled her in.

"You're going to go and gather some intel for us, Sam. Daytime information that will help us set our nighttime strategy."

Sam gulped. "You mean . . . spy?" This made her think of Byron, and her mist heart did a flip and sink. Why was Madalynn asking her to do the exact same thing she had criticized the Roamer for?

"Sam, when justice is being served, it's not called spying, it's called surveillance. All you'll be doing is listening for the weaknesses in their nasty little bond so that we'll know how to use them to our advantage. In the spirit of fairness, our goal is to do to Jaida exactly what she's done to . . ." And there was that interesting mini silence again, this time accompanied by the briefest appearance of Madalynn's pretty pink tongue as she licked her lips. ". . . *you.* She made sure you were blackballed. She made sure you were friendless. And that's exactly what's going to happen to her. It's called recompense."

"Recompense," a voice echoed. Bree had crept up behind

them and was now towering over Sam like an overgrown corn husk that had been left baking in the sun too long.

"Bree understands that word. Don't you, Bree?" Madalynn sounded downright maternal. "All those people who made you feel invisible in the daytime. We adjusted their eyesight, didn't we?"

"They got recompensed," Bree snarled. That word was making Sam a little uneasy. But at the same time, she couldn't help feeling some pity for the beige behemoth who was now staring longingly at Madalynn's vibrant pink dressing gown as if it represented all her hopes and dreams.

Madalynn smiled. "Don't worry, Sam, you'll do more than monitor, of course. You'll be a big part of the nighttime avengement, too. We wouldn't take that away from you."

Sam grimaced. *Busted.* She spit out her confession as quickly as possible: "But I don't know how to be solid yet."

Madalynn dismissed Sam's revelation with a wave of her misty hand. "No worries. You'll be solid when you need to be. It always happens at just the right time."

"Are you sure? Because Byr—uh, somebody told me that the only way to be solid is to believe in the weight and possibilities of your soul."

"Really? Interesting." Madalynn shrugged, then winked at Sam. "Well, if that's true, you're in luck. 'Cause nothing weighs down a soul like payback."

It was already light out, but Sam was still pace-hovering by the bed, where her body slept peacefully. Weezy seemed to be getting used to seeing her in two different places; he glanced back and forth between the Sams with a resigned expression on his pancaked snout.

"Don't look at me like that," Sam grumbled. "You're just a dog; you don't know what it's like out there in the real world." Weezy did a head tilt, which made Sam realize she must be whining. "Oh, come on! Jaida's been torturing me for months! It's not right!" Weezy snorfled, a common pug noise that Sam was suddenly taking very personally. "Fine! Be like that! I don't need your approval! I know what I'm doing!"

"Honey?" Her mother's voice came from outside the bedroom door, and Soul Sam snapped back into her waking body like a retractable measuring tape. She groaned.

I seriously will never get used to that.

Margie stuck her head in. "Morning! So, guess what? Slight change of plans today. You're not going to school, you're having a follow-up with Dr. Fletcher. I already okayed it with the principal—"

"What?" This news shocked Sam out of her funk, and her reunited selves sat straight up in bed. "Why? What does he want to see me for?"

Margie looked startled. "Oh! I don't know, exactly, but it must be important because he called at five a.m.—"

"No! No way. I'm not going! I'm—I'm sick!" Sam burbled.

"Oh no, what's wrong, sweetheart? Do you have a fever?" Margie hustled over and did that Mom-thermometer thing, pressing her lips to Sam's forehead.

Sam started praying, *Please be fire-hot, please be at least 106 degrees, except, no, I have to go to school today because I'm supposed to be gathering intel on Jaida, ohhhhhh, please get me out of this, Fletch knows, I know he knows, I know he knows I met with the Dreams because By the Spy ratted me out—*

And that's when Sam saw it: the fine patch of fuzz in Margie's bald spot. The evidence of four full days without a trichotillomania episode, the stubble of relief and deep sleep, the bristles of refreshment and renewal.

The regrowth that was going to guilt Sam into a follow-up appointment with a maniac sleep doctor and his assistant, Mole Mother.

✳   ✳   ✳

Dr. Fletcher was waiting at the door to the clinic when Margie dropped her off, bouncing nervously on the balls of his feet. "By St. Dymphna, you made it! Wonderful! How do you feel? Did you eat? I can have Jo run over to the Seven-Eleven and get you a muffin! Or we have some granola bars from the Super Dollar close-out that are only just expired and still quite tasty!"

Jeez, Fletch, did you take a bath in coffee this morning? It wasn't until Sam had turned down the toxic breakfast offer and was safely inside the dimly lit office that she realized the real reason he was motormouthing.

Joanne was there, but there were also four new faces gazing at her apprehensively.

"Yes, well, you're probably wondering what's going on and who all these people are and why I called you in and took you out of school and what we're going to ask you," prattled Fletch. "Sam . . . meet the *SSSS.*" He said it like a snake hiss, gesturing grandly to the four strangers sitting in a semicircle.

Sam was pretty well flummoxed, but she made an attempt. "The . . . *sssssssss?*"

"No, the *SSSS.*" Fletch chuckled at her mistake.

Seriously, dude, I'm making the same sound you are. It was a little early in the day to feel this annoyed.

She was rescued by a handsome elderly gentleman wearing glasses with greenish-tinted lenses. "It's our code name, Samantha. The S-S-S-S." Green Glasses Guy said the letters separately, followed by a somewhat weary sigh. "Dr. Fletcher feels that an acronym just isn't clandestine enough."

"And he's right! Our work is too important to be upended by a clumsy cryptograph!" This from a middle-aged man who was chewing gum so strenuously, his jaw muscles should have been rocking a six-pack.

"I really think we're fine," said a kind-faced woman shyly, pushing back her hair with a wrist full of extremely jingly bracelets. "Who in the world could figure out that S.S.S.S. stands for 'Secret Society of Sweet Sleep'?"

"Well, *someone* has, obviously." Delivered dramatically by a heavyset man with a lumberjack beard, the statement threw the room into a bit of an uproar.

"We don't know that," chided Green Glasses Guy.

"It's the only logical explanation!" barked Gum Man.

"Let's not jump to conclusions," soothed Bracelet Lady.

"We *should* jump to conclusions! All of us, jump, now!" thundered Lumberjack Beard.

As usual, it was Joanne who took control of the room. "SSSS! Shhh!" she hiss-hushed. "You're scaring Samantha."

Necks snapped as the S.S.S.S. turned to look at Sam. "I don't know," mused Green Glasses. "I think she looks more angry than scared."

"That can't be right," Fletcher said, peering into her face with his oblivious sclerae. "Why would she be mad?"

"For real? Why would *she* be mad?" Sam was outraged. "Okay, let's see. How about you talking about me in the third person like I'm not even here, dragging me in for a 'follow-up' with a room full of people I don't know, who are yelling about stuff I don't understand, *and*"—she pointed at Joanne—"siccing her hunky son on me!"

Joanne's stern face melted into a goofy smile. "He *is* good-looking, isn't he? Takes after his father."

"Yeah, a good-looking *snoop*!" Sam cried. "Why are you spying on me, anyway?! I didn't ask to have my soul cut loose, so I'm probably not gonna be out there plotting an evil takeover of the world!"

"No, Sam, you're not. But you've put yourself in league with someone who might be." Bracelet Lady stated this so directly and yet so gently that it had the effect of shutting Sam right the heck up. She gawked at Bracelets, unable to complete her rant.

"This is Dr. Karen Hopkins, Samantha," said Fletcher, and then—Sam would have sworn it—*he blushed*. "From Bismarck, North Dakota, sector of the Clutch, and a very fine polysomnographist. One of the best, really."

"Oh, you're too generous, Dr. Fletcher." Sure enough, Dr. Hopkins also turned as red as an heirloom tomato. "I can't hold a candle to your circadian rhythm research!"

Sorry to interrupt your parasomnia sweet talk, but— "What's the Clutch?" Sam really wanted to know, but she also wanted to steer the conversation away from the topic of just who might be planning to take over the world, since she already had an uneasy inkling.

"The tribe that seems to have mysteriously gravitated to my sector," said Dr. Hopkins, attempting to nonchalantly cool her burning face by pressing the metal of her approximately twenty-five noisy manacles against her cheeks. "During the day, they're loners and keep to themselves, but their Waker souls desperately want to be in relationship; they spend the whole night hugging and talking and trying to make emotional contact." She peeked at Fletch and then ducked her head shyly.

Hmmm, wonder why they're drawn to you, Doc. Sam's inner sarcasm seemed to have backup in Gum Guy's barely audible mumble "Yeah, big mystery."

"That's Dr. Gopal Madhav, guardian of the Pranks and the Numbs," Dr. Fletcher said pointedly at Gum Guy, who waved as he jammed another piece of Hubba Bubba in his mouth. "Dr. Joseph Thomas, New York City, keeper of the Broadways." Fletch gestured to Lumberjack, who was gloomily stroking his massive beard into a sharp point. "And my mentor, overseer of the Roamers and the Extremes in New Rochelle, and foremost expert on the silver cord, although nobody knows it because we are a *secret* society after all . . . Dr. Richard Knavish." Fletcher beamed at Green Glasses Guy, who received the praise with a gracious nod. "And we called this special *SSSS* meeting because we have reason to believe, Samantha, that you've fallen in with a dangerous element."

Sam only had a split second to decide if she was going to play dumb or play defense; she settled for "neutral silence." Which immediately backfired.

"See? She admits it!" cried Dr. Thomas, trembling with indignation.

"Admits what? I didn't say anything!" Sam responded angrily.

"Joseph, calm down," said Fletch. He gently took Sam's shoulders in his hands and spoke softly. "Samantha, listen. I know you're a loyal person. But we feel the need to tell you that the MeanDreams are not what you think, and Madalynn Sucret, while being a very lovely girl, is also Satan's handmaiden."

"Oh, come on!" Sam wriggled away in exasperation.

"You may have hit that a little hard," Dr. Hopkins murmured to Fletch.

"You think?" Fletch murmured back.

"Why are you bashing Madalynn? She's been, like, my only friend," Sam said with the vehemence that comes from trying to convince oneself of a shaky truth. "And what the *Dreams* are doing isn't dangerous, it's just—just—" She couldn't really find the word, but she knew it was in her head somewhere and it was just going to be soooo, *uh, definite. No, definitive! Yeah!*

Dr. Knavish had been silent so far, even yawning at one point, but now he leaned in and said with relish, "You see, everyone? There it is. If a *Helper* can be swayed, then *any* SleepWaker can. There's no nefarious physician out there detaching the enemy! The enemy is within. It always has been."

"What?" Sam was more confused than ever, and also a bit terrified; she wasn't sure what "nefarious" meant, but it sounded pretty darn dastardly. "What's a Helper? And who's the enemy?"

Dr. Mahdhav stood up and removed his gum for emphasis. "With all due respect, Richard, that is bogus bullhockey. We have a running tally of the souls we've detached and the numbers just don't add up! There is a devious detaching doctor out there and we all know it!"

"'Devious detaching' . . . are you people serious?" Sam's voice had risen to a hysteria octave. She grabbed the handset of Fletcher's rotary phone and held it up by the spiraling cord, the blaring dial tone adding to the drama. "Somebody better explain exactly what's going on or I swear I'm calling the cops! Or, or, the FBI! Or, like, the AASM!"

"NO!" The doctors all yelled simultaneously; apparently, the American Academy of Sleep Medicine was a far more serious threat than the feds.

Dr. Hopkins stood and carefully removed the phone from Sam's kung fu grip. "Samantha . . . I know how overwhelming all of this must be. And we'll get to the topic of the, uh, devious detaching doctor." She snuck a mildly disapproving look at Madhav, who defiantly stuck his gum back in his mouth and commenced mastication. "But first and foremost, you must trust that Dr. Fletcher is deeply committed to the happiness and well-being of his patients, of all sleepwalkers, actually. That's why the S.S.S.S. even exists. He reached out to each one of us at great personal and professional risk because he could recognize that we cared deeply, as well."

"So . . . what? He taught all of you how to split kids in two?" Sam said.

"In a way," Dr. Hopkins continued with a small smile. "But to be honest, we're still not completely sure why it works for us and not for others."

"Others? You mean other doctors?" Sam turned to Fletcher. "Dude, how many people did you try to recruit?"

"Only the ones I thought would be able to handle the responsibility. It was safe, though. I merely, well, *advised* them on methods for the sleep studies of their most challenging cases. Then if their patients' souls detached, I could ease the doctors gently into the *SSSS*. If not . . . well . . ." Fletcher's face darkened.

Dr. Hopkins got a bit misty-eyed. "Dr. Fletcher tried to help by intervening with the suffering children who *didn't* detach. For his troubles, he was accused of trying to steal patients and banished from the AASM."

Dr. Thomas chimed in, "But he found the four of us. And we've been able to help so many."

Dr. Mahdhav chewed out, "This is all very heartwarming, but we need to tell Sam the rest, the part that's not quite so *kumbaya*."

Fletch moaned and dropped his head into his hands. "Foolish! I'm so foolish! I should have trusted my theory, trusted my instincts!"

"What's he griping about?" Sam didn't want to feel sorry for Fletcher, but she did, which was super annoying and inconvenient.

Dr. Hopkins awkwardly patted him on the shoulder and said with great solemnity, "He detached Madalynn Sucret." The rest of the S.S.S.S. sighed deeply, and Fletch moaned again.

"Yeah? So what?" Sam barked defensively, not really wanting to know so what.

"Everything about her sleepwalking episodes warned me, but I was taken in by her angelic daytime demeanor! I think she hypnotized me!" yelped Fletch.

You and everyone else, Sam thought, and immediately felt like a BadFF. "What was so terrible about her sleepwalking? I mean, I did some crazy stuff, too—"

But the members of the S.S.S.S. were already shaking their heads. "She was destructive, Samantha. Driven." Dr. Hopkins pressed on. "She would sleepwalk halfway across town, and her parents would always find her in the same place, trying to break into someone's house."

Sam's heart started drumming so loudly, it felt like it had relocated to her ears. She had a sneaking suspicion if she asked *Whose house?* she was not going to like the answer. Instead she protested, "Big deal! I broke into a *synagogue,* people!"

Joanne was grim. "Trust me, Madalynn was not trying to get into that home to light a menorah."

"I should have known!" wailed Fletcher.

"It could have happened to any of us, Fletch," Dr. Thomas said gruffly. "At least we know now and we've taken the pledge."

"Yeah, and a big fat lot of good it's done us," grumbled Madhav.

Dr. Hopkins explained, "The S.S.S.S took a pledge not to

detach anyone who exhibited anything aggressive or antisocial in their sleepwalking."

Madhav chomped furiously. "And yet the MeanDreams tribe keeps growing!"

"I told you, Gopal, she is infiltrating the other tribes and gathering SleepWakers to her cause," counseled Knavish. "We all know how manipulative Madalynn can be." He gave Sam a sideways glance. "Did you see any Wakers from other tribes who seem to have been coerced into joining the MeanDreams?"

The image of a girl in red flannel pajamas immediately popped into Sam's mind. *No! Kyra wanted to be there! She said it was better!* Sam crossed her arms over her chest and pressed her lips together.

Fletch sighed. "Loyal . . ." he mumbled to himself.

Madhav was still on a roll. "I'm going to say it one last time, the numbers are off! Mad Madalynn might be soulnapping, but I'm telling you, we *also* have a rogue doc out there who's releasing teenybopper misanthropes into the night!"

Misanthropes? Dr. Hopkins intercepted Sam's perplexed look. "Haters," she said, with a jangle of bangles for emphasis. "Just a fancy way of saying 'bullies.'"

That word again. Rage filled Sam's breakfastless stomach with heat.

"Okay, I think we're done here. Usually I'm not one of those kids who's like, 'Oh, you're old, you don't understand my generation,' but I'll tell you one thing: I know bullies. Let's just say I know them personally, 'kay? Bullies start fights for *absolutely no reason* and pick on people who haven't done anything to deserve it. That's not Madalynn and it's not the Dreams. They have reasons, and I have reasons, and my soul, or SleepWaker Sam, or whatever you want to call that thing I am at night, is doing what it needs to do to fix stuff for the daytime me. None of you are out there, so you don't really get it. So back off. Because *I've found my tribe.*"

The tension in the room was so thick, you couldn't have cut it with a full-tang ninja sword. Then Dr. Hopkins, a hand placed over her bracelets for maximum quiet, spoke in her devastatingly gentle voice:

"If that's true, then why haven't you been able to be solid yet?"

The flame in Sam's gut was extinguished so quickly, it was as if a bucket of sand had been poured down her throat. She wheeled around and hightailed it out of the office, blinking back tears.

Well, this is ironic.

If Byron's theory were right, tonight she probably *would* be able to become solid. Because her soul had never felt heavier.

* * *

By some miracle, the security desk was empty when Sam arrived at school, which was a major relief. The formidable security guard, Claudia, who was known for her salty catchphrase of "Are you flyin' on me?" was not someone Sam was up for tangling with this morning. She slipped past the desk and tore down the hallway, certain she was going to hear an "Are you flyin' on me, comin' in without a late pass?" over her shoulder at any minute. Somehow, she made it to the rear stairwell and paused inside briefly, waiting until her heart slowed down a fraction before attempting the steep stairs to the fourth floor.

Madalynn had told her exactly where the old faculty restroom was, thankfully, because Sam couldn't remember ever having been on the fourth floor of Wallace. Left over from a time when the school population had been bigger, and students and teachers were not as lazy and would actually climb four flights of stairs, it was now mostly locked up and used for storage. She recalled that for a brief period, the Banana Splits support group had met up here, but eventually it was decided that kids with divorced parents felt isolated enough, so gathering in a dusty, abandoned science lab was probably not the best thing for their mental health.

Sam scooted down the eerily silent hallway to the

farthermost corner, stopping in front of a door upon which some former class clown had done a bit of scraping, so that the *Faculty* sign now read *Fa tty*, the extra *t* having been added in with a Sharpie. As Madalynn had promised, the lock was broken, and Sam dashed inside, briefly turning on the light to get her bearings.

It was every bit as disgusting as she'd expected a long-abandoned, tightly sealed, windowless bathroom-to-be.

Don't puke, don't you dare puke, Sam ordered herself.

Swallowing back the bile rising in her throat, she quickly took note of the double bathroom stall, taped shut with an *Out of Order* sign, then turned off the light, plunging herself into utter blackness. She felt her way over to the stall, took a shuddering breath, and crawled under the partition—*don't think about your hands touching the floor, oh God, don't think about your hands touching the toilet*—and stood up quickly inside the stall.

Okay. Breathe. She had survived the initial launch into intel gathering. If Madalynn's calculations were correct, within the next twenty minutes, Jaida and her band of brats would be cutting gym class and entering this exceedingly smelly room to plot out their next evil plan.

It was the perfect location, since their deeds stunk to high heaven. Sam wallowed in her righteous indignation for a good few minutes; it helped to quiet the sneaking suspicion that what she was doing right now was not a whole lot better than the crap Jaida pulled every day. And even though Margie had gotten her excused from school for the morning, it had been for "medical" reasons, not "vengeance" ones.

When she finally heard the giggles and fumblings at the door, Sam started trembling like a poodle in a pen full of pit bulls. She quickly climbed up on the commode and braced herself, but the sudden brightness of the light and the nearness of her enemy was so overwhelming, she almost pitched off her precarious perch right into the putrid potty.

"Don't be an idiot, we can't do that one unless we break into her house." Sam immediately recognized Gina's voice.

"Yeah, but my sister knows her brother, so we could probably work it out." That sounded like Amy, but— *Wait. Are they talking about me? They want to break into my house?* Now Sam was shaking so hard, she was certain the stall was vibrating. If only she could have done this in her insubstantial soul body instead of her quaky physical one!

"Oh, that makes sense." This sarcasm was definitely Jaida's. "We're gonna tell Daisy's brother that we want the keys to their house so we can get in to mess with her. Super smart."

Daisy? The same Daisy from the bubble tea shop? What had she done to piss off Jaida's posse?

"Oh. Right." Amy again, sheepish now. "Too bad, though. For serious, you have to see this."

Sam heard a video start to play on someone's phone and resisted the impulse to peek her head over the top of the partition to watch.

"Oh, come on!" Amy groaned. "The reception sucks in here."

Jaida sounded bored and irritated at the same time. "Well, *duh*, Ames, it's a school. You think they want us watching Netflix between classes? Just tell us what it was, and we'll see if we can pull it off."

"The site's called Mad Girlz Prank, like 'girls' with a z, which is kinda uncool, I know, but they did this great one where they put plastic wrap over the doorway of the sister's bedroom and then made this freaky loud noise so she jumped out of bed and ran into the plastic wrap 'cause she couldn't see it, so she bounced off and fell on her butt—" Amy was laughing so hard by this point, Sam could hardly make out the words, but she got the gist: This was a humiliating and painful practical "joke."

Gina barked an obnoxious guffaw, but Jaida's voice was dismissive. "It's pretty good, but not for Daisy. She needs something a little more, like, obvious. She's not the brightest bulb in the chandelier."

"Is that why you're mad at her? Because of her stupidality?"

Gina said this casually, but Sam could hear the burning curiosity beneath her breeziness. So even the minions themselves didn't know why one of them had been axed.

"Really none of your business, G." Jaida sounded just as casual, but *her* underneath tone was "back off or suffer the same fate."

"Oh, no, I know! I didn't mean—"

Jaida cut Gina off. "Chill." Apparently, Gina obeyed this command, because Jaida continued on, her voice thoughtful now. "So, we need something else for Dumbsy, but you know who this prank would be *perfect* for? The Snoozing Loser."

Amy and Gina went completely nuts with "OMG, totally!" and "Yes, YES!" while Sam clapped a hand over her mouth so as not to outright scream.

"Too bad we can't pull it off. Oh, well, life is full of disappointments," Jaida said flippantly, as if not being able to break into Sam's house to torture her was on the level of your mom forgetting to buy your favorite cereal on her grocery run.

That's it. Any guilt she'd felt about eavesdropping was gone; Jaida deserved whatever she got. Sam wished she'd checked her phone before entering the Toilet of Terrors; then she would know how many hours before she could spill everything to Madalynn. *I don't know if I can wait that long.*

There was so much rage and hurt bubbling inside her, it threatened to boil over into the world's longest ALL-CAPS text—her fingers twitched and quivered above the phone in her pocket. But there was no way a text was going to do this whole terrible scene justice.

Justice.

There was that word again.

And now Sam couldn't wait to see it done.

twelve

UNFORTUNATELY, by the time Sam was a soul hovering in front of the enemy's abode that night, she wasn't quite as fired up.

There were a number of reasons for the drop in her enthusiasm level. One was her conversation with Kyra, or lack thereof, when the Dreams showed up. Kyra was still wearing her red flannel pajamas, but even the bright color didn't stop her from blending into the tribe, much more so than the night before. And when Sam tried to talk to her, Kyra didn't have much to say. Or anything, really; she just slid farther and farther into the mass of bodies until Sam almost couldn't make out her shape. And when Sam tried to peer in, Bree played gatekeeper with a most unfriendly beige smile.

Another thing that cooled Sam's avengement rage was the discovery of Madalynn's plan for the evening.

Queen Dream, tonight decked out in a vivid purple chemise with matching marabou mule slippers, put her arm around a short boy whose bucktoothed face was freckled with zit cream. "Meet our new Prank pal, who's going to help us out tonight. Arthur, this is Sam. Sam, Arthur."

"S'up?" Arthur whispered, scratching his head, which was immediately almost obscured in a glitter bomb of soul dandruff.

"Help us with what exactly?" Sam asked, trying not to sound as apprehensive as she felt.

Madalynn smiled and held out her manicured mitt, in which rested a container of plastic wrap and a roll of tape. "Who's going to be the Snoozing Loser tonight?" she purred.

Sam stared at the items, confused. "But—"

"But what?"

"When I texted you . . ." Sam was trying to make sense to Madalynn, but she was also trying to sort out in her own head why she was having to state the obvious. "I told you how mean that prank would be. That's why I was so upset. Because it's, like, really . . . mean."

Madalynn looked at her curiously, like Sam was speaking

a foreign language. "You're still not understanding 'recompense,' are you, Sleep Sis?"

Sam's mist stomach dropped to her floaty feet. This time she was hearing that word differently; this time she heard *wreck*-ompense.

"Oh, I get it! You're worried because she didn't *actually* do it to you," Madalynn continued.

"No, I—"

"Just 'cause she didn't do it don't mean she didn't wanna do it." Bree had lumbered into their conversation and was now staring Sam down with her freakily colorless eyes. "It's the same. Don't matter who did what first. Backward and forward, it's the same, and deserves the same." Sam was struck once again by how very vibrant was the venom of this virtually vanishing girl.

Madalynn obviously thought everything was settled, because she motioned for Sam to put her hand out for the goods. Feeling helpless, Sam complied, but the tape swished through her skin, hit the ground, and bounced away, striking the side of Jaida's dark house with a sad little *thwunk*.

"Sorry," Sam mumbled.

Madalynn sighed deeply, conveying all the angsty responsibility of being a highly attractive mentor to a deeply dull apprentice. "Don't stress it!" she said perkily, then turned to Arthur. "Prank, counting on you to pick up the slack!"

Arthur looked like he might just expand the capabilities of a released soul by physically vomiting. He disappeared through the wall and opened the window from the inside. Bree passed him the plastic wrap and tape, and Zac reached in to noogie Arthur for good measure.

"Dreams, tell our friend Sam that she's got this," Madalynn commanded.

"You got this, Sam," the Dreams all spoke together.

"Tell her she's going to *feel* the justice." Madalynn patted her heart on the word "feel."

"You're going to *feel* the justice, Sam." The Dreams patted themselves.

"Say 'Avenge yourself, Samantha!'" Madalynn crowed.

"*Avenge* yourself, Samantha!" they repeated.

"A comeuppance for the oppressor!" Madalynn was getting seriously worked up.

"A comeuppance for—"

"Hey, guys?" Sam jumped in. "Uh . . . good enough. Thank you." She attempted a confident, avenging smile and slipped through the wall into the oppressor's bedroom.

The room was shabbier than it had appeared through the window, and even without a body, Sam could tell that it was cold. Because under the thin blanket, Jaida was sleeping in her coat. The sight made Sam feel queasy and uncertain, so she forced herself to focus on Jaida's face, hoping to find evidence of the usual arched eyebrow and nasty curled lip. Unfortunately, all Sam saw was Jaida's breath making little clouds of condensation in the chilly air.

She turned away sharply and glided over to Arthur, who was almost finished taping long sheets of plastic wrap over the outside of the bedroom door.

"Hey . . . it's not gonna actually hurt her, right?" Sam whispered, glancing back at the window to make sure Madalynn hadn't sneaked in to witness her avengement wimpiness.

Arthur also took a preemptive peek before he muttered, "Nah . . . least I don't think so. She's s'posed to just bounce on her tailbone."

The thought of her nemesis ricocheting off her coccyx did not help Sam's jitters. She willed her brain to conjure up images of Jaida's multiple abuses, particularly her enemy's desire to play this very same practical joke on Sam. It helped a little; as long as she didn't have to turn around and face the abuser herself, looking all shivery and vulnerable in the narrow bed.

Arthur put the last piece of tape on the doorframe. "Oh, almost forgot." He dug around in his pajama pocket and pulled out a small index card. "Madalynn says you're s'posed to put this on her bed for after." He held it out to her.

Sam gritted her teeth and pawed at the paper helplessly. "I can't—"

"Oh, right, I forgot. 'Kay, I'll just do it." He went to tuck it back in his pocket.

"Uh . . . what is it, anyway?"

Arthur shrugged, then held out the card for Sam to read:

Love & Kisses,
The Mad Girlz

"What the—?! Is she serious?!" Sam was horrified.

"As a heart attack," Arthur said gloomily.

"But—but that's, like, so, so . . . *incriminating*! Jaida's parents are gonna call the police, and Jaida's gonna pin it on Gina and Amy!"

"Nah. Madalynn said the cops don't bother coming anymore. 'Sides, it's part of the gag, right? That's the name of the website, but her friends are mad, too. Get it?"

Never was the closing line *"get it?"* delivered more morosely.

And Sam *didn't* get it, didn't even hear it, because she was stuck on the words *"cops don't bother coming anymore."* It was repeating in her head, in concert with Dr. Hopkins's voice, *"always find her in the same place, trying to break into someone's house."*

In that moment, she could longer ignore the truth: Madalynn wasn't trying to help *Sam* make things even with her bully; Madalynn had her *own* score to settle with Jaida. *And I'm her bootlicking lackey minion.*

Also in that moment? Madalynn stuck her head through the wall next to Jaida's bed, screamed "FIRE!" and all H-E-double-hockey-sticks broke loose.

Jaida leapt up with a shriek, ran for the doorway, hit the plastic wrap, and rebounded tragicomically, falling on her butt just as Arthur had promised. The Prank himself shrieked, dashed right through the plastic and down the hallway, hurtling through the closed front door like some kind of soul ninja. The Dreams watching through the window cheered in a joyless, thundering monotone. And then there was a loud *SLAM!* as a burly man in sweatpants and a dirty undershirt threw open his bedroom door and roared:

"WHAT IS GOING ON?!"

Sam knew he couldn't see her, but she still cowered in abject terror, sinking behind a bureau. Her head was screeching *Run! Run!* but her soul was frozen, inert. *Come on, idiot! This is the one and only thing that's good about not being solid! You could walk right through him and he'd never know!*

The man strode over to the doorway and angrily ripped down the plastic.

"Dad . . ." The sound was so tremulous and thin, Sam had to peer around the corner of the bureau to prove to herself that it was Jaida speaking. Her nemesis was still on the floor, pulling the coat around herself as if for protection. And very quickly, Sam understood why.

"Shut up!" The contempt in the man's voice was like a physical blow. "I can't take this anymore!"

"I'm sorry—" Jaida whispered.

"You said this kinda stuff was gonna end when they caught that sleepwalker girl! What, are you such a loser that other kids are messing with you now?" he snarled.

"Please . . . Dad . . ." Jaida was breathing hard. There was a rasp, almost a rattle as she sucked in air, her tortured inhale grating through Sam's wispy being with sharp metal prongs.

Jaida's father lumbered over to the bedside table and picked up the glittery fanny pack. "Here. I pay enough for this crap. Use it so I get my money's worth." He threw the pack on the floor next to Jaida and the contents spilled out.

An asthma inhaler. Two EpiPens. Benadryl. A medical alert bracelet.

Sam gasped.

Jaida's head snapped up, and she looked around wildly. Sam yanked back behind the bureau. *Oh please please please don't feel me.*

"Don't be stupid, use it!" the man growled. "I'm not taking you to the ER again!"

As Jaida took a long drag off her inhaler, all the pieces of the puzzle started to fall into place for Sam in the worst ways possible. The fanny pack wasn't a fashesty; it was a lifeline. The fact that Jaida never ate in the cafeteria wasn't because she was stalking Sam; it was because she had bad enough allergies to need an EpiPen—all the food was a possible threat. And the vicious words that she'd used against Sam weren't Jaida's own; they came from her father.

Who now stalked through the room, pausing only to kick angrily at the downed plastic, and then disappeared with a slam of his bedroom door. Which left Sam alone with her tormentor, witnessing the one thing that every persecuted soul is supposed to desire: tears streaming down the face of her enemy.

So why was it making Sam feel so wretched?

✳ ✳ ✳

She knew it made no sense, but as Sam crept through the construction zone, she tried to hide behind pylons and heavy machinery. *Like that's gonna fool Madalynn.* But when she'd escaped Jaida's house to find the Dreams gone, Sam suddenly nursed a crazy hope that she was done, that Madalynn was going to let her off the hook now, and the worst thing that could still happen that night was if the Broadways appeared and sang a tragic ballad about how avenging yourself can backfire in a big, ugly way.

"Now where are you going, you sneaky little Dream?"

So much for crazy hopes. Madalynn was seated in the bucket of a hydraulic excavator, her sapphire eyes sparkling down on Sam, her purple-marabou-muled feet swinging as if she didn't have a care in the world. Standing behind her were Bree and Zac, their ominous largeness silhouetted against the night sky.

"Who, me? Uh, nowhere really, just gliding along, minding my own business," burbled Sam.

"Minding your own business? That is *adorable*." Madalynn descended from the bucket like a falling angel. Her henchpeople plopped down beside her, much less gracefully. "No such thing, right? At least not for girls."

Sam's eyes shot around wildly, looking for a tribe, any tribe, to rescue her. She'd even take a drunken Later right now.

"Sam, don't you get it? This is the way it works for us. We're not allowed to be honest. Nobody wants girls to be all confrontational and in-your-face. So, we have to take care of everything behind the scenes. In the dark, where you can see what's really going on."

Sam hated that the words struck something in her. She

hated that Bree was nodding in agreement. She hated that enemies sometimes were sad, and perfect girls sometimes were cruel, and even cruel girls sometimes made sense.

Why can't light always be light and darkness always be dark?

"Anyhoo . . ." Madalynn breathed. "As I said before, the key is to make everything even. If things work out as planned, Jaida and her minions will have the argument of the century tomorrow, since, *obviously*, they were the ones who pranked her. 'Cause *nobody else* knew about their bathroom conversation, right?" Madalynn seemed delighted by this line of thinking. "Boom! Unfriended."

"Uh-huh." Sam's mind was whirling. Maybe it wouldn't be too bad. They'd have a big fight, and it would be over. Maybe it *would* be good for Jaida to get a little taste of her own medicine, as long as this was the end of—

"Of course, just to make sure . . ." Madalynn's silky voice stopped Sam's defensive reasoning cold. "We do want to be *certain* Jaida learned her lesson. So, we reboot tomorrow night."

Sam gulped. "Reboot?"

Madalynn nodded. "Arthur found another fab practical joke on that website your surveillance so kindly provided— what was the name of it again, Bree?"

"Mad Girlz Prank. With a *z*." Bree drew out the *z* with a little snarl, displaying her pointy beige teeth.

"Right! So adorbs! Tomorrow night we're going to take a bottle of Tabasco and drip it into Jaida's mouth while she's sleeping and leave a note that says, 'Watch your tongue from now on.' Perfect, right?"

Um, yeah, perfectly evil. Well, at least *this* was clear and obvious. "We can't do that. I just found out that Jaida has food allergies and asthma and stuff. It's too dangerous."

And then the creepiest thing happened, because seriously, how creepy is it when someone is still smiling at you warmly and using a silky-smooth voice when a super-creepy threat comes out of her mouth?

"Not as dangerous as saying no to me, Samantha." Madalynn leaned closer, her fragrant soul breath caressing Sam's face. Bree and Zac leaned in as well, their halitosis pretty much canceling out any sweetness. "There are just so many ways I can make your life unpleasant. Your nighttime life *and* your daytime one."

On this dismal note, Madalynn and her disciples turned and hyper-crossed into the darkness like high-speed specters, leaving a residue of creepy behind that made all the construction machinery look like hulking monsters and demons. Before the walking harvester could pick Sam up in its mega claw and crush her into soul dust, she took off in the opposite direction, pushing like mad for her own hyper-cross, but pretty much only achieving sorta jacked-up crossing. All the while hoping that By the Spy was roaming somewhere in Fletch's sector and could forgive her for being so incredibly stupid and naive, since Sam needed his help to stop a teenaged demon and her satanbabies.

How could I have trusted Madalynn? She wanted to rest on the fact that even Fletch had been hypnotized by the Dream Queen's seeming sweetness, but Sam's annoyingly loud conscience wouldn't let her. *Madalynn didn't use me; I used her. I ignored all the signs so that I could get back at Jaida, plain and simple.* Her soul stomach knotted up in shame.

When Sam reached the Juvenold's park, she immediately knew something was up. The Juvies were still swinging and seesawing, but their laughter and play was muted, like someone had put a foggy filter over the scene. Sam found Alyssa sitting glumly on top of the monkey bars. "Alyssa?"

Alyssa brightened slightly at the sight of Sam; she grabbed a handful of blue hair and waved it. "Hi there, you. Gonna join our tribe?"

"Oh, uh, no."

"Aw, too bad. 'Cause, we lost one of us. Lost, lost, lost." She made a mimed crying motion with her hands.

"Lost?" Sam felt shivery in her middle. "What do you mean?"

"A big tribe of nasties swooped in, and next thingy we knew, Minnie got sucked off the slide. Poor, poor Minnie

Mouse . . . they sent her back." Alyssa stuck her bottom lip out sadly.

"Sent her back? *Back where?* What does that mean?" Sam was trying not to panic, but it was pretty obvious who the "big tribe of nasties" was, and "sent her back" sounded like what you do to bad food in a restaurant. But Alyssa was now twisting herself into a pretzel trying to get a better peek at her pouted bottom lip, so Sam decided to move on.

"Alyssa, remember Byron, that Roamer I was with a few nights ago? Have you seen him?"

"The one with the dimples?"

Sam gritted her teeth. *We're having an existential crisis here; please don't remind me of the cuteness.* "Yeah, that one."

"I haven't seen him tonight. You should check with the OCDeeds."

"Um, okay. They're in this sector, right?"

"Oh yeah. They're usually over on Turner Avenue at the Container Store." While Sam was processing this odd information, Alyssa leaned too far forward in the quest to ogle her own orifice and fell off the monkey bars right onto her blue noggin. "I think I broke my neck." She erupted in giggles.

Sam wasn't sure this was actually possible due to a soul body's lack of bones, but she didn't have time to wait around to see if some kind of SleepWaker ambulance was going to pull up. She took off in the direction of Turner Avenue, misting indiscriminately through trees, traffic, and Later Zones, loudly cursing her sloth-cross speed all the while. Finally she slid through an underpass and came out across the street from the Container Store.

Sam gingerly approached the window, sliding her face an inch or two through the glass. She blinked a few times, trying to make sense of the worker-bee buzz she was witnessing.

Against one wall, SleepWakers were stacking Tupperware lids, file folders, and wastebaskets according to color. A small girl in ragged pajamas, her matted hair hanging like two dirty oven mitts on either side of her head, shouted, "Robin's egg! Midnight! Navy! Cornflower! Cerulean! Cobalt! Teal! Turquoise!" as the stack of infinitesimally graded shades of blue mounted, while a chubby boy silently directed the progress of a tower of interlocking bins from petal pink to deep rose. In the middle of the showroom floor, three multi-pierced goth girls positioned and repositioned and re-repositioned bento boxes, carefully inserting the plastic sushi, foam sandwiches, and wooden juice box samples into their respective pockets. Just left of the window, a boy with a sleep dent in his massive Afro painstakingly organized a display spice rack alphabetically, murmuring, "Vindaloo curry . . . West African pepper . . . yellow mustard seed . . ."

"Excuse me, I'm looking for—" Sam whispered.

"Noooo!!" he wailed. "All I had left was za'atar! Now I have to start over at achiote powder!"

"Oh! I'm so sorry—" Sam gulped.

"Dev, don't yell!" yelled one of the goth girls. "You made me mess up my bento!"

"Well, *you* yelling about *Dev* yelling made me forget what comes after fuchsia!" yelled the chubby stacker of pink bins.

Dev grabbed his dented Afro in anguish. "Get out! Get out!"

Sam yanked her head back through the glass, barely missing getting bonked in the head with the Hungarian paprika the boy slung like a throwing star.

"Shoulda told you, you don't want to be messing with OCDeeds while they're organizing."

Sam felt more relief than annoyance at Byron's voice, but she still whirled around with a considerable amount of 'tude. "Yeah, that would have been good information *pre*-concussion!"

Byron snorted. "How's that gonna happen? You have to be able to be solid before anyone can hurt you."

"First of all, thanks so much for reminding me what a failure I am, and secondly, totally not true, because I'm already feeling pretty beat-up, dude!"

"Yeah, well, whose fault is that?" Byron was ticked and it

looked like he wasn't about to let her off the hook. "Didn't I say you weren't ready to be on your own?"

"Well, maybe if you didn't go all bossy boy on me, I would've listened!" Sam cried. "And maybe if you'd told me the truth from the beginning that you were spying on me and reporting back to your mom, we could have avoided all of this!"

At least Byron had the decency to look sheepish. He stared at the ground and cleared his throat. "Okay. That's fair." And then, with the faintest trace of dimple, "But I didn't have to report back on how awesome you are. She already knew that."

All the ethereal blood rushed to her pretend face. Now *she* was staring at the ground. They remained in eyes-down silence for a moment.

"Sam?"

"Uh-huh?"

"Do you mind if we move on? Because this is the kind of awkward that usually makes the Broadways show up, and I just can't deal right now."

She had to smile. "Moving on."

"Great." He gave her full dimplage this time, causing some swooniness that she chose to ignore since they were officially moving on. "So, I think we should go see Fletch."

Sam knew she needed the doctor's advice, but the thought of confessing her SleepWaker sins to those judgy sclerae was almost too much for her. "Can't you just help me with this? You're, like, King Roamer, he who sees all and knows all."

"Sees and knows *some*, not all. Like, I can tell you that the OCDeeds have messy, screwed-up daytime lives, which is why their souls are so touchy about order, and that info might help you avoid getting clubbed with spices. But when it comes to the MeanDreams, I think we're both in over our heads."

Sam grimaced. "Okay, but I hope he's not having a pajama party with the S.S.S.S. I don't think they're too thrilled with me."

Byron nodded. "To be safe, we're gonna do an indoor cross and that can be a little weird. Try to just keep . . . you know, moving on."

An "indoor cross," as it turned out, was pretty much what it sounded like. Instead of gliding through the streets, they traveled through buildings, store to store, house to house, trying to stay inside as much as possible and away from an encounter with the MeanDreams. And it was definitely more than a little weird. The eeriness of the empty post office or an echoey Starbucks minus baristas and hipsters was nothing compared to the freaky presence of gym rats pumping iron in the 24-Hour Fitness or solitary figures trying to pick up spares in the all-night bowling alley. But the journey through the deep night of people's homes was the thing that almost did Sam in. A kid crying out with a nightmare, a couple screaming at each other in their bedroom, a man chain-smoking while staring out a window—it was all too lonely. Too much.

People show who they really are in the darkness.

They finally misted through the wall of the clinic to find Dr. Fletcher sound asleep on his examining bed, snuggling a bundle of electrodes.

"Fletch. Wake up," Byron said gently.

The doctor's eyelids peeled back slowly to reveal the glowing whiteness. "I hope you're a Waker. I'm too young and too sane to be hearing voices."

"Oh, sorry. Forgot to be visible." Byron made a quick, grim face that Sam thought looked more like he was trying to poop, but it seemed to work. Fletch jumped up excitedly.

"Byron! You found her!"

Sam gasped. She and Byron spoke at the same time:

"Can you *see* her?"

"You can *see* me?"

Fletcher deflated slightly. "No, I can't. But I can feel that she's here."

"Oh, great," Sam said sarcastically. "Everybody on the

stinkin' planet can 'perceive' me, but I'm still invisible. Story of my life."

"Don't be a crybaby," Byron said briskly. "You want to try again?"

"Not really." The last thing she wanted was to become solid just in time to have Fletch give her an "I told you so" white-eyeballed look.

"Is she going to try to be solid?" Fletch sounded hopeful.

"No, she's feeling sorry for herself now," Byron announced.

"Dude. Not helping."

"Just tell me exactly what happened with the MeanDreams, and I'll repeat everything to Fletch. And try to cut to the chase, we don't have all night."

Sam was still irritated. "Maybe we can get the Broadways in here to rap about all my issues, how about that?"

"Shut up. Talk."

"Fine, bossy boy."

Sam took a deep breath and started to explain, slowly at first, but soon the words tumbled over each other, words of confusion and fear about Madalynn and Jaida and Kyra and the MeanDreams stealing Minnie Mouse and sending her "back," whatever that meant, and Sam's own part in their scheme, and just plain old *who the heck am I in my soul?* really, because everything was laced with yelling thoughts of *What do I do? Why do I care? Why can others feel me, and why do I feel what they're feeling?*

"And how come, even in the darkness, I can't just be *normal*, like, a normal SleepWaker who can recognize her tribe?!"

When Byron relayed this last sentence, Fletch pointed a bony finger in Sam's general direction and cried, "Ah! That's it! You *can't* recognize your tribe because you don't have one! Because you're *not* normal!" He delivered this like it was the best news in the world, even ending with his arms thrown out in a V for victory.

Of course, this was a terrible thing to say, but the cheerleader move was the straw that broke the Waker's back. Sam flushed with anger.

"Uh, Fletch? She's looking pretty ticked." Byron added hesitantly, "Maybe you could elaborate?"

"Haven't you figured it out yet, Sam?" Fletch toned down his verve and spoke softly. "You're a *Helper*. The first of your SleepWaker kind. And the one who's going to take down the MeanDreams."

Shocked into silence, Sam looked over at Byron for some kind of lifeline. He shrugged with a half nod. "I told you. Remember? I said you were something else."

"Yeah, something else, but what? What is a Helper?" She

felt like she was going to cry again, and it was super annoying. Byron finally cut her a break and threw her a bone of compassion.

"Fletch, you gotta explain it better. We're losing her."

Dr. Fletcher nodded, then continued gently, "I want you to think, Sam. Think about all the things you did when you were sleepwalking. Try to remember the pattern."

"I've thought about that a million times! There *was* no pattern. It was just all . . ." Sam couldn't even say what she was really thinking. *My long list of crazy.*

Byron translated. "She says it was random."

"Random shmandom! Let me show you something." Fletch leapt up and ran to his file cabinet, digging around and tossing papers with wild abandon, then ran back, brandishing a notebook and a folded newspaper. "Your mother kept a journal for a while, a record of your walks, back when one of your specialists was trying to establish some sort of pattern. When you were living in Wayne, while you were in the fourth grade, you sleep-stole a wheelchair from a Mrs. Buckley in your neighborhood, who your mother says was a rich, albeit nasty, old lady. That happened on"—he flipped the pages of the notebook—"October eighth. Now look at this!" He slammed the newspaper article down and pointed at a headline.

"'Oktoberfest kicks off in South Jersey'?" Byron read.

"Oh, whoopsie." Fletch peered down at the newspaper and moved his finger to a tiny article on the bottom of the page. "There!"

"'Happy Heart Nursing Home Seeks Assistance,'" Sam read. "Huh?"

Byron scanned it quickly. "The article asks for supplies and donations for a rest home that was struggling financially."

"Specifically . . . *wheelchairs*," said Fletcher passionately.

"That's pretty awesome, Sam." Byron grinned. "You were a girl Robin Hood, stealing from the rich to give to the poor."

Sam shook her head, agitated. "But . . . I don't remember knowing anything about this place."

Byron looked doubtful, too. "You really think she saw this, Fletch? I mean, who reads newspapers anymore, especially a ten-year-old?"

"Well, I don't know how or why she read it, I only know that it couldn't have been a coincidence. Her mother found her on Dey Boulevard, three blocks from Happy Heart." Fletch turned in Sam's direction, his sclerae burning. "Think, Sam, think! Remember, and find the pattern. You just have to look through this new lens!" He flipped the pages of the notebook. "Pick any of these and push your mind back!"

March 21. Sam baking brownies in her sleep. Burned herself badly. ER visit.

March 22. Found Sam in recycling bin at Short Hills mall. Covered in garbage.

March 23. Found Sam on Dodie Drive in the intersection, sleep-directing traffic in a rainstorm. Almost got hit by a car. Walks are getting more dangerous. So scared.

Sam stared at Margie's loopy handwriting, her heart aching for her trichotillomaniac mother. *Think. Think.* They'd moved out of Wayne after the wheelchair incident and were living in Parsippany in a tiny apartment. Jax had to transfer in the middle of eighth grade and was starting to hate her. *Think, Sam.* She liked her new fourth-grade teacher, Miss Calabria, better than mean Mrs. Burkee at her old school. *Think, Sam, think!* Margie had gotten a job waiting tables at a diner. Where the cook was the owner's brother-in-law, which meant he sucked in the kitchen, which meant the diner was struggling, which meant Margie was struggling, which meant—*oh my God*—

"Desserts . . ."

Fletcher went pale. He gawked, his sclerae so wide and

white, his pupils looked like two ravens that had crash-landed on an iceberg. "Sam . . . I can *hear* you now. . . ."

Byron whirled around to face her. "Keep going! Keep talking!"

Sam spoke slowly, her voice shaky. "My mom . . . My mom said . . . maybe if the diner she worked at had good *desserts*, people could ignore the disgusting food. She would make better tips."

"So, you sleep-baked brownies . . ." whispered Fletch.

She pushed her mind back, grabbing at shreds of memory. "Jax was trying to make friends at his new school. One of them, Sage . . . his father worked in sanitation. He would curse out people who didn't separate trash from recycling, and when he was mad, Sage would get mad, and then he would be a jerk to Jax."

"Recycling bin . . ." murmured Byron.

Sam was shivering now. "My teacher, I mean, my new teacher . . . Miss Calabria. I remember . . . she told us that she wouldn't drive in Parsippany in a storm because the traffic lights would go wonky on Dodie Drive. That's the word she used, 'wonky.' I thought it was funny; *she* was funny. I liked her, way better than my old teacher because . . ." It came to her in a flash and now the words flew out. "Because Mrs. Burkee was moody, and when she was grumpy, she would give us really annoying assignments. . . . And one of those assignments was writing about current events in the newspaper!"

Byron laughed, clapped his soul hands. Fletcher grabbed all the papers on the desk and threw them in the air. "By St. Dymphna! I would hug you if I could see you!"

That came pretty close to killing the thrill for Sam. "You *still* can't see me?"

Fletch was racing around the office, looking for more random celebratory papers to throw. "It'll come!"

"But—"

"It will come, Sam, trust me!" He gave up finding more papers and instead threw Joanne's stethoscope jubilantly. "It'll come when you—!"

"*Please* don't say when I believe in the weight and possibilities of my own soul. It sounds like an Instagram meme," Sam grumbled.

Dr. Fletcher shrugged buoyantly and flopped into a chair. "Well, I have no idea what an instant Grammy is, but if it's an old lady who suddenly appears to give advice, maybe you should listen."

Byron looked confused. Sam decided to just let that one go.

"Okay. So, let's say that I'm a . . . Helper." The word felt strange in her mouth—too far-reaching—arrogant almost.

Like calling yourself president when you were really only student-body treasurer, and that only because you got the least votes of anyone who'd been running for president. "There's still not much I can do about the MeanDreams until I can be solid. So . . . maybe I can try to fix this tomorrow at school. You know, while I have working hands and, like, a visible body. I'll just, I guess . . . *talk* to Jaida. Maybe I can warn her."

Byron and Fletch exchanged a look that said "that's so not gonna work," but what else could Sam do? The Helper definitely needed help, but like fairy godmothers, instant Grammies were hard to come by these days.

thirteen

SAM MEANDERED down the hallway, gnawing on her cuticles. Which was basically all she'd had to eat the entire day, since she felt so nauseated about approaching Jaida she'd skipped both breakfast and lunch. The one saving grace had been that Madalynn was MIA; she'd never been out sick before, so Sam could only assume that she'd overslept or that the faculty had declared a Madalynn Sucret Is Awesome holiday and sent her to a spa. Whatever the reason, Sam was relieved not to have to face Madalynn *and* Jaida in daylight hours.

As she neared her locker, Sam saw exactly what she had hoped for yesterday but dreaded today: Jaida and her posse in the midst of a heavy-duty argument. She wasn't close enough to hear what was being said, but there was much pointing, hand-wringing, and a few tears. Finally Gina and Amy stalked off in different directions and Jaida turned and slammed her books into her locker. Madalynn's silky voice echoed in Sam's mind: *Boom! Unfriended.*

Talking to Jaida at this moment was pretty much number one on Sam's un-bucket list, but she didn't know if she would get another chance. Jaida whirled around at her approach and the first thing Sam noticed was the dark circles under her eyes. But of course, Jaida didn't register Sam's look of compassion, she only cared about Sam noticing the *second* thing—the infamous sparkly fanny pack, the broken zipper now held closed with a safety pin.

"What are you looking at, Fiashco?" Jaida snarled. *Um, Fashion Fiasco, I'm guessing?* Jaida was staring her down so viciously, Sam had to quickly conjure up the image of the fragile girl in the cold bedroom or she never would have been able to do what she did next. Which was walk over to Jaida's locker. Yeah, your basic death wish.

"Jaida, I . . . Jaida, you . . . I . . . you . . ." This was a really bad start. But at least it had the advantage of being *so* bad, it shut Jaida up for a few seconds in eyebrow-raised awe. Which was all Sam needed to get the ball rolling.

"Okay, this is gonna sound crazy, but you were right

about me, I mean, I'm not a narcoleptic, I'm a sleepwalker, and my doctor detached my soul, which is what you can do with certain sleepwalkers, so there are all these souls wandering around in the night, they're called SleepWakers and they form tribes, and some of the tribes are not so nice, and, and, and, aaaaaand—"

Aaand she *did* sound crazy. Loony. Completely unhinged. Mondo bizarro. The ball was definitely rolling, but it sounded more like it was rolling around the empty corridors of Sam's brain.

So, she blurted it out: "I know what happened at your house last night!" And then she watched as the thunderclouds on Jaida's face whipped into a hurricane of rage.

"How do *you* know what happened?" Jaida demanded. "Did they *tell* you? Did you *help* them?!"

"No! I mean, yeah, I did, sort of, but they didn't—"

"I'm gonna hurt you!" Now Jaida was backing her up against the lockers, so enraged Sam could literally feel heat rising off her face. "I'm gonna hurt you so bad your grandchildren are gonna end up in the ER!"

"Wow, uh, that's a little harsh—"

This really is not going well.

"I'm gonna—gonna—rip your large intestine out of your mouth and your small intestine out of your butt and I'm gonna use you as a jump rope!"

"Okay, that one was actually pretty creative—"

Creatively psychopathic, that is.

"I'm gonna—! I'm gonna—!" Jaida was obviously search-ing for something more gruesome than disembowelment, but before she could drum it up, a melodious voice was heard.

"Oh, my good goodness. Did you hear that, Principal Nussbaum?"

Sam and Jaida whirled around to see an outraged school administrator accompanied by a glowing Madalynn Sucret, who had indeed taken a spa rest day, as evidenced by her luminescence and the goodie bag of moisturizer samples she was carrying.

"Come with me, Miss Coakley." Principal Nussbaum's voice was icy.

And even though Jaida shot her a look that promised future evisceration, Sam was sorry to see her go. Because that left her alone with Madalynn, who leaned her shiny vis-age toward Sam and whispered, "See? I got your back. And I know you'll have mine. Or else. See you tonight, Sleep Sis." She flounced away, her ringlets bobbing up and down like towheaded toddlers in a bounce house.

Overwhelmed, Sam leaned back against the lockers. Compared to what lay ahead, disembowelment was looking pretty appealing.

What the—

For a moment, Sam wasn't sure why everything looked so ripply and there were ducks swimming through the air. Then she groaned.

She was staring through the shower curtain. Because her soul had woken up hiding in the bathtub. *Great.* Not only did she have a cowardly consciousness, but she also had a dumb one. *Are you really gonna hide from Satan's handmaiden behind a clear plastic shower curtain?*

Sam pulled her mist body into a fetal position in the bottom of the tub. She just wanted to disappear and not face anything. What good was a rested body in the other room when her soul was so torn up inside? Her mind and her essence were on call 24/7, and she just didn't know how to turn them off. *Some kind of Helper I am. I can't even help myself.*

She heard the water before she felt it, a tremendous swoosh of sound. Sam unwound herself to see Arthur putting the stopper into the bathtub drain as the faucet gushed.

"Turn it up higher, Prank!" Madalynn sang out as she yanked back the shower curtain. "I think Sam needs a nice wet lesson!"

"What are you doing?!" Sam instinctively grabbed at the hot and cold knobs to turn off the water, but of course, her hands slid right through. She turned to Arthur, who couldn't meet her eyes. "Arthur?"

Madalynn smiled. "Oh, Sam, don't worry. He'll turn it off. Right after you finish your business with Jaida."

Dread filled Sam's soul. "What? The whole house will flood!"

"Not if you hurry." Madalynn gestured grandly with the bell sleeve of her leopard-print robe. "Come on, Sleep Sis, I'll help you hyper-cross. We'll be there in a jiffy, and be back before you can say, 'Oh no, we don't have homeowners' insurance!'" She laughed, a terrifyingly tinkly sound.

Be solid, be solid, you idiot soul hands! Sam clawed at the stopper in the drain, but the idiot soul hands just kept misting through. The tub was already halfway full. *I'm not a Helper! I can't even help my family not drown in their beds!*

"Samantha, you are wasting time." Now Madalynn's voice was chillier. "Prank, tell her."

Arthur gulped. "C'mon, Sam. Let's get it over with." He was so pale, the spots of pimple cream on his face resembled snowflakes on an ice rink.

Sam leapt out of the bathtub. "Fine! Just go!"

They slid through the wall into the living room and then

out onto the lawn. Before the "blur" could start, Sam cast one agonized look back at the house and a tiny movement caught her eye. It was Byron, gesturing "I got this" from his shrub outside the bedroom window. She whipped her head back around, praying that Madalynn hadn't seen, but Queen MeanDream just barked, "Stop stalling!" Sam nodded and took off, feeling a flood of relief in proportion to the tsunami that was about to be halted in her bathroom. *Thank you, God, for By the Spy.*

Since they were only hyper-crossing to the other side of town and not across the Great Lakes, the blurred journey took mere seconds. In front of Jaida's dark house, the even darker MeanDreams formed a clump. Bree stood guard like a malevolent signpost, but Zac was skirting the outside of the tribe, giving out violent wet willies. Madalynn paused only long enough to bark, "Zac!" and then blazed right through the wall of the house, disappearing from sight. Sam looked at Arthur, who was shaking so hard, little fireworks of dandruff were exploding off his scalp.

"Since you can't go solid yet, she said she's gonna help out," Arthur quavered.

"Oh, I guess Madalynn's a Helper now," Sam mumbled acidly.

"Huh?"

"Nothing. Arthur, we can't do this! How do we stop her?"

Sam whispered urgently, casting a quick glance at Bree and Zac, hoping they didn't have super-evil superhuman hearing.

"There's no way out, Sam. The bathtub's on at my house, too, and I don't have a Roamer to turn it off!" Arthur whispered back.

He saw Byron. "Thanks for not tattling on me, Prank," she said softly.

Arthur shrugged, a wisp of a smile showing off his rather impressive buckteeth. "Come on, let's just get this over with. I've got gerbils at home who definitely can't swim."

He turned and zoomed into the house. Just as Sam was about to follow, it came to her: *Arthur knows how to be solid. Why didn't he turn off the water at his house himself?*

"He's afraid." The voice came from within the group of MeanDreams.

Bree whirled around, growling, "Who said that?"

She was met with silence.

But Sam knew, even though she had only heard the voice a few times. Kyra was somewhere in the middle of the tribe, probably wearing her bright red flannel pajamas but still invisible to the naked eye. Sam wasn't sure what was more disquieting, the entire group just staring at Bree mutely, or that Kyra had read Sam's mind, knew the truth, but seemingly had no way to escape this melded mass of souls.

Sam turned slowly back toward the house, and as she

glided through the wall, a new feeling came over her. A feeling of protectiveness for Kyra, for "Minnie Mouse," for the missing Achieve, and especially for Arthur. Seriously, who was low enough to scare a sweet, goofy kid with a flaky scalp and front teeth that were practically at a right angle to his gums? Only the lowest of the low. Only a bully. *And I know what a bully is*. A person who hurts someone else for *absolutely no reason*.

"Finally!" Madalynn rolled her eyes so strenuously, the pupils actually disappeared briefly. "And just in time . . ."

Madalynn was standing next to Jaida's bed, holding on to Arthur with one hand, and her other hand was turning, tilting a bottle of Tabasco over Jaida's open mouth.

Suddenly everything was in slo-mo, like a movie, the Bully laughing, the Victim sleeping, the Prank shivering, the Tabasco pouring . . .

. . . and the Helper helping.

Sam didn't even think, she just stuck her hand out and caught the flow. In her *solid* hand.

Madalynn's perfect lips made a little o of surprise.

Then Sam knocked the bottle of Tabasco away from Madalynn. With her *other* solid hand.

Madalynn's perfect lips made a capital O of shock.

Then Sam used *both* solid hands to grab Jaida by the shoulders as she screamed, "WAKE UP! RUN!"

Jaida jumped up, totally disoriented, shrieking, "WHAT? WHAT?"

Sam grabbed Jaida's hand, solid-body-slammed Madalynn to the floor, and ran out of the room, dragging Jaida behind her. They dashed down the hallway, and Sam misted right through the front door, stopped only by the nasty sound of the entire front of Jaida's body hitting the wood.

THWACK!

Crap! Sam turned and slid back through. Jaida was doing a *Looney Tunes* sort of stumbling reel, so Sam quickly unlocked the front door and dragged the cold-conked girl through, dashing past the entire MeanDreams tribe, who stood there watching with their mouths in capital Os so similar to Madalynn's it was freaksome, and out to the street. Which is when Jaida fainted, right into Sam's solid arms, and Sam was pretty much out of ideas.

Just then, like a melodic cavalry, she heard it.

> *Run away with me!*
> *Let me be your ride out of town . . .*

And Chadney raced up on a motorcycle, one burly arm maneuvering the handlebars and the other extended up above his red head in the quintessential soaring Broadway ballad pose.

Let me be the place that you hide!
We can make our lives on the go . . .

Sam did not need to be musically invited twice. She threw Jaida over the seat of the hog and jumped onto the back. Chadney peeled out, still singing, except now Sam couldn't really hear him over the sound of the MeanDreams yelling, and the motor, and the wind whizzing by, and her own heartbeat, and, eventually, the police siren.

The squad car tore up right behind them and Sam was in the perfect position to see the stunned, openmouthed face of her old pal Officer Stanhope as he chased a speeding motorcycle whose only visible passenger was a body hanging limply over the passenger backrest.

"Chadney! Go faster!" Sam screamed.

Chadney put the pedal to the metal while changing songs.

So long, farewell, auf Wiedersehen, good-bye!

He lurched onto a highway and Sam held on for dear life, praying fervently that her new solidity wouldn't suddenly fail her, leaving her essence to fly away like a released helium balloon. Besides, she was the only thing anchoring Jaida's comatose form to the bike, as Chadney was too busy trying to outrun the cops while singing all seven von Trapp children's parts from *The Sound of Music*. There weren't many cars on the road at this time of night, but the few Later drivers that they passed gawked, honked, craned a neck or two out a window, and one woman screamed soundlessly and let go of the steering wheel, causing her Honda to fishtail across two lanes of traffic. It was at this point that Sam closed her eyes.

Chadney swerved wildly off the highway onto a side street, the squad car in hot pursuit and gaining ground. *We're road toast.* There was no amount of inspirational singing and maniac driving that was going to get them far enough ahead to shake the police. *And then what?* Just as Sam was raking through her memory, trying to recall what Byron had said about how the Pranks dealt with the cops at the Galloping Ghost, Chadney pulled a hard left and drove up over a lawn and in between two houses.

"FENCE!" Sam shrieked, but Chadney had already veered right toward an open gate. They plunged through the backyard, scattering sports equipment and sandbox toys, and then Sam flung her quivering, barely solid body onto Jaida's knocked-out one as Chadney did a spectacular flying jump over a swimming pool. When she had the nerve to raise her head again, Sam gasped; they were speeding down her street.

As they screeched into the front yard, Byron popped out of the house with a dumbfounded expression. He raced over and they yanked Jaida from the motorcycle, dragging her across the lawn by her pajamas. The sirens grew closer as Byron shouted, "I forgot to unlock the door!" Sam did a split-second time calculation and jammed Jaida's head through Weezy's doggy door, then leapt through the wall and yanked Jaida's body the rest of the way into the house. They heard Chadney hit a triumphant B flat above high C and peel out. Sam collapsed to the floor as the sirens wailed past and there was sudden, blissful silence broken only by the slight rasp of Jaida's asthmatic breathing.

"How did you know? To send Chadney?" Sam knew her soul couldn't sweat, but she was suddenly tempted to sniff her armpits for stress stink.

"Well . . . I didn't, exactly. I just cornered him at school and said there might be trouble tonight. Of course, he totally acted like he didn't know me. As usual. What, did he just, like, pull up in front of her house?" Byron slid down the wall and sat next to Sam.

"Yep. Swooped in like a singing knight on horseback. I've never been so relieved to hear a cheesy ballad in my life." Sam finally allowed herself a small smile.

Jaida shifted and moaned slightly.

"Help me." Sam pulled herself to her feet, and together

they lifted Jaida. Byron carried her into the bedroom and put her under the covers, next to Sam's physical body. Weezy opened his pop eyes, surveyed the situation, and snorted, which was Pug for "You gotta be kidding me."

Sam and Byron stood, staring down at the strangest of bedfellows. After a moment, Byron spoke.

"Now what?"

"Not a clue."

Byron nodded, then shoulder-bumped Sam. "Guess you finally believe."

And, yep, she shoulder-bumped him back. "I believe."

fourteen

SAM WOKE UP the next morning to a very daunting sight: her nemesis sitting on the bed with a pug in her lap and an expression on her face that can only be described as "I've been watching you sleep and remembering all of my disembowelment threats."

Sam gulped and launched immediately into the scheme she and Byron had hatched the night before. "Hey there, good morning, Jaida! How did you sleep?" She had intended for this to sound all confident and happy, but it came out all shaky and *please don't hurt me.*

"How. Did. I. Sleep." Jaida parsed out the words with spaces of loathing in between.

"Yeah! 'Cause that's what you ask somebody after a *sleepover*—how did you sleep?" Sam burbled.

She's never gonna buy this. Good-bye, intestines.

The look Jaida gave her was reminiscent of someone stepping over vomit on the sidewalk. "Are you trying to tell me that we—*you and I*—had a *pajama party*?"

"Well, yeah! I mean, what do you call that?" Sam pointed to feathers littering the floor. "From our awesome pillow fight!" She held up a sheet of paper with pink and purple alternating script. "And here's the list of the guys we think are cute! And"—Sam drummed up her best acting chops for this one— "I found my bra in the freezer! Good one, Jaida! Ha-ha-ha-ha!"

The enemy stared at her in utter disbelief as Sam forcibly paralyzed her own facial muscles to retain their enthusiastic grin. Finally, by some miracle, Jaida actually looked slightly confused. "I had a wicked nightmare . . ." she mumbled gruffly.

"Yeah?" Sam said, not sure if it was wise to let Jaida relay her "nightmare" about being yanked out of bed by an invisible force and running face-first into a door.

She needn't have worried; Jaida was obviously not in the mood to share. Her eyes bored into Sam's for another long, agonizing moment before dropping away, which freed Sam up to lose her own forced smile. She resisted the temptation to rub her overworked jaw.

There was a supremely awkward silence as they both contemplated their next move. Jaida looked down at Weezy, who stared back in kind, his ginormous eyes unblinking. They stayed like that until Weezy sneezed, nailing Jaida with a direct hit of pug mucus.

"Oh jeez, sorry!" Sam jumped up to retrieve Weezy, but Jaida just shrugged, wiping her face on her sleeve.

"It's okay. I used to have a dog." Her voice was barely audible.

Was this a tiny opening? Sam ventured tentatively through the midget doorway of civil conversation. "Really? What kind?"

"A Yorkie, 'cause they're hypoallergenic. But it's actually mostly cats that I—" Jaida immediately realized her mistake, and her face hardened into an angry mask.

Sam knew she was basically taking her life in her own hands, but she couldn't stop herself. Maybe it was the newly discovered Helper in her, but she just had to know. "Why do you keep it a secret?"

The mask tightened. "Keep *what* a secret?"

"It's so not a big deal, you know." Sam was fairly horrified to hear herself continue talking. "Lots of kids have allergies and asthma—"

Now Jaida used that voice, the bitter, awful, threatening one that had kept Sam in a prison of fear for months. "I swear . . . *I swear*, if you keep talking, you're gonna regret it."

But suddenly, that voice lost its immobilizing power. Not because it was any less bitter, awful, or threatening, but because of the new thought that popped into Sam's head: *I'm such a hypocrite*. Hadn't her whole life been about keeping her *sleepwalking* a secret? Did she really need to ask Jaida *why*? Sam knew the answer already. Because it made Jaida different. And she didn't want to be different. How many times had Sam wished and prayed to be normal? Wasn't it possible that Jaida had wished and prayed the same thing? Maybe if Sam told her the truth, even if it sounded totally psycho, Jaida would know that she had a freak soul mate.

"I'm sorry," Sam said softly. "I understand how you feel—"

"Listen, just shut up, okay?" Jaida bit out. "Can you just shut your mouth? Please?"

Except she's not ready.

"Yes. I can. I can do that." The truth was going to have to wait. But not because Sam was afraid. She wasn't afraid anymore. And Jaida could tell, because she dropped her head onto her hand, obviously overwhelmed by the shift in her status.

"We should go," Sam murmured.

Jaida nodded.

"There's your stuff." Sam pointed to the clothes Byron

had retrieved from Jaida's house. "That, uh, *you* brought over. 'Cause, you know, we decided to have a sleepover."

On a school night, right after I got you sent to the principal's office, and after months of hating each other. Sam bit her lip, suddenly tempted to laugh.

Jaida shot her a look, then set Weezy gently on the bed and grabbed her clothes, stopping when she saw the fanny pack lying underneath her jeans.

"Thanks," she grunted over her shoulder.

Sam nodded. Maybe things that were born in the darkness really could venture into the light.

✳   ✳   ✳

Sam definitely wasn't a selfie snapper, but for once she wished she'd had her phone ready; she would have loved to have taken a video of the scene when she and Jaida showed up at the breakfast table. Margie gasped, burned herself on the waffle iron, and stuck her entire hand into the butter dish. Jax froze, his fork halfway to his mouth, and gawked at the unprecedented sight of his sister with what appeared to be someone of the buddy persuasion.

"Hey, guys, this is Jaida, from my school." Sam knew the next few moments were going to be weird, but somehow it just didn't seem to matter anymore.

"Are you freakin' kidding me?" Jax didn't even register that his utensil was still poised in midair. "You have a *friend*?!"

"Well . . . let's not push it." Sam couldn't resist shooting a rueful grin over at Jaida, and it almost seemed, for the briefest of seconds, that she might receive one back.

"JAIDA!" Margie threw a dish towel over her buttery hand and ran over, crushing Jaida in a giant hug. "WELCOME TO OUR HOME!"

"Jeez, Mom, don't break her ribs," Sam protested, but to her astonishment, Jaida's face melted into a genuine smile, and now Sam was the one rubbernecking.

"Thanks," Jaida sort of whispered.

"DO YOU LIKE WAFFLES?" Margie was still hugging and still shouting.

"Um, Mom?" Sam instinctively swooped in. "Can you show us the ingredient list? We're, uh, doing a project at school where we have to record everything we eat. It's for science. About . . . GMOs . . . and that kind of stuff."

And then the miracle of Jaida's genuine smile was bestowed upon Sam. It was exceedingly brief, morphing quickly to her usual closed-off expression, but still, it was a bona fide marvel.

✳ ✳ ✳

Margie kept up a steady stream of chatter on the drive to school, for which Sam was grateful; it somewhat deflected the weirdness of Jax's repeated looks of shock and awe from the front seat. Unsure of what was going to transpire between them when she and Jaida finally emerged from the car, Sam was trying to mentally prepare herself for any scenario.

Well, except for the one that actually took place.

Jaida got out first, and as Sam slid across the seat to follow, practicing her "Bye!" variations in her head—*friendly? casual? meaningful?*—she ran smack into Jaida, who had stopped abruptly right outside the car door. Sam grabbed on to Jaida's arm to steady herself, Jaida put out a hand to catch her, and that's exactly the position they were in, two girls obviously helping each other, when Madalynn saw them.

She was standing on the Wallace steps in her cheerleading uniform, and she was staring at them. And she was alone. Which immediately made Sam think of the first time she had seen Jaida all by herself and how it had put the thought in her mind that aloneness was a particular weakness. *Or a particular strength.* Sam logged this observation into her memory bank for later use, because, at the moment, it was being crowded out by *Seriously, how can Madalynn look that stunning even when she's obviously contemplating a double murder?*

And then, with one of her signature blazing-noonday-sun smiles, Madalynn whirled around and was gone, leaving

Sam and Jaida holding each other in a truly uncomfortable half embrace.

"Hey, dorks. You okay?" Jax rolled down his window to deliver this caring question.

They quickly split apart, embarrassed. Sam made a decision to let Jaida off the hook; there was no benefit to be had in forcing them to walk into school together. "I'm just gonna—" She motioned to her family.

Jaida looked relieved and, possibly, even a little grateful. "Yeah, okay." She took off toward the front door, her head down.

"'Kay, bye, guys." Sam slung her backpack over her shoulder.

"Have a great day, sweetie!" Margie crowed.

"She seems pretty decent. Try not to scare her off," Jax drawled.

Sam had to smile. *If you only knew.* But at the same time, she was strangely touched; it seemed like her brother actually wanted her to have a friend. It was sweet, no matter how unlikely the candidate was.

✳ ✳ ✳

Madalynn made numerous cameo appearances throughout Sam's day, and in every one, her gleamy daytime demeanor intensified, leaving sighing faculty and besotted students in her glittery wake. And the shinier she became, the more nervous Sam got. It was almost as if Madalynn were storing up as much happy energy as possible to better power her dark soul through the night.

By the end of school, Sam was a jittery train wreck. The one piece of good news was that in a stroke of medical irony, half the cast of *Flo! The Musical* had come down with strep throat and Mr. Todorov was reluctantly canceling rehearsal, which meant she wouldn't have to face Madalynn at set crew. Sam was slated to start building the pieces for the Renkioi Hospital scene, and somehow, constructing patients' beds and inserting battle paintings of the Crimean War into the window frames was strangely therapeutic. In fact, the challenging physical labor of sawing and hammering so helped Sam not think about vengeful SleepWakers that she kept going for hours, way past her scheduled time, and finished up the entire hospital set. It was nearly nine p.m. when she stood back, both to admire her work and pray she had so exhausted herself that her soul would just be too pooped to pop out of her body that night.

Of course, that was not the case.

In fact, her pooped soul not only popped, but apparently had the foresight to prep for battle in Margie's tool chest, because SleepWaker Sam woke up in front of Jaida's house clutching a big silver staple gun in her solid hand.

She groaned. *Seriously? What am I gonna do, staple Madalynn's essence to a tree?*

She quickly peeked into the bedroom. Jaida was sound asleep on the narrow bed, wearing a wool cap. Sam groaned louder. *Stupid Helper consciousness!* This compassion thing was exhausting, no matter how much rest her body was getting. She peered around anxiously, hoping to see Byron materialize through a fence or one of the many rusted cars lining the street, but no such luck. It was painfully quiet and still; not even one brave cricket. The silence was unnerving. Sam held the staple gun up like a revolver and shot off a couple of rounds of flying staples just to put a little bit of noise into the soundless darkness. *Where is Byron?* After all the times she told him not to stalk her without asking, he picked *tonight* to listen?

Without warning, the cloud of preteen evil materialized out of thin air, led by Queen MeanDream herself, in an adorable aquamarine babydoll nightie. As scared as Sam was, the first thought that crossed her mind was, *How many pairs of pajamas does this chick have?* Too bad Madalynn was too small to lend something to Bree—the beige giant was wearing the same faded nightgown for the fourth night in a row, and she didn't look particularly happy about it. In fact, the expression on her monochromatic face was downright murderous.

"Well, Sleep Sis," drawled Madalynn. "I thought we might find you here." She turned to Zac. "Now that our friend is able to be solid, I think she needs a big hug, don't you?"

Before Sam could process this command, Zac lunged, catching her in a crushing embrace. Her initial reaction to the pain was to wisp out, think herself un-solid, but something stopped her. *You can't force me to be nothing again.* Instead, Sam endured the supposed lovelock, gritting her teeth, compelling her soul to push back with all the weight and possibility she could muster.

Madalynn laughed. "Okay. If that's how you want to play it. Let her go, Zac." With a grunt of regret, Zac released her and Sam stumbled away, breathing hard. "So, Sam. Last night was something, huh? I'm not sure protecting your enemy counts as justice."

"Which means you don't get to be a Dream," Bree said hostilely. "You're out."

Sam quickly decided that yelling "Yay!" would be unwise, although she was sorely tempted. She arranged her features into as pleasant and bland an expression as she could manage. "Oh, well, guess I'm just not cut out for your tribe. But listen, thanks for everything and hope to see you around the streetlights sometime!" Sam gave what she hoped was a winning smile.

"Oh, Sam, if only it were that easy." Madalynn sighed. "Unfortunately, in the process of trying to restore balance between you and Jaida," she continued, "I'm afraid things

have gotten a little out of whack with . . . you and me."
She sighed deeply, conveying all the angsty responsibility of
being a highly attractive bearer of bad news.

Her earlier bravado waning, Sam felt her soul heart start
to bongo. "Oh . . . really? Because I feel like we're good.
All . . . even and level. And, like, horizontal and, uh, linear
with us . . ."

"Oh, Sam, come now. Did you or did you not push me
down in front of my entire tribe?" Madalynn questioned,
turning to the MeanDreams. "What did you guys see?"

"She knocked you flat," said the MeanDreams flatly.

"Not to mention friending the enemy at school today,
after all I went through to render her friend*less*." Madalynn
shook her head. "You've disrespected me, disrupted the
course of justice, and disheartened my tribe. That's a few
too many disses, Sam. So now I'm going to have to respond
in kind."

"What does that mean, exactly? 'Cause, it sounds a little
Mafia." Sam tried for a chuckle, but instead horrified herself by doing an exact imitation of Margie's wedged-hairball
laugh.

And then it all happened so fast.

Madalynn snapped her fingers, and her tribe parted to
reveal a few members of the Broadways, who, although looking utterly terror-stricken, still managed to pull off a decent

overture in three-part harmony. A shivering Arthur struck a triangle with a beater, while Bree and Zac kneeled in front of Madalynn and flicked on two bright flashlights, the combined beams creating a very convincing spotlight.

And Madalynn attacked. Her first note, that is.

Listen...

Then she launched into a showstopper, the eleven o'clock number, the soul barer, in an alto belt that shook the sidewalk.

No one's going to tell me how to live
I don't think so
"You get a little and so you give"
My heart says no
I'm the one who pulls the strings
of the guitar
in my song

You think you've got me figured out
I don't think so
Want to see me filled with doubt
My shrink says no
I'm the one who pulls the strings
of the guitar
in my song

Madalynn was singing so loud, the force of her voice blew Sam's hair back from her face. She was no music expert, but it reminded her of that song from *Frozen* mixed with what it might sound like if *Texas Chainsaw Massacre* was made into a musical.

You want me just to ignore
I don't think so
That I was lying on the floor
I don't think so
Yours was the first shot of the war
You destroyed our great rapport
So, I declare that heretofore
I plan for vengeance, payback galore
Hard-core
I will restore
A level score
The Waker world has a door
That will be shut forevermore
For
I'm the one who pulls the strings
of the guitar
In my soooooong

Madalynn held her blaring final note for a good twenty seconds, her mist arms stretched into the air. Silence. Sam wasn't quite sure what to do, so she awkwardly applauded.

Then Bree and Zac lunged forward, hauling a stumbling body between them, a slender dark-haired girl who looked vaguely familiar. "Take a peek into your future, darlin'," Madalynn purred to Sam, who stared in disbelief.

It was Minnie Mouse.

The Juvenold that Alyssa said was "sent back."

And now Sam knew what "sent back" meant, because Minnie's eyes were half-open, her face was blank, and there was a noticeable absence of a silver cord floating behind her.

Minnie was no longer a SleepWaker; she was, once again, a sleep*walker*. Somehow, Madalynn had taken the darkness, the night, and the freedom of her soul away from Minnie Mouse.

Madalynn and the MeanDreams started to drag Minnie away. And just before they disappeared into the night, Minnie woke up and started screaming.

"Noooo!" Sam screamed, too. She would have charged after them, hyper-crossed like an essence on fire, if Byron hadn't suddenly materialized and blocked her.

"Stop! Sam, stop!" He held on to her, one solid soul grasping another.

"Let me go! I have to—!" Sam pummeled and kicked, her misty heart throbbing in terror. *How did this happen? How* could *this happen?*

"You can't go up against them all by yourself, Helper or not!" Byron shouted, and she finally stopped pushing, reeling back, remembering Minnie's slack expression, the slightly open mouth, the dead eyes. *That's what I looked like.* All that time, that was what her mother and Jax had been seeing, had been dealing with. *I can't go back to that. I can't.* Joanne's words rang in her head. *That one desperate, exhausted life.*

"Sam. Look at me." Byron shook her, trying to get her attention.

"They . . . they had some of the Broadways," Sam whispered.

"Yeah. I heard the power ballad on my way over," Byron said grimly.

"And Minnie . . . did you see her? Did you see what they did to her?"

"I didn't really see much of anything. I only heard you scream and—"

"Where were you? Why weren't you here?" Sam wasn't even able to pretend anymore. And she was glad when he looked shamefaced.

"I'm sorry, I was . . . Listen, I know you've never been happy about me being By the Spy, but my mother asked me to do it. I mean, not to be a spy, but just to make sure new Wakers are okay," Byron said, visibly agitated. "Knavish detached a new Extreme tonight, and I was supposed to show her the ropes. Literally. Their souls like to do stuff like zip-line between skyscrapers."

"Well, just . . . bad timing, okay?" was all she could manage. Sam reached down and grabbed her staple gun, felt the weight in her hand, trying to ground herself in this nightmare.

"Tell me."

"Minnie . . . she's a sleepwalker again. That's what Alyssa meant when she said the MeanDreams 'sent her back.'" As Sam expected one type of reaction from Byron—the same horror she felt—it hurt a lot more to see his confusion and disbelief.

"That's not possible. They don't have that kind of power. They can't."

She almost dropped her wimpy weapon. "I know what I saw."

"But . . . come on . . . you've never actually *seen* someone sleepwalking before, right?" Byron was shaking his head, obviously completely closed off to this possibility. "We *were* sleepwalkers, but I never *saw* anyone else in the act, did you? So how do you know for sure?"

"Byron." Sam felt sick to her soul stomach. "There was no silver cord."

"You must have missed it. You missed it the first time I showed you, remember?" Sam looked into his eyes. She could see that he was not going to budge, but for the life of her, she couldn't fathom why.

"Okay. If you say so." She looked down at the staple gun, turned it over and over in her hands. There was a dead silence between them.

"What are you gonna do now?" Byron asked uncomfortably.

"I'll stay here. Just to make sure Madalynn's not coming back to, like, drown Jaida and her dad in tap water."

"I'll stay with you."

"Nope, I'm good." She gave him a smile that signaled his release from duty. "If they come back, I'll shoot staples into their eyes."

"But—"

"I'm good."

Byron nodded, hesitant.

And then he was gone.

Well, he was a Roamer, after all. What did she expect?

More. Her inner voice never failed to tell the annoying truth. *I expected more.*

fifteen

O W W W W W W.

This was the first thought that passed through her waking mind the next morning. Ever since she'd been a SleepWaker, the mornings had been revelatory for Sam— the feeling of a rested body, relaxed muscles, renewed cells, and all that good stuff—it was mind-blowing. But today . . . not so much.

Sam raised an arm to rub her crusty eyes and immediately noticed the scratches on her hand. *What the heck?! Did my body fall out of bed onto a porcupine?* She looked over to see if Weezy had somehow gone rabid in the middle of the night, and immediately moaned—her neck was painfully stiff. What in the wide green world was going on? This was what it felt like when—

No. Sam didn't even want to complete that thought, but her independent brain forged ahead without her permission. *When . . . I was sleepwalking.*

Of course, this was impossible. She had a clear memory of her soul enduring the awful events of the night before. There was even physical evidence, for Pete's sake; the staple gun rested heavily on her blanketed leg. "So, yeah, impossible, right?" she said out loud to Weezy, who opened one googly eye and snorted gently. He then commenced to give Sam an early morning lick-down, which was both disgusting and comforting. As his rough tongue caressed her ouchy flesh, she said it to herself again and again: *Impossible. Right?*

✳ ✳ ✳

As she limped over to Wallace, Sam tried to focus on solving the mystery of her achy body and not on the cryptic phone call she had received from Principal Nussbaum requesting her presence at school on a Saturday morning. She tried to convince herself that he wanted to compliment her in person on how much she'd changed recently, what with the staying-awake-in-classes-and-answering-a-question-here-and-there thing, but when he met her at the doors to the auditorium with a confused/enraged expression on his face, that fantasy went right out the window. Mr. Todorov stood next to him, weeping, "If you wanted us to do *Fiddler on the Roof*, why couldn't you just say so?!"

Sam felt a familiar sense of dread. Whatever was going on, she knew it was going to be big and messy and hard to explain. And probably expensive. Definitely expensive.

Principal Nussbaum flung the auditorium doors open and Sam gasped.

The entire set that she had built the day before was on the ceiling.

Under the ceiling? On the floor of the ceiling?

What am I looking at?

Renkioi Hospital, with its beds and Crimean War pastorals and Florence Nightingale's nursing station, was *nailed to the ceiling of the auditorium and hanging upside down.*

"How is that even possible?" Sam whispered.

"I was hoping *you* could tell *me*," said Principal Nussbaum icily.

"What do you mean?" She couldn't seem to raise her voice any louder than a guilty-sounding mumble.

He pointed a finger violently behind her at the security station. Sam turned slowly as Claudia, the security guard, pressed "play" on the video system at her desk. Sam approached, her terror mounting, as a grainy figure moved across the screen.

"Are you *flyin'* on me?" Claudia said in disbelief.

Because the grainy figure on screen was Sam.

My body is still sleepwalking. Even with my soul freed, my body can't rest.

The grainy-screen Sam opened a ladder.

I'm not a Helper. I'm not even a MeanDream. I'm worse than that.

The screen-Sam grabbed a hammer and nails and started up the ladder.

People show who they really are in the darkness. In the darkness, my body is still destroying things.

The screen Sam reached the top of the ladder, turned, and very deliberately looked into the camera.

And smiled.

A very familiar, very shiny, gleamy, megawatt smile that was not Sam's at all.

Payback galore had begun.

✳   ✳   ✳

"I'm telling you, Madalynn is hijacking bodies!" Sam yelped.

"Not scientifically possible," Fletch said with utmost conviction.

"But I *saw* her! I saw *her* face in *my* face! And look at my hands!" She displayed her scratched, bruised fingers. "How do you explain that?!" Sam had never understood her mother better than now, because all she wanted to do was tear her own hair out.

"A few boo-boos does not an upside-down castle make." Fletcher was being maddeningly confident. "How could Madalynn possibly have done that all by her lonesome?"

"I don't know! She probably had the whole tribe with her, but she was the only one who decided to be visible! Because she wants me expelled, or, like, hauled into juvenile court!" Sam's voice was so shrill by this point, she was surprised the clinic's windows were still intact.

"Samantha, calm down," said Joanne, briskly grabbing a tube of ointment and applying the goo to Sam's wounds. "We realize this is a very emotional time for you, but nothing is to be gained by ranting."

Sam submitted to Joanne's gooing with gritted teeth. "Okay. Listen. Queen MeanDream has figured out how to hop into a soul vacancy, and she's also turning Sleep*Wakers* back into sleep*walkers*, and those two things have to be connected somehow, and you don't think that deserves a rant?!" Her voice rose again against her will. "Besides, how can you say 'not scientifically possible,' when *you* were the ones who told me that scientists pretty much know zip?" Joanne sighed rather dramatically and wrapped Sam's hands in gauze.

"Well . . . she makes some good points, Jo," Fletch said, his conviction obviously wavering. "We really don't know what we're talking about half the time. Except, of course, for Knavish, who's a genius."

"Just the sort of thing one likes to hear during one's entrance," came a voice from the doorway, and in walked Dr. Richard Knavish himself, his green-tinted glasses sparkling with raindrops.

"Richard! Thank you for coming!" Fletch looked over at Sam. "I hope you don't mind, Samantha, but I called him right after Joanne received your textual this morning." He grabbed a tissue and extended it to Knavish. "Would you like to dry your—"

"No!" Knavish recoiled as if Fletcher had tried to hand him a live snake. Then, more calmly, "No, I'm perfectly fine."

That dude is so strange. But Sam was desperate for any kind of help at this point, even from a man whose eyes looked like lime slices. "Dr. Knavish, what is happening?!"

Knavish tossed his raincoat onto a hook. "That's what I'm trying to ascertain, child. You are absolutely certain it was Madalynn?"

"I'm sure," Sam said strongly. "It was my body, but her smile."

Knavish murmured, "Hmmm, I wonder . . . 'Before the

silver cord is severed, and the dust returns to the ground it came from' . . . the Tanakh, 450 BCE."

"What does *that* mean?" Sam exclaimed.

"You're not thinking that her cord will be severed?" said Joanne, aghast.

Fletch turned to Sam. "Did your principal mention that Madalynn was disembodied or dead today?"

"Uh, no. But I don't get it, why would jumping into my body sever her cord? Doesn't it go through anything? Mine went through cars, for crying out loud." Sam heard herself and shuddered.

Knavish shook his head. "It's about intent. Passing one's silver cord through the worldly flesh of another in order to possess and subjugate . . . It's against human nature, and in theory, should result in death. But it appears that death is not immediate . . . hmmm . . . Perhaps she's figured out how to inhabit other bodies only temporarily." Knavish was pacing back and forth, almost talking to himself at this point. "But it's very dangerous. Repeated bodyhopping will fray the lifeline beyond recognition, eventually causing it to snap, and Lord knows what it might do to the host. Fascinating . . ."

The host. That would be me. Sam felt like something black and slimy was crawling inside of her. "This is too much. I can't do this anymore. I thought sleepwalking was the worst life ever, but . . ." She turned to Fletch in despair. "I'd rather sleepwalk off a cliff than go through this."

"Oh, honey . . . don't say that."

Her mother was standing at the door, and her appearance made Sam gasp for two reasons: first of all, Margie had her arm around Jaida. But also, Margie had cut off all her hair and was sporting a half-inch buzz that matched the regrowth in her bald spot, showing off a perfectly shaped head and a lovely face with just a trace of dark circles under the eyes.

"Mom . . . you look amazing." Sam knew she sounded way more stunned than she should, but *come on*, how many kids can brag that their mother looks awesome nearly bald?

Margie smiled as Fletch made a stab at hospitality. "Come in, come in! Do you need a cup of tea? I can send Jo to the Seven-Eleven." Joanne must have reached her 7-Eleven excursion limit, because she pursed her lips in annoyance.

"No, thank you." Margie closed her umbrella as Sam approached Jaida tentatively.

"Hey."

"Hey." Jaida looked guarded. "This place is weird."

Despite her black sludge emotional state, Sam almost smiled. "Total understatement."

The door opened again to reveal a soaking-wet Jax. "I thought you were coming back with the umbrella," he said to Margie.

"Oops! Sorry, honey. My mind . . ." She fluttered her hands around her sassy 'do.

"Jax?" Sam looked back and forth between her brother and Jaida. "Why are you guys here?"

"Celebrating a brand-new holiday." Jax grabbed a hospital gown from Fletch's exam table to dry himself off. "I'm dubbing it Upside-Down Day."

"Jax!" Margie hissed.

"How did you find out?" Sam said dully. "Was it on the news?"

"Instagram. You already have over six thousand likes."

"Great." Sam flopped down in a chair, overwhelmed.

"Well, now, I don't think we all know each other! Introductions all around!" Fletch launched back into his role of amiable master of ceremonies. "Have you met my mentor, Dr. Richard Knavish?" He waved in the general direction of Knavish, who was rubbing his eyes and mumbling to himself. "And this is . . . ?" Fletcher peered closely at Jaida, who had the normal reaction to such expansive sclerae.

"Whoa!" She stared for a moment in awe, then had the grace to look embarrassed. "Sorry. I'm Jaida."

"Of course, of course. So! What should we all talk about?"

Fletch used his brightest voice for this ridiculous question, and everyone in the room just looked at one another for a long moment. Finally:

"We could talk about this. I found it under my bed." Jaida held up an empty bottle of Tabasco.

"We could talk about this. I found it stuck in Weezy's doggy door." Margie held up a clump of wavy hair that quite obviously belonged to the girl bearing the hot sauce.

"Hmmm, all very interesting." Jax made a mock-thoughtful face. "But I'm thinking maybe we could talk about *this*." He held up his phone, with the Instagram photo of the hospital set debacle, which now was at over seven thousand likes and climbing.

Sam winced. "We'll get to all of those. But first . . . we should talk about *this*." She turned to Margie and took a deep, shuddering breath. *Here goes.* "Mom, I'm sorry that I got suspended. Again. But I'm more sorry that I've been lying to you. I just didn't think that you would believe the truth, or maybe . . . that you could handle it. And the truth is"—Sam looked at Fletch, who nodded his permission—"Dr. Fletcher has figured out a way to release the souls of sleepwalkers so that they can resolve whatever it is that makes them so restless at night. I know, I know, that sounds off-the-chain bonkers, but it's true. And he says that *my* soul is a Helper, and that's what drove me to do the crazy things I did all my life. And I'm finding out that being a Helper is hard and scary and dangerous, and that people can do bad things to you while you're trying to help, or even *because* you're trying to help, and I don't know if I can do this. All I've ever wanted was to be normal, and this is really, really far away from normal." Sam was crying now. "And I'm also scared that you won't be able to stand it, because you're afraid of losing me like we lost Dad, but I don't know what else to do. I can't go back, but I can't seem to go forward, either. I need your help. I'm a Helper that needs *your* help." This last bit was a sob, a downright snot-laden ugly cry.

Margie was still, silent, staring at the ground, listening. When she finally lifted her head, it seemed lighter and not just because of the hair-free haircut. "Sam. I do believe you. Because . . . I think your father must have been some kind of Helper, too."

This was the last thing she'd expected to come out of her mother's mouth, and it dried up Sam's tears like a cosmic Kleenex. She and Jax looked at each other, then gaped at Margie, and in unison, exclaimed, *"What?!"*

"Fascinating . . ." breathed Knavish, pulling up a chair to listen. All he needed was a container of popcorn and his moviegoing persona would have been complete.

Margie spoke slowly, haltingly. "Your dad . . . he was like you. I would always find him sleepwalking in dangerous

places, doing things I couldn't understand. The night he . . .
we were living in Point Pleasant at the time. You and Jax
were little and Grandma was with us; I needed her because I
was always chasing him in the middle of the night. But that
time . . . he got out without me knowing. When I caught up
to him, when I saw him, he was standing by the Manasquan
River, it seemed almost like he was waiting, almost like he
knew. And then a car went straight off the bridge into the
water. And your dad walked . . . he walked right to the edge
and I realized, *He's going to go in, he's going in after the car,* and
I ran and I grabbed him, I was screaming, I held him as hard
as I could as the car sank lower and lower, but he got away,
and he went in, swimming, he went under, for such a long
time, and I knew he was still asleep, and when he finally
came up—it wasn't him. It was another man, the man who
had been driving, and your dad . . . your dad . . . he didn't
come up. He never came up." Margie took a moment to com-
pose herself, then continued, pushing the words out. "And
I thought, it's because of me. It was because I tried to stop
him. Because I held him for so long, the car sank so low, he
had to go so deep . . . if I hadn't stopped him, if I had let him
do what he needed to do, he wouldn't have died. And I . . . I
kind of lost my mind and I ran. I ran home and I hid under
the covers. Until the police came to the door a few hours
later to tell me what had happened. They found the car and

they found . . . your dad. But they never found the man he saved. No one ever found out if he actually survived."

Margie stopped then, not because she was necessarily done, but because Sam was hugging her, hugging her so hard Margie probably couldn't get enough air to utter another word, and then Margie was hugging back, gripping Sam with the same gridlock squeeze, and they probably would have stayed that way until one of them passed out, if not for the quiet voice that interrupted their fierce embrace.

"He survived."

Sam and Margie drew apart, and Jax turned slowly.

"I survived." Dr. Fletcher spoke again, his face bewildered and astonished and afraid, all at the same time.

A million questions hung in the air, and no one seemed to know which to ask first. The fragile silence hung like a soap bubble, short-lived but full of wonder.

And then Knavish popped it, leaping from his chair and applauding. "Bravo!" he shouted. "Oh, this really is too wonderful!" He blew kisses up to the heavens. "Great Muses, what perfection! I couldn't have written it better myself!" Knavish danced about, even clicking his heels at one point, but after what had just happened, it only seemed mildly loony.

It was Jaida who finally tried to make sense of something that made no sense. "So . . . you didn't know?" She looked at Margie, at Fletch, at Jax and Sam. "Come on. You didn't know . . . *any of you*? For real?"

"Aquaphobia . . ." breathed Joanne. "No wonder . . ." She grabbed the tissue that was still crushed in Fletch's hand and wiped the perspiration from her forehead and the back of her neck.

"I ran away, too." Fletch faced Margie. "I'm sorry."

Margie nodded, somewhat understanding, but not really. "Why?"

"I was a different man in those days." Which sounded very dramatic and heady, so Fletch clarified. "I mean, literally. My name is not really Baptiste Fletcher. It's Bob Flemkowsky. And I wasn't always a sleep doctor. I was a podiatrist."

A communal gasp led to very individual reactions.

Knavish crowed, "Marvelous! Delicious! Bob Flemkowsky the podiatrist! Bobby the foot doctor becomes Baptiste the rogue parasomnia specialist! Brilliant!" He extracted a tiny notebook from his breast pocket and feverishly began taking notes.

Margie remained steady, listening intently.

Joanne dug inside the collar of her crisp white uniform and mopped the tissue in her armpits, murmuring, "I should have known. I mean, who names their kid Baptiste?"

Jaida took a very public hit off her inhaler.

Jax said in a dazed voice, "Feet are gross."

Sam, for her part, was trying to remain open. She wasn't exactly thrilled at the thought of her eternal soul being released by a dude who used to shave warts off people's lower digits, but if there was anything she was learning from this whole experience, it was that things are not always what they appear to be. And despite the rampant labeling in both the daytime and Waker worlds, Sam was becoming a big believer in the concepts of change and possibility.

Fletcher continued, "As you've probably noticed, my visage is rather unusual. So, imagine me as a child with these same-sized eyeballs on a much smaller body. I was the object of terrible scorn, so vicious and inhuman that I learned to never raise my head to look others in the eye. Therefore, it was a natural progression to becoming a podiatrist; I could use my scientific skills while always looking downward."

"Makes sense," mumbled Jaida.

Knavish sighed in origin-story rapture.

"But I was a very angry man. Dishonest. I stole from my patients. I charged them for procedures they didn't ask for and didn't need. I knew I had hit rock bottom when I started to think about amputating people's pinky toes just for fun. Did you know that the pinky toe balances the entire body? I did. And I wanted everyone to be off-balance, as they had made me feel for so many years." Fletch shook his head sadly. "The best thing that ever happened to me was driving off that bridge. I took it as a sign to begin again, to start my life anew. I saw it as a baptism, hence my new choice of name: Baptiste."

Everyone in the room was hanging on each word. "And what about 'Fletcher'?" Sam whispered. "Why did you choose that?"

Fletch looked mildly surprised at the question. "Oh. That was just because 'Flemkowsky' is such a heinous last name. It sounds like a farm animal hacking up sputum."

"It really does," said Jax. Everyone nodded.

"I never meant to cause you pain." Fletch now addressed Margie directly. "When I read in the newspaper that it was a sleepwalker who drowned, I dedicated myself to helping those with parasomnias. Your husband saved my life, a life that wasn't really worth saving. But I determined that I would not receive his gift in vain. I ran away so that I could leave everything, absolutely all of my old self, behind."

"I understand," Margie said softly.

"Jax?" Fletch held out a skinny hand, which Jax eyed for a moment before he shook.

"Okay, Flemkowsky," he said quietly.

Then Fletch peered at Sam, his sclerae vulnerable and questioning. "Do you forgive me, Samantha?"

Before she could answer, the door slammed open to

reveal Byron; it was strange enough for Sam to see him in daylight hours, but the weirdness was totally exacerbated by his wearing of an extremely nerdy rain poncho. If Byron was startled by the cast of characters in the room, he didn't show it; his eyes were focused on Sam.

"Byron?" Joanne questioned. "How did you—?"

"Instagram," said Jax.

"Yeah." Byron pulled off his poncho hood. "Sam. Obviously, I was totally wrong last night and you were right. I'm sorry. Do you forgive me?"

Before Sam could answer, Jaida jumped up. "Okay, you know what? There seems to be a theme here, so I'm just gonna get this over with. Sam, I'm sorry about . . . uh . . . well, there's a lot. But I really am sorry, about all of it. I can explain more later. I think I can, anyway . . . but do you think you could ever forgive me?"

Sam was tempted to laugh. Or cry. Here she was, being asked for forgiveness, from her SleepWaker sort-of crush, her daytime sort-of enemy, and the man her father had pretty much died for—the man who, in turn, had truly given her a new life. Maybe it wasn't the life she had desired or planned for, maybe it wasn't "normal," but at least it was genuine. Genuine and right and utterly bizarre, just like she was.

Helper.

That's what her dad was. And who she was. And now

she could feel it, she could feel the change, her essence dropping into place at last. Samantha Fife was herself, finally,
body and soul. And ready to do what she was destined for:
to help rescue the SleepWaker world from the clutches of a
beautiful bully.

"Forgiven," she said softly.

Time to bring some light to the darkness.

sixteen

IT'S NOT EVERY HEROINE'S QUEST that begins
in the middle of the night at the SuperSlide Amusement Park
in Bismarck, North Dakota, but Sam was not every heroine.

She and Byron were searching for the teacups ride,
which shouldn't have been difficult considering they'd been
told that there was a giant red-and-yellow teapot in the
middle, but no matter what ride they misted through, they
kept ending up at either the Go-Kart Roadway or the batting
cages. Finally they slid through the SuperSlide and spotted
the objects of their hunt: SleepWakers packed into all six
of the circular cups, arms around each other's shoulders,

leaning forward in total face lock, talking in hushed, urgent tones. This was the Clutch.

"They look pretty intense," Sam whispered. "You think they'll be open to this?"

"Well, hopefully from you," said Byron. "I don't know why, but they've never been very chummy with me."

"Okay. Here goes." Sam approached the teacups tentatively. "Excuse me? Can we talk to you guys for a minute?"

The murmuring at Teacup #1 subsided, and a number of faces turned to look at Sam and Byron. One rather elfin-looking girl with a sharp chin and pointy ears stood very slowly, both her hands still held by other Wakers.

"Are you Clutch?" Her voice was hesitant, suspicious.

"Uh, no, we are not . . . Clutch," said Sam. "I'm Samantha, a Helper. You probably don't know what that is, right?"

Elf Girl leaned in to her teacup and whispered with her fellow . . . *Clutchers? Clutchees?* Sam looked at Byron, who shrugged.

Elf Girl turned back, tilted her pointy chin up. "We do not know what that is." She said it with finality, an air of "we're done here."

"Listen, um, what's your name?" Sam stepped forward and the Clutch did what the Clutch apparently does, which is Clutch one another. "Hey, it's okay! We're not gonna hurt anyone!" Sam tried to sound soothing. "Dr. Hopkins told us where to find you."

Elf Girl leaned in and whispered again to her tribe. Sam was starting to feel a bit agitated. How the heck were they going to persuade any of these guarded, secluded souls to help them battle the MeanDreams? They couldn't even get them to step out of their stupid teacups. But Hopkins's name must have carried some weight, because Elf Girl turned back.

"I am Wichachpi."

Byron and Sam looked at each other. "Sorry?" Sam said. "Can you repeat that?"

"Wichachpi."

"But your jacket says . . . Lauren," said Byron, narrowing his eyes.

She tilted her chin again. "My Clutch name."

"Oh! So, you all have, like, different names at night? Is that what you mean?" Sam was trying, but Wichachpi Lauren wasn't making this easy.

"Our souls are our true selves. They have their own names, not stamped by a parent's expectations." This, from an extremely short boy with extremely long arms who held Wich's left hand, even though he was seated on her right.

"Huh. O-*kay*," Byron muttered.

"So, are you the leader here? Because I have something very important to tell you," said Sam.

"I am sorry, Helper, but the Clutch does not recognize your right to speak here, because of your association with a Roamer." Wich spoke with authority. "Their tribe does not believe in connection. It only exists for the individual. Therefore, your words are to be disregarded."

Byron looked completely taken aback, and Sam sputtered angrily, "Hey! You can't do that! That's judgy and, and . . . tribe-ist! You have no idea who this person is, and what he's done for the Wakers! He's more connected than anyone!"

The short long-armed boy declared, "If this is so, then he is not a true Roamer. But perhaps it is just that he has not yet been put to the test. When he is, he will save himself, not others. That is the Roamer's way." Long Arms and Wich turned away and were absorbed back into the human knot.

Perhaps it was the slight rise of unease in her stomach, or Byron suddenly looking kinda busted, but something drove Sam to seriously overreact. She march-misted right through the ticket turnstile and invaded the Clutch's personal teacup space, knocking sharply on the red plastic to get their attention. "Listen, *Lauren* and—" She pointed at Long Arms.

"Odakotah."

"And Odakotah, you think just because you can do a group hug, that makes you relationship experts? Let me tell you what real 'connection' is! It's hyper-crossing half-way across the country to freakin' North Dakota, which is, like, practically freakin' *Canada*, just to warn you about a dangerous tribe that's messing up our world! *How* danger-ous? Well, let's just say that my body is currently tied down and guarded by a group of Laters to keep it from getting snatched by a psycho SleepWaker! So, you can take your fancy soul names and your weird no-contraction sentences that you think make you sound all mysterious, and you can stick them right up your—"

"Sam?" Byron gently tugged on her pajama sleeve. "I think you're losing them."

He was right. The Clutch was rising and silently filing out of their teacups onto the gravel path.

"Hey! Hey, where are you going?" Sam barked.

"We are retiring to the Bouncy Bounce House," Wich said stiffly. "It is an enriching communal experience. We wish you well with your physical-body-robbing dilemma." Long Arms stood on his tiptoes and mumbled something into one of her pointy ears. She nodded and with a slight bow to Sam and Byron, intoned *"Wakan tanan kici un,"* then glided away arm in arm with a Waker in boxer shorts and a half tee.

"What do you think *that* means?" Byron muttered.

"I think she just told us to go hug a moving train," Sam muttered back, gritting her teeth. The Clutch was about to disappear through the SuperSlide and Sam just wasn't up to navigating the Go-Kart track again, so she called out, "Wait! Please wait! *Wichachpi!*"

Wichachpi stopped and slowly turned around. Boxer Shorts tried to whisper something, but she held up her hand. "So. You *do* know how to say my fancy soul name."

Sam smiled slyly. "Are you messing with me, Wich?"

"I do not mess," Wichachpi said formally. "But remembering and correctly pronouncing another's moniker is a bridge to true relationship. Therefore, I grant you one chance to explain the nature of your visit. And this time, do not quibble and say you only came to bring a warning. It is obvious you desire something from us."

"Whatever, *Lauren*," Byron mumbled sourly.

"Let me handle this, 'kay?" Sam said out of the side of her mouth.

"Knock yourself out. I'm just gonna go be a disconnected individual over here." Byron walked to the SuperSlide and flopped down on his back in the green section, putting his hands behind his head and staring up at the insanely starry sky, which was one of the few good things about being in practically freakin' Canada.

Sam observed the way the Clutch was like an unbroken chain, each one in contact with another by way of a held hand, an arm around the waist, a half hug, and she sighed. *This is either gonna be really tough or really easy.*

"We want you to come to an emergency meeting of all the SleepWakers. In Dr. Fletcher's sector. Tonight. We have to figure out how to stop Madalynn and the MeanDreams before they destroy our nighttime lives and our daytime lives, too. And we have to figure it out together. You, of all Wakers, should know that we can *only* be strong together. Will you come?"

A buzz of voices immediately rose up from the Clutch. Wichachpi put up her hand for silence.

"We did not know it was the MeanDreams you spake of. They are a danger to all Wakers." Wichachpi seemed tentative for the first time.

"That's why we were spaking of them!" Byron called out from his prone position. "Maybe you should pay attention when people spake!"

Wichachpi shot Byron a dirty look.

"Okay, thanks for your input!" Sam called to Byron, then turned to Wich again. "We need you. Please."

The Clutch murmured as they Clutched even closer. But Sam was watching only Wichachpi, knowing that if she'd won her over, the rest would follow by nature, for they couldn't bear to be apart. The elfin girl tilted her pointed chin upward, listening, as if her sharp little ears were antennae.

"And where is Dr. Fletcher's sector?"

Sam breathed a massive sigh of relief, then grinned. "See ya in Jersey, dudes."

✳ ✳ ✳

But before she could see anyone in Jersey, dudes, Sam and Byron had one more stop to make. New Rochelle, New York.

"A real castle? In America?" Unfortunately, Sam was hyper-crossing through Niagara Falls when she asked this question, so apparently all Byron heard was pounding water. It wasn't until they were buzzing through Buffalo that he was able to answer.

"Yeah, it's called Leland Castle, built in the nineteenth century by some crazy old rich guy. The Extremes love it."

It was easy to see why. As soon as they approached the imposing palatial mansion, Sam spied a figure balanced precariously atop a granite cross at the very tip-top of the structure, a hundred feet in the air. But only for a second, because then the figure jumped.

"HEYYYY!!" Sam screamed, her Helper spirit spontaneously spurring her soul body to hyper-hyper-cross toward the hurtling SleepWaker. Before Sam could even get into rescuing range, however, the Waker's head came within probably an inch of the ground, and then her misty form rubber-banded back up in the air with a shriek of triumph.

Byron was relaxed. "I told you the Extremes love to bungee jump. It's not like she's actually gonna crash, right? She can just make her head un-solid—"

"Give me a minute," Sam gasped. "Can't listen to Waker logic when I can't even breathe." She turned away from the nauseating sight of the Extreme bouncing up and down the entire height of the edifice, but whirled back when she heard the sound of glass shattering.

"Emmy!" Now Byron was annoyed. "I told you, you can't be solid when you go through windows!"

"Don't be such a buzzkill, By." The Extreme poked her head back through the obliterated window, picking a shard of glass from an elaborate set of multicolored braces on her teeth.

"That's Emmy, the new one," Byron said to Sam, shaking his head. "Even as far as Extremes go, she's pretty extreme." He yelled back up to the roof, "Guys! Can you come down here?"

The groans and catcalls came from far above, and Sam had to crane her neck back to see the outline of a group of SleepWakers balancing on turrets atop the castle's west wing.

"Seriously! I need to talk to you anyway, so come down to earth, please!" Byron shouted.

One by one, the Extremes made sickening leaps from the turrets into nearby trees, shimmying to the ground. Emmy, of course, chose to rappel down the side of the castle on her bungee cord, which almost immediately gave way, plunging her at a wicked speed toward terra firma. She landed on her feet like a particularly nimble cat in pajamas.

Byron addressed the small group. "Guys, this is Sam. She's gonna tell you what's going on. This is right up your alley, trust me."

Sam spoke in her most "we're in grave danger" voice. "Extremes, we need your particular skills to combat a force of evil in our world. There is a meeting of all the SleepWakers tonight in Fletch's sector—"

"*Bo*-ring," Emmy intoned.

Byron sighed loudly.

"Come on, Emmy," coaxed a girl with messy dreads. "Fletch is in New Jersey. We can street luge down the Garden State Parkway."

Emmy made an exaggerated yawn face, patting a filthy hand over her multi-braced mouth.

"Lela's right, that would be awesome," said a bristly-haired boy with a parachute strapped to his back. "And after the meeting, we can go to Manhattan and BASE jump off the Freedom Tower."

"Been there, done that, Charlie," Emmy said, pulling out a giant hunting knife from somewhere on her person and cleaning her grubby nails with it.

Charlie shrugged apologetically to Sam and Byron. "Emmy's pretty much afraid of her shadow during the daytime."

Suddenly Sam had a brilliant lightbulb-over-the-head idea. "Emmy . . . how would you feel about gathering intel?"

For the first time, the Extreme looked slightly intrigued. "You mean, like . . . spying?"

Sam did her best Madalynn smile. "Oh, Emmy. When justice is being served, it's not called *spying*. It's called *surveillance*. . . ."

✳ ✳ ✳

Sam stood at the vertical steps of the monkey bars, her face pressed against the metal, preparing herself mentally.

"You can do this, Helper." Byron's voice penetrated her fog.

She gulped. "Yeah, 'Helper.' Not 'Speech Maker.' And definitely, *definitely* not 'Warrior Girl.'"

"Eh, warriors are a dime a dozen." Byron shrugged. "Just be your own soul. It's enough."

Sam couldn't resist a tiny "yeah-whatevs" look in his general direction before turning and climbing to the top of the monkey bars. She paused, wishing for just a moment that she had the slightest shred of Extreme in her essence, and then crawled onto the horizontal struts and stood up slowly, wobbling and dizzy. And what she saw below made her even dizzier.

All the tribes of the SleepWaker world were gathered in the park, following their soulish agendas: The Achieves were building a lean-to from fallen branches while practicing tai chi; the Numbs were simulating a game of *Tetris*, using their bodies as the pieces; the OCDeeds were measuring the length of the grass with rulers in the soccer field and trimming where the growth was a quarter of an inch too high; the Pranks were carefully following the OCDeeds and re-cutting their carefully trimmed patches of grass into silly shapes, giggling all the while; the Clutch had stuffed themselves into a tiny play castle and were huddled in a massive embrace; the Juvenold were running from tribe to tribe, trying to coerce everyone into a giant game of Red Rover; the Extremes, minus an intel-gathering Emmy, had unscrewed the giant bulb at the very top of a lamppost and were taking turns sticking their hands into the electrical socket; Chadney led the few Broadways who had not been soul-napped by Madalynn in a heart-wrenching rendition of "Left Behind" from *Spring Awakening*; and the Roamers wandered on the outskirts of the park, each one alone and remote from the others.

Sam balled her fists, trying to give her soul as much weight and possibility as it could stand.

"SleepWakers!" Intended to be a holler, it sounded more like a mouse fart. *"SleepWakers!"* Slightly better. Heads started to turn toward her. "Uh . . . We called you here tonight to discuss—"

"Can't hear you!" called an Achieve who was in the middle of his tai chi forms, moving through Wave Hands Like Clouds.

Sam cleared her throat. "Sorry! To discuss—"

"Red Rover, Red Rover, let Nina come over!" A Juvie (Nina, presumably) ran madly from her line of Wakers and rammed into the opposing line, bouncing back and falling on her bum. Both lines screamed with laughter.

"Discuss the situation we are all in—"

"Yes! Lela just electrocuted her soul!" The Extremes high-fived Lela, who was sparking like a metal fork in a microwave.

"WE ARE IN MORTAL DANGER, PEOPLE, PAY ATTENTION!!!" Sam bellowed.

An entire parkful of essences looked up in sudden star-tled silence.

"Okay, then! You're listening! That's good! Yes!" Sam plunged forward bravely. "Some of you know me already, but for those of you who don't, my name is Sam and I'm a Helper. And it seems like I'm the first one of those, so I don't exactly have a tribe." She moved on quickly, before anyone could get suspicious or question her loyalties. "And we are here tonight to discuss a threat that is common to all of us: the MeanDreams tribe."

Immediately, there was a furious buzz of voices, some fearful, some angry, and one who was an obvious fan of out-standing middle school fantasy literature: "They who should not be named!!!"

Sam forged ahead. "The night has been a safe haven for us. But if we don't act now, that will be taken away. Many of us have been bullied in the light, haven't we? Aren't we tired of it? Can we allow someone to come into our world and bully us here too? Remember what we've learned in all those anti-bullying rallies in school, 'If you see something, say something!'"

"That's the slogan for spotting terrorists," Byron whispered.

"Oh, sorry, right. Uh . . . 'Stand up! Speak out!' That's it!" Sam mustered her best fighting spirit. "Look at us!

Look at our numbers! If we all stood together against the MeanDreams, they would back down!"

"*Or* they would fight back!" yelled an Achieve. The rest of the Achieves murmured their agreement.

"Yeah! What are we supposed to do, challenge them to a rumble?" mocked a Prank. Chadney perked up at this mention, and the Broadways switched to the "Tonight" quintet from *West Side Story*.

"No! We're not going to fight, we're just going to present a united front! There's power in numbers!" Sam winced. It sounded so wimpy all of a sudden, especially with a 1950s musical as background.

"Oh, *puh-leeze*." An OCDeed eyerolled. "Like confronting a bully *ever* works."

"And even if we did take them on together, what happens when we separate back into our tribes? They'll find the smaller groups and punish them!" a Juvenold wailed.

"Not if they know we have each other's backs!" Sam forged on valiantly. "We just have to show them that we care about each other!"

"Except I *don't* really care about the rest of you," a Roamer said flatly. "Sorry to be a downer, but I have enough to deal with in the daytime. I don't need to be picking fights at night."

"We will take care of our own." This came from somewhere in the Clutch clutch. "There is no need for cross-tribing."

"Taking care of your own is not working!" Sam was getting heated. The "inspire unity" approach was floundering, so now she was going to have to inspire some fear. "How many of the tribes have lost Wakers to the MeanDreams?"

This caused more buzz, even angrier and definitely more fearful.

"They went because they wanted to go!" yelled an Achieve.

"No one can force a SleepWaker to do anything against their will!" called out another Roamer from the farthest edge of the park. "In the night, we are our essential selves, and in control of our own destiny!"

Suddenly there was a little voice from the seesaw. "No! No! That's a fib!" Alyssa stood up on a frog head while another Juvenold held the plank in balance. "Minnie Mouse didn't want to go! The nasties stole her off a slide!"

The Numb with the soul patch, Noa, jumped up. "They took Kyra, too! During her highest-scoring game!"

A Prank shouted, "And they snatched Arthur right out of the grocery store! While he was putting up a sign that said 'Mini Cucumbers' on the jalapeños!"

These revelations had the effect of causing near pandemonium.

"So, what are we supposed to do about it? If we agitate them, they'll come for us, too! None of us would be safe!" a Roamer shouted.

The long-armed Clutch, Odakotah, called out from the play castle, "How fitting! A Roamer's essential purpose is to save himself! And to blame the remainder of the SleepWaker world for his selfishness!"

A different Roamer hollered from behind the baseball diamond backstop, "Leave it to a Clutch to blame a Roamer! Hide behind your mommy's tribe, why don't you!"

Now it was legitimate pandemonium. Tribes started yelling insults from every quarter of the park.

"Pranks are evil clowns!" yelled an OCDeed.

"Oh, go organize your silverware, O-C-Dee-generates!" bellowed a Prank.

"Numbs?! More like *Numbnuts*!" shouted an Achieve.

"Did you Achieve your degree from Doofus University?!" squawked a Numb.

"Juvenold are cold and full of mold!" screeched an Extreme.

"You are Extremely pathetic!" bawled a Juvie.

"*Can you hear the Wakers sing, vile and mean and insulting . . .*" warbled the Broadways.

Wichachpi burst forth from her circle of hand-holders. "You dare to butcher the Clutch's favorite musical, *Les Misérables*?! Heathens!"

"STOP! STOP!" shouted Sam. "Can't you see that the MeanDreams are winning already?! They're dividing us without even being here! SleepWakers! You don't understand what you're dealing with! It's more than just the soul-napping. The MeanDreams are also—!"

The sound of a war cry cut Sam off, and Emmy appeared at the top of a huge oak tree across the street. She jumped approximately twenty feet from the topmost branch onto an old power cable, dashed down the length of the wire like a manic tightrope walker, flung herself over the electrical pole onto a fire escape, rode the ladder down, jumped on top of a moving minivan, leapt across to a Prius, and bounced off the soft top of a convertible like a trampoline, landing next to Sam on the monkey bars. There was a stunned silence, broken only by Lela's *"Nice!"*

"I got you some intel, Boss Lady," Emmy said, saluting Sam with a grubby paw. "You want it straight up"—she cast a glance at the listening SleepWakers—"or on the down low?"

Sam made a split-second executive decision. "Tell us—all of us!—what you know."

Emmy gave her an admiring look, and Sam immediately

knew this was going to backfire. "You got guts, Boss Lady."
Emmy turned to the waiting crowd. "So, I was dangling
above the MeanDreams on a zip line I made out of fishing
wire and an old seat belt—"

One of the Extremes raised his hand. "Awesome! How'd
you do that?"

"DIY tutorial later, bro," Emmy continued without pausing, "and I heard what they're planning. You guys already
know that Madalynn's been hijacking sleeping bodies—"

There was a huge, collective gasp from the SleepWakers.

"Actually," Sam whispered frantically, "we were just getting to that."

"—and tooling around town in 'em—" Emmy just kept
muscling through.

There was a huge, collective *"WHAAAT?!"* from the
tribes.

"Probably shoulda gotten to it sooner," Byron gritted
through his teeth.

"—and now we know why! 'Cause she's walking 'em
over to some mysterious sleep doc who does a little hocus-
pocus mojo and reattaches their souls so that they can never
again be a SleepWaker!"

A stupefied silence fell over the crowd.

"So *that's* how they do it," Byron whispered shakily.

"*What* mysterious sleep doc?" Sam whispered dazedly.

But her question was lost. Because suddenly there was a screaming, hyperventilating, hyper-crossing mass exodus off the lawn. Tribes disappeared faster than hot wings at a Super Bowl party. Within seconds, the park was completely empty, except for one ruler left lying on the grass by an OCDeed whose terror had trumped his neurosis.

"Oh, and, Boss Lady? You're her next victim, by the way." Emmy peered out at the vast emptiness. "Huh. Maybe if I'd said that sooner, everybody wouldn't have bailed."

Sam felt like a blimp that had accidentally flown into a commercial airliner and was now hurtling, airless, toward the earth. She would have sat right down on the monkey bars and cried, if not for one thing.

Alyssa was still standing on the frog head, which had thumped to the ground when her Juvie compadres abandoned the other end of the seesaw. She looked up at Sam, her mascara-free eyes filled with despair. "Minnie Mouse? They did this to her?"

Sam nodded.

"Then . . . I say we get those nasties."

Before Sam could respond, Noa the Numb reappeared, hitching up his too-short pajamas. He nodded to Sam.

Then a Waker came out from behind a tree. It was Dev,

the alphabetizing OCDeed who had almost concussed her with a bottle of spices. He grabbed the discarded ruler and raised it to Sam.

"Solidarity, Boss Lady." Emmy pulled out her giant hunting knife—*where the heck is she keeping that thing?* Sam wondered—lopped off a chunk of her hair, and handed it to Sam. "You might want to put that in a pendant."

And Byron.

Byron was still there.

A Juvie, an Extreme, an OCDeed, a Numb, a Roamer, and a Helper coming together to form a new tribe?

Only in the darkness.

seventeen

THE THREE FACES staring back at Sam were aghast. Even the fourth face, flat as it was, somehow looked flabbergasted. And furry. Flat, furry flabbergastation.

"Absolutely not." Fletch was the first one to speak. "That is an unacceptable solution."

Weezy snorfled. It sounded like an agreement.

"I know it could be dangerous—" Sam began.

"*Could* be?!" Fletch hugged his bundle of electrodes convulsively. Being that this visit to Sam's house was his first excursion out of the sleep clinic in close to ten years, one could not fault him for bringing along a security blanket of sorts.

"I'm with Flemkowsky," said Jax, his mouth set in a straight, grim line. *"No bueno."*

"What other way is there?" cried Sam. "Are you gonna tie down my body and sit by it every night and never sleep again? Don't you remember what exhaustion does? It makes you a machete-wielding despot!"

"Don't use my own words against me, young lady," Fletch sniffed. "Gandhi would *not* approve."

"Then how else are we going to find out who the mysterious Dr. X is?!"

"I'll activate the *SSSS!*" Fletch got so worked up, his snake hiss was accompanied by a spray of saliva. "We'll find the rapscallion!"

"Fletch, that's gonna take too long. Who knows how many Wakers she'll send back while you're all searching? You don't know what it's like out there! These people—these *kids*—we can't let them be lost again. . . . Don't you get it, I have to stop this dude for the sake of the whole nighttime world!"

Her superhero-worthy speech was met with mulish stares. Frustrated, Sam looked at her mother for help. "Mom?"

Margie reflexively raised her hand to the right side of her head; luckily there wasn't enough hair there to pull. "Let's see if I've got this right. You want me to let an angry soul bent on revenge come into our house, steal your body, and walk it to God knows where so your tribe can follow and discover the identity of a madman and hopefully grab your body back before he hooks it up to machines and electrocutes it back to sleepwalking?"

Sam winced. "Well, yeah, but you don't have to be so graphic—"

Jax cut her off. "And you want *me* to hold on to Mom so she doesn't go chasing after your body like a mother lion trying to protect her cub."

"Yes, but—" Sam attempted.

"Because you think," Jax continued, "that *I* wouldn't go chasing after you myself? That I would just let you, or your body, whatever, be hurt."

"What?" Now Sam was confused. "No, that's not what I—"

"Because all those times I came after you in the middle of the night when you were sleepwalking didn't mean anything."

"Jax." Sam protested. "No—"

"Because . . ." Jax sat forward for this one, looking straight at her. "Because the way I treated you during the day made you feel like I didn't care. I made you feel like you were a burden. A freak. A loser."

Sam's eyes suddenly burned with tears. She wanted to say no again, but the word stuck in her throat.

"I'm sorry. I'm sorry, Sam. I know I'm kinda the caboose on the asking-for-forgiveness train, but . . ." His face was once again that of an eight-year-old boy defending his sister and her relentlessly immature central nervous system. "That thing you said, that the darkness shows who you really are, I hope that's true, because the guy who chased down his sister in the middle of the night is who I am. Or, at least, who I want to be."

Now they couldn't really look at each other, just clumsily grasp hands.

"So . . . I don't think I can let her take you. I won't be able to do it. We gotta think of another way." Jax's plea was so pained that it effectively shut the door on Sam's plan.

"Oh. Sorry to interrupt, the front door was totally wide open. . . ." Weezy went nuts at the sound of Jaida's voice, barking joyously and tossing his squat body off the sofa like a pug kamikaze. "Hey, buddy," she said as he danced in little circles around her feet.

"My badness," said Fletch sheepishly. "I left it open in case I needed to run screaming back to the clinic."

Margie got up and squashed Jaida in a hug. "You should know, Weezy is crazy about you. He doesn't get off the couch for just anybody." Jaida smiled shyly and crouched for some slobbery kisses.

"S'up, Jaid?" Sam asked, composing herself.

Jaida kept her focus on Weezy. "Hey. Just wanted to know what happened last night."

Sam shot a glance at Fletch and her family. "You got a couple hours?" she asked wryly.

"Yeah." Jaida looked up for this. "I do, actually."

"Oh." Sam hoped she didn't sound as startled as she felt. "Cool."

There was an unnatural silence as all the parties looked at one another for clues on what to do next. Sam finally chose to go with the obvious.

"Wanna take Weezy for a walk with me?"

✳ ✳ ✳

The initial awkwardness of being out in public with someone who had threatened to use her guts as a jump rope just a few days earlier was thankfully smoothed over by Weezy's absurd excitement. Sam and Jaida had to stop numerous times in the first half block for him to scatter-pee or collapse in puggish reverse-sneeze paroxysms. By the time they had gotten to an actual walking rhythm, the words were flowing more freely.

"But how can you hide a hunting knife in your pajamas?"

Sam sighed. "Emmy's a wild card, for sure."

Jaida was silent for a moment. "That reminds me . . .

well, it doesn't *really* remind me, but it's kind of about clothes, so . . . awkward segue . . . I'm sorry about all the 'fashesty' comments."

"Oh. Okay." Sam decided to dive into the deep water. "Can I ask you something?"

Jaida looked straight ahead, seeming to brace herself. "Yeah. Do it."

"Why did you . . . do you . . . did you hate me so much? What did I do? 'Cause, you know, I'm not really sharp about this kind of stuff. So, probably it's just better if you tell me, like, super straight up, if I did something to make you hate me or if you just . . . hated me all on your own."

They walked a full block in silence, broken only by the sound of Weezy's happy rasps. It was so uncomfortable, Sam had to force herself to not just turn around and run, focusing instead on short-leashing a pug who kept weaving back and forth like a drunken sailor with a corkscrew tail.

"You didn't do anything." Jaida's voice was so quiet, Sam almost missed it. "Well . . . I mean, you did do *something*, but it was actually a nice something. Your first day at school, I dropped my . . ." Jaida motioned to her fanny pack, now held closed with two safety pins. ". . . and you picked it up for me. And I thought maybe you saw what was in it, 'cause the zipper was already toast, and I was in a pissy mood 'cause of my dad and . . ." She blew out a frustrated breath. "You remember doing that?"

"I don't." The well-worn mental video of her encounters with Jaida had already played through in Sam's head. This memory was not on the tape.

"Probably 'cause you're a Helper." Jaida shot her a sideways glance, with a slight twist of her lips. "You probably do stuff like that constantly."

Sam shrugged.

"Anyway . . . that's it. That got me rolling and then I couldn't seem to quit. So I guess I don't have any excuses. I'm just mean."

"Don't say that!" Sam was possibly more surprised at her own strong response than Jaida, but she couldn't help herself. "If there's one thing I've learned from this whole bizarro experience, it's that telling people what they are, or *who* they are, is a crap idea. So, we shouldn't do it to ourselves, either."

Jaida crossed her arms tightly across her chest and stared at the ground. Weezy seemed to sense that she was struggling, and he responded by plopping his chunky behind down on her foot.

"You saw my dad that night, didn't you?" Jaida was almost whispering. "The night with the plastic wrap thing."

"Yeah." Sam spoke just as quietly.

Jaida nodded, swallowed. "He wasn't always like . . . how you saw him. He got like that after my mom left."

Weezy was panting now, his tongue hanging out so far, he was in danger of stepping on it. Jaida unlocked her arms and crouched down, giving him a drink straight from her water bottle. It was a sight to behold.

"I'm sorry about your dad. *And* your mom. That's a lot." Sam had to speak slightly louder than she wanted to, because of the slurping noises.

Jaida glanced up at her. "Yeah, well. Everybody's got stuff, right?"

"Yeah." *Everybody's got stuff.*

Wait.

Everybody?

Everybody, including the most perfect girl in the light who was so perfectly evil in the darkness?

Suddenly it all started to come together in Sam's head, images and thoughts and sentences—Kyra in her red pajamas slipping further and further into the MeanDreams tribe—*there's power in numbers*—Madalynn standing on the steps of Wallace, looking so alone—*render her friendless, like she did to you*—Bree with her angry invisibility, Zac with his desperate roughhousing, and the sound of Gina's voice in the skanky bathroom, so afraid that she might end up like Daisy, torn out of her place and drifting away—*we take care of things in the darkness, where you can see what's really going on—I do want to belong—somewhere—*

"Jaida." Sam knew she must have sounded commanding, because Jaida stood right up, dropping her water bottle. Weezy tried to chase it, unsuccessfully, on his shortened leash. "I need some backstory. About you . . . and Madalynn."

eighteen

SAM'S SOUL WOKE UP in her body to the sounds of a heavy rain outdoors, and Weezy's growls indoors. He was tucked in a sleeping Jaida's arms and doing a saucer-eyed stare-down of Emmy, who was playing Five-Finger Fillet with her hunting knife on the nightstand. Byron was pacing, but when he saw that Sam was awake and separating from herself, he snatched the knife away. "You sure took long enough to detach, Helper," he said rather grouchily.

"And good evening to you, too, Roamer," Sam retorted, pulling the blanket up over Weezy's head, then over Jaida's. *Might as well give her a few more minutes of oblivion before the madness starts.*

"Roam's been super edgy ever since we got here," said Emmy, punching out a pane of glass from Sam's window and biting into it. The rain blew in through the open space.

"Will you knock it off! It's pouring out!" Byron snatched the glass and tried to replace it, but the rain still dribbled in through the giant bite mark. Emmy sighed dramatically and spit a mouthful of chewed window into the wastebasket.

"Brah, we know you're stressin' your senses about tonight," Noa drawled. "But Sam's plan is a righteous one." He and Alyssa were sitting cross-legged on the desk; the blue-haired girl was wearing a sapphire nightgown that perfectly matched her noggin.

"Wow, Alyssa," Sam breathed. "Those pajamas are perfect."

"Yay!" Alyssa squealed. "Bright bait for the beige babe!"

But Byron looked doubtful. "You really think that's gonna work?"

"I'm with Mr. Doom on this one. Your plan seems kinda talky." Emmy pouted. "I think we need more action. How d'ya feel about crossbows?"

"Don't worry, Emmy, there'll be plenty of action," Sam said, swallowing nervously. "So, everybody's clear on what they're doing?"

"Crystal." The voice came from the closet, where Dev was lining up Sam's shoes according to lace length.

"Oh, hey, Dev?" Sam ventured. "I really hate to mess up your system, but I want to put something on my feet. Just in case . . ."

"Nooooo . . ." moaned Dev, looking at his perfect shoe queue.

Byron shook his head, now even more agitated. "Madalynn's not gonna get through us. And there'll be four people holding on to your body, one of whom is my mother. Have you seen her biceps?"

"I said, just in case." Sam very gently extricated a pair of sneakers from Dev's grasping hands and slipped them onto the feet protruding from the end of the mattress. "You know I totally trust them, and you guys. But Madalynn is . . . Madalynn."

Emmy nodded in agreement. "Can I have my blade back?"

"No," Byron said flatly.

"Yeah, no knives, okay, Emmy?" Sam pleaded. "Just 'cause, you know, there are a couple of people here with stabbable flesh."

Emmy sighed dramatically again.

Alyssa jumped off the desk and clapped her hands excitedly. "Let's wake up the allergic girl with the butt purse!"

"Jaida," Sam supplied. "And it's called a fanny pack."

"Whatever! Her!"

"Okay. Remember, guys, you're going to get visible slowly so we don't completely freak her out." Sam leaned over the blanketed lumps in the bed.

"Oh, wait!" Alyssa stuck her hand straight up like she was in a classroom.

"Um . . . yes, Alyssa?" Sam felt a little foolish.

"Is it bad that our tribe doesn't have a name yet?" Alyssa questioned. "Shouldn't we have a name when she meets us?"

"How 'bout the Randoms?" suggested Noa.

"Now's not a good time, guys, but, Alyssa, going forward, you're in charge of fielding suggestions." On this note of diplomacy, Sam pulled the blanket back gently just from Jaida's face, leaving Weezy snoring in his muffled tent. "Hey . . . ready to wake up?"

Jaida opened her eyes slowly, nodded. Then, with a dawning realization on her face, she turned her head slightly to look at the other Sam, the one sleeping beside her. Jaida looked back and forth between the two Sams for a moment, then shivered.

"That's . . . pretty challenging," she croaked.

"Yep. Imagine how I felt the first time I saw her," Sam said. "So, everybody's here. Do you want 'em to be visible all at once or one at a time?"

Jaida sat up. "Just do it all together. Not sure my lungs can take the suspense." She quickly reached over, grabbed her fanny pack from the nightstand, and held it tightly as if to steel herself.

"Okay, guys. Really slow," Sam said to her nameless tribe, then fought back hysterical laughter as they all made the pooping face and slowly materialized for Jaida's eyes.

Jaida's mouth dropped open. "Whoa . . ." And then by some miracle, her lips curled up in a slight smile. "Hi, every-body." Her voice was soft and full of amazement.

The tribe responded with rather shy greetings, except for Alyssa, who squealed, "Howdy, Butt Purse!" and went to hug Jaida around the waist. Sam snagged her just in time. "What? Too soon?"

"You've probably seen Alyssa around Wallace," Sam said as Alyssa hugged her instead.

"Yeah. But you sure look . . . different," Jaida said.

"Because I don't wear pajamas to school, silly," Alyssa giggled.

"Uh, yes, that's definitely why." Jaida bit her twitching lip.

"May I?" said Dev as he started rearranging Jaida's wavy hair.

"That's Devon," Sam said to the startled girl. "He's an OCDeed."

"Ah," Jaida murmured as Dev gently corkscrewed her bangs. "Got it."

"And that's Noa, and Emmy." Sam pointed to the two Wakers, who had quickly digressed into a somewhat violent round of Thumb Wars. "And . . . Byron." The Roamer still looked fairly surly, but managed a small wave.

"So . . . you guys are actually all asleep right now? In your beds?" Jaida shook her head in wonder, accidentally dislodging one of Dev's spirals. "I just can't. I feel like I'm dreaming."

"Yeah. I get that." Sam gazed at her tribe, realizing how quickly she'd gotten used to seeing their hovering souls. They filled the night with life, with promise. Did the real world, the world of bodies with souls firmly entrenched, the world of Laters and those who slept soundly, did they realize what was swirling around them in the darkness?

"Are we ready?" Byron still sounded anxious and irritable.

Sam forced herself out of her reverie. "Jaida, will you take Weezy and go wake up my mom and everybody else?"

"Sure." Jaida got out of bed and gently extracted the drowsy pug from the covers. Crossing to the bedroom door, she stopped and looked at Sam. "Good luck, 'kay?" Weezy sneezed his blessing. "I'll see you soon."

Sam nodded. "There's an umbrella by the front door." She choked up suddenly, barely getting the word "door" out. Who would have ever guessed that Jaida would be her partner in busting up a clique? Her former enemy ducked her head and disappeared quickly into the hallway, obviously overcome as well.

She knew that Byron was fretting, but Sam had to take a minute to look down at her sleeping self. She remembered how frightening and otherworldly it had been the first time she'd experienced this SleepWaker thing, the strangeness of observing her own face as if in a warped mirror. Now that she knew how to be solid, she was able to touch the face of Sleeping Sam, push her choppy bangs to one side, feel the warmth of her flesh and blood. Knowing that someone was going to try to cross into her skin tonight made her feel protective, like a mother sending her child into unknown danger. Sam quickly bent over and kissed her own forehead.

"Let's do this."

Noa and Alyssa looked at her with compassion. Emmy gave her an arm punch that was almost gentle. Dev tenderly adjusted the laces on Sleeping Sam's shoes so that the loops were symmetrical.

"You know what would be super cool?" Alyssa bubbled. "Let's hold hands!"

The tribe "awww"-ed. Except for one.

"That's a little Clutchy for me," grumbled Byron.

"Hey, crab apple," Emmy said. "Read the room." Truthfully, the rest of the tribe were giving him some pretty grimy looks.

"Fine! Fine, we'll hold hands." Byron crankily stuck out his to Dev, who was busily applying hand sanitizer. "You see this? Souls don't have germs! I can't work with this!"

"You don't know that," Dev protested. "Are you a cosmic microbiologist? Huh?"

"That'd be a sweet video game. *Cosmic Microbiologist*," mused Noa.

Alyssa started chanting. "Cos-*mic*, Cos-*mic*, Mic-*cro*-biol-*igist* . . ."

"Cosmic germs are for wimps," stated Emmy as she grabbed Dev's hand sanitizer and drank it.

"Hey, guys? Can we focus, please?" Sam was about ready for a cosmic night guard, since she was grinding her soul teeth by this point. She grabbed Alyssa's hand, and Alyssa squealed happily and grabbed Dev's. He nodded and grabbed Noa's. Noa took Emmy's hand. Emmy sighed dramatically and held a reluctant hand out to Byron. After a moment, he grabbed it.

It worked. As they stood, linked together, a feeling of SleepWaker solidarity passed from soul hand to soul hand. And possibly some cosmic germs as well, but that comes with the territory of togetherness.

Sam waited until she heard voices outside her door. "Let's go," she said, suddenly afraid that if she had to see Fletch and Joanne, or watch Jax pull Margie's hand away from her buzzed hair, it would all be over; Sam knew she would just want to hide herself behind their always solid bodies.

The nameless tribe misted through the wall out onto the lawn as the group of vigilant Laters circled Sam's body inside.

The rain was pounding, and it felt like a continuous pressing weight on Sam's heart. She tried to ignore the foreboding heaviness, motioning to Emmy and Noa, who rapidly misted through a spruce tree to hide. Alyssa hugged Sam ferociously around the waist, and Dev patted her on the back, somehow managing to adjust her collar at the same time. They morphed into Margie's Toyota as Byron stepped up next to Sam and took her hand. She looked at him in surprise.

"What can I say?" Byron managed a smile. "I read the room."

Sam gripped Byron's hand back so tightly she nearly crushed the solid right out of it.

They turned back to stare out into the squall. The rain was so heavy, coming down in blinding sheets, they didn't see or hear the MeanDreams until they popped up right in front of them, which is a very unpleasant way to start a showdown. But there was something far more unpleasant in store.

At first, Sam thought it was the storm obscuring her

vision, but she could clearly see Zac and Bree looking primed and ready for battle, and the dark mass of souls behind them—*and* the empty space where Madalynn usually stood.

"Where is she?" Sam demanded.

"Sorry, Dream Reject, you don't get to ask the questions," Bree growled.

"Sorry, Dream Reject!" echoed the MeanDreams.

Byron dashed to the bedroom window, looked in, and dashed back so fast, he was his own blur. "All good. You're still in there and so are the Laters," he whispered.

"Is *he* your whole tribe? Pitiful." Bree lurched toward them like a faded Frankenstein's monster, Zac hulking behind.

"Pitiful, pitiful," chanted the MeanDreams.

Sam stepped back, so disoriented by Madalynn's absence and the menacing presence of Beige and Bullet and their parroting, monotone tribe, that all memory of her plan flew right out of her head. Until she heard the *slap!* followed by a yelp of pain.

Emmy and Noa had reappeared in front of the spruce, and they were playing Red Hands. Noa hovered his hands, palms down, above Emmy's, wincing in agonized anticipation as she swung her hands up and over—he tried to pull away in time, but she smacked him, hard. Noa yelled "OW!" at the top of his lungs.

Bree immediately saw the danger. "Zac, no!" she shouted, but it was too late. Zac's eyes lit up, and he charged over to them, knocking Emmy out of the way and sticking his meaty mitts under Noa's spindly fingers. Noa only had half a second to gawk at the size of those hams before they flew up and over and walloped his digits so vehemently, Noa's entire soul body followed the downward direction of the smack. Like a nail being whacked by a hammer, his legs shot into the ground up to the knees.

Sam heard Byron behind her. "Whoa!"

"What?!" She turned to him.

"I didn't know a Waker could go into the ground." He looked troubled. "Something wrong about that . . ."

But Noa rebounded, jolting out of the earth like a yanked lawn dart, and came back for more. He defiantly put his hands out again, palms *up* this time. Zac grunted in savage delight and stuck his buffet slayers out, palms down, waiting happily to get thwacked.

Bree turned on Sam and Byron in beige rage. "You think you're so smart, don't you, distracting Zac? You think you're . . ." Her voice trailed off as her faded eyes lifted above their heads and widened.

Alyssa was standing in front of the Toyota now, her electric-blue hair and matching nightgown positively incandescent as she posed in the "brights" setting of the car's headlights. She looked like some kind of ultramarine angel as she gestured to Bree with a gentle sweep of her brilliant-blue arm. Dev appeared next to Alyssa with handfuls of color swatches that he'd obviously, uh, *borrowed* from the Container Store. He held them up and fanned out the swirling, vibrant palettes.

And Bree, the beige behemoth, the tan titan, the invisible Goliath, who was really just a sad little girl, after all, couldn't help herself. Especially after Alyssa reached into the car and pulled out a glowing magenta robe, big enough for even the most colossal colossus. This put the colorful nail in the coffin for the colorless girl. She gave Sam a bland side-eye.

"You suck," Bree muttered, and lumbered off to Alyssa and Dev like a clumsy moth to the flame.

"You suck," echoed the remaining MeanDreams, but Sam could feel the slight shift in their demeanor, a hint of confusion, a tinge of "who are we supposed to follow if no one is leading?" A tiny crack had opened, and Sam jumped in.

Literally.

"Wish me luck," she whispered to Byron, only waiting for his "Luck!" before she took a flying leap, right into the dark mass of souls.

nineteen

I CAN'T BREATHE.

Sam knew this was ridiculous, a soul didn't need air.
But she still felt suffocated. The sensation of being inside a
small space—shut and locked in—was overwhelming. She
forced herself to see clearly, to distinguish the separate bodies, the individual essences, fighting her way through the
swarm, looking for holes, gaps through which to pass, but
everything and every*one* looked the same, and not just iden-
tical, but blended together into a continuous moving wall
of SleepWakers. Sam put her head down and kept going,
determined to succeed at her task.

"Arthur!"

In what she supposed was the center of the tribe, although it was so dim and full of flailing limbs it was hard to tell, was the Prank. Sam's heart sank, as he looked paler, skinnier, and itchier than ever.

"Come with me!" Sam grabbed his hand, but when she turned to go, it suddenly seemed like there was no way out, as if the souls had completely melted together around them. Sam felt that clutch of consciousness claustrophobia again, and she forced the panic down, afraid she might start screaming like a lunatic.

"Arthur, we'll have to mist out! Don't you remember? You can do that! Make yourself un-solid and we'll go right through!" As unpleasant as it was to pass through another Waker, it had to be better than enduring this stifling, soul-sucking swarm. Sam tightened her grip on Arthur's hand, took a deep breath, and made herself as insubstantial as possible, a gossamer girl made of vapor.

But as they permeated the mass around them, "unpleasant" turned to "ghastly." Every soul Sam passed through was so dark, so angry, so *trapped*, that by the time she reached the edge of the tribe, all her energy was sapped and replaced with the binding weight of hopelessness.

Oh, Madalynn, what did you do? What did you do to them?

Sam finally crossed the border, limping out of the tribe,

but Arthur bounced back as if he'd hit a brick wall. She lost her grip on him, and he started to disappear again, sucked back into the throng.

"No . . ." Sam wanted to scream, but all that came out was a moan. Byron caught her and held her upright as she strained to remember what was supposed to come next. There was a plan, right? She could hear Byron calling her name, but it seemed so far away.

I'm so tired. It was so nice and dark in there. I wouldn't have to think so hard, or help anyone. . . .

"SAM!" Byron's voice finally pierced her fog. At the same time, over by the tree, Zac smacked Noa's hands and roared, "HURTS, DON'T IT?"

Sam jolted alive again, a charge of adrenaline stiffening her soul spine. She quickly looked over to make sure that Bree was also still distracted, breathing a sigh of relief when she saw Alyssa and Dev wrapping the hue-hypnotized Waker's beige hair in a brightly patterned turban. Sam turned back to the tribe. "Dreams! I have a request!"

The tribe drew together, looking communally suspicious. "What?"

"I have some*one* here who would like to talk to *one* of you." Sam leaned into the "one," shading it casually, but purposefully. "One-on-*one*. You know, mano a mano."

The MeanDreams started to shift uncomfortably, and

when they spoke again, their chorus was a bit ragged. "We . . . You . . . Who . . . What?"

"It's working," Byron spoke right into her ear. "Keep going!"

"Yeah, *individually*." She hit the word hard. "You know that word. After all, it's *individuals* that make up a tribe, right? Otherwise, you get that groupthink mob mentality and then you start doing things you never thought you'd do, like, oh, I don't know, maybe . . . stealing SleepWakers from other tribes?"

At this, the MeanDreams went into a collective tizzy. They started to jostle, bump, collide. The outlines of separate Wakers started to come into focus and this started a chain reaction of events: one MeanDream accidentally stepped on another's foot and there was a yelp of pain. Another MeanDream apparently forgot to be solid momentarily and misted through his neighboring MeanDream, who did not appreciate the essence intrusion and muttered a nasty rebuke. A shorter MeanDream got elbowed in the eye and retaliated with a mighty shove. His taller tribemate tipped backward, and that's when Arthur came into view, his pale face hovering just inside the invisible, yet seemingly impassable border of the tribe.

"There he is!" Sam pointed excitedly.

Byron turned back to the house and shouted, "Jaida!"

The front door opened and an umbrella bloomed. This caused an uproar among the MeanDreams, as they knew that only a Later would need rain gear. Jaida dashed over to Sam and Byron, the storm streaming down around her circle of protection, looking panicked.

"Sam, I can't see him. I can't see any of them!" Jaida cried.

"I know, but they're there!" Sam exclaimed. "You can do this, Jaida! Just call him. Quick!"

"Arthur!" Jaida shouted over the downpour. "I know you're the one who did all that stuff to me! The things you did, they were dangerous and wrong! I almost drank something that could have really hurt me! So I want you to hear this!"

The Prank's white face became downright ghostly, looking horrified and guilty and terribly sad. The MeanDreams started to wail and thrash, becoming one pulsing organism again, drawing him in farther.

"Hurry!" Sam shouted.

Arthur was almost gone, almost disappeared into the mass of souls, only a wisp of light in their overwhelming darkness, when Jaida cried:

"I forgive you!"

And everything stopped. A hush. A standstill.

Except for Jaida, who kept on.

"I forgive you. Because I know what it's like to do bad

things to people who didn't do anything to me. Who didn't deserve the way I treated them." Jaida reached out a hand without looking. Sam swallowed hard and took it, coming up to stand beside her. "But they forgave me. So, I can forgive you."

Suddenly, out of nowhere, a low, melodic hum pierced through the storm. Byron groaned, "You have *got* to be kidding me."

"*Forgiveness, is the mightiest sword . . .*"

Emmy, who was now delivering some Red Hands torment to Zac, yelled, "OMG, seriously?"

"*Forgiveness of those you hate will be your highest reward . . .*"

"I thought the meanies soul-napped the Broadways!" squealed Alyssa, who was busy putting magenta maribou slippers on Bree.

Byron roared, "Not enough of 'em!"

The Broadways materialized through a fence, but Jaida seemed unaware of their unwelcome ballad, her focus being on the MeanDreams. "I was a bully. I guess I did it because I was being bullied, too, and I thought it would make me feel better. But it never did."

The MeanDreams were rapt, listening intently. Arthur's skinny form started to reappear.

"It's like, it just keeps going, like this endless cycle of

being mean, 'cause what's gonna stop it?" Jaida looked at Sam. "You need someone to help you stop it. You need a Helper."

The Broadways began to soar.

"*You must never lose faith! You must never lose heart! Be willing to be brave! Brave enough for love!*"

"Dude, what is this song?!" Sam hissed to Byron.

"'Forgiveness' from *Jane Eyre: The Musical*," Byron hissed back. "They've already sung it at me five or six times. Makes me want to poke my eyes out with a fork."

"Okay, Sam, bring it home!" Jaida whispered.

Sam grinned at her and called out, "Arthur! MeanDreams! You have to help us stop this! I know you all have stories, you all have things to forgive and be forgiven for! But we've started a new tribe, made up of SleepWakers from other tribes, and we're coming together, even with our differences, and we're ending the cycle! We're closing the loop! It can stop here if you join us!"

"*Forgiveness . . . is the mightiest . . . SWORD!*" the Broadways wailed.

Never underestimate powerful words with tear-jerking vocals as backup. Arthur un-sucked himself from the MeanDreams and broke free, racing over to Sam's line of Wakers like a lovefest version of Red Rover.

Jaida gasped. "Arthur? I can *see* you!"

"I'm sorry, I'm so sorry," he implored. Jaida caught his visible, solid body in an embrace as the mass of MeanDreams boiled and burbled and belched out another soul.

"Kyra!" Noa shouted joyfully. He raced away from Zac and Emmy to catch Kyra as she stumbled, just snagging her red flannel pajama top in time before she fell. Kyra held on to him, gasping out, "My parents . . . they never did anything wrong . . . they weren't ignoring me, they were just worried about my brother—"

"I know, I know," Noa soothed her. "It's okay."

And then three Wakers grand-jetéd out of the MeanDreams and did a jazz run over to Chadney and the Broadways, bursting into an emotional rendition of the title song of the Civil War musical *Reunion*.

The spell was broken, the MeanDreams shattered. SleepWakers were reeling out of the throng, each talking loudly as if to reassure themselves that they still had their own voice, each with a story of how they had been sucked in, taken over, crushed by the weight of their own anger and fueled by the anger of others.

Sam and Jaida turned and stared at each other in wonder. They moved closer and might have ended up in the first hug of their bizarre relationship, if it hadn't been for the scream.

Margie's bloodcurdling scream that came from inside the house and stopped everything on the lawn. Dead.

twenty

SAM DIDN'T THINK, she just ran, jumped, sailed through the wall into her empty bedroom.

Empty?

Not quite empty. Sleeping Sam was still Sleeping peacefully on the bed, but her mother, Jax, Fletch, and Joanne were gone. Soul Sam looked around wildly, registering that the bedroom door was wide open and she was alone in the room. Her nameless tribe had not followed her for some unknown reason, and she was now the only one there to protect her—

Body.

Of course.

It was already too late.

She turned slowly to face the bed.

Just in time to see her body sit up and smile at her.

And even though Sam had expected it, the sight was so horrifying, so macabre, that she lost her balance and fell backward.

And downward.

And inward.

The very thing she had feared the very first time she had detached was now real. Sam lost all of her solidity, or perhaps relinquished it, and she just kept falling, through the bedroom floor, though the foundation of the house, feeling the differing molecules rush through her essence, unable to stop, unable to right herself, all the feelings of falling tied up with the feelings of failing, she had failed her family, she had failed herself, her own body, and it would just be easier to quit now and let the earth swallow up her soul—

And then, suddenly, something stopped her.

And reversed her, yanking her back with an invisible hand, enveloping her in an ethereal embrace, a father's embrace, and rushing her back to the surface, as the voice in her head cried out, *You came, you helped, you didn't let me drown, thank you, thank you . . . Dad . . .*

All at once, she was back on her misty feet in the empty bedroom, where she stood, panting and trembling and wondering.

Did I imagine him?

It was far too much to take in, the glimmer of a world beyond even this second world of the night. Overwhelming, and she was already far too overwhelmed, so Sam stuffed it down, shook it off, banished it from her mind, and turned to the task at hand. Which was rescuing her body, as Madalynn had disappeared with it. *In it.*

Sam barreled through the wall, back out into the storm, and into complete chaos. The rain, the lightning, wailing souls everywhere; she didn't know where to look, how to even begin.

"Sam!" It was her mother's voice, followed by a muffled shout. Sam turned toward the sound frantically.

"Where are you?!" Sam screamed.

Finally the moving wall of essences cleared enough for her to see Margie. She and Jax, his mouth covered with a bright cloth, were being roughly restrained by Wakers, most of whom were unfamiliar, but there was one she would know anywhere. The sharp chin, the pointed ears—

"*Wichachpi?!*" Sam gasped.

The Clutch leader's elfin face contorted in anguish as a figure emerged from behind her.

Madalynn/Sam staggered out, her pajamas drenched, her hair plastered to her head. Her gait was odd, jerky, like a marionette on loose strings, Sam's familiar face twisted into a humorless and loveless, but extremely toothpasty, grin.

"You tried to break up my tribe, Sleep Sis. Good thing I brought backup. Always smart to have some new friends waiting in the wings." It was Sam's own voice, but the words were so very Madalynn's. She staggered toward Sam, and it was like looking into a fun-house mirror, seeing herself stretched and distorted, devoid of her spirit and occupied by something alien and almost inhuman.

"The whole Clutch came on board!" Madalynn/Sam crowed. "They're very loyal to their leader, and you know how I value loyalty." This cryptic statement was directed at the shamefaced team of Beige and Bullet. Bree hung her head, still swathed in the magenta robe, which Madalynn/Sam promptly ripped off and handed to Zac. He looked at her in misery, then tore the robe right down the middle. Bree whimpered.

"Where is my tribe? How did you—how did you—"

Sam stuttered, unable to force out the words "How did you brainwash the Clutch?"

"Well, I will say it was a lot easier sneaking *into* your house than it was for Wichachpi to get those pesky physical bodies out. Seriously, *four* locks on the front door? Isn't that overkill, even for a sleepwalker's house?" Madalynn/Sam shook her borrowed head. "And as far as your tribe is concerned . . . Bring him!"

Byron was roughly pushed out of the crowd by Odakotah. The long-armed Clutch snuck a regretful peek at Sam.

"Byron!" Sam cried out in relief, but the Roamer just stood motionless.

"I'm sorry, Sam," he said, barely above a whisper.

"Are you wondering why By the Spy doesn't fight back, why he's not defending you?" Madalynn/Sam continued, crossing over to Byron with that eerie, unbalanced step, peering into his grim face. "Has his Roamer soul finally caught up to him? Maybe he's just going to check out now, and let you take care of everything. People do show who they really are in the darkness, after all."

Sam felt her spirit start to return. No way was she going to fall for this. "That might be true, but even in the darkness, we can make choices."

Madalynn/Sam laughed, the sound grating and joyless. "Oh, Sam, you are as adorable as ever. And you're right, of course. The only reason your tribe isn't trying to stop me or, like, gut me with that Extreme's super-scary knife is 'cause I've got something on them. Because . . . I've got something on *you*."

Sam looked around at the Wakers covering the lawn, their heads bowed, their faces blurred by the streaming rain. She saw Dev and Alyssa and Noa, and even Emmy, staring at the ground. Sure, they were being restrained by Clutch, but there was something else immobilizing them as well. What information or plan could Madalynn possibly have that would handicap all these brave souls?

"What do you want, Madalynn?"

"It's more of what I *don't* want. I don't like the ideas you're putting in the Wakers' misty little heads. Forgiveness is for fools, Sam. Suckers. And all your gooey garbage about 'being an individual'"—Madalynn/Sam did air quotes and then grimaced at Sam's un-manicured nails—"well, that's just going to make it harder for me to recruit. I want control of the night back and the only way *that* can happen is if the Helper is gone."

"No!" It was Fletch's voice. Sam spied her doctor, locked in Margie's Toyota and guarded by more Clutch. Fletch's eyes were so wide and wild that Sam could see his sclerae from across the whole lawn as he pounded on the window, yelling, "Don't listen to her, Sam! I can fix this!"

Madalynn/Sam continued as if she hadn't just been interrupted by a hostage situation. "Gone from the night and back to your old, miserable, dangerous, sleepwalking self. So! Here's the plan: You're going to let me take your body to my special friend—what did you call him, Dr. X?—and he's going to zap you back in *here*." She patted her chest, Sam's chest, with a little grin. "And you're going to do that because . . . well, I'll just admit it, I took Wichachpi's body for a little spin tonight and right now it's waiting on an exam table to be reattached if *your* body doesn't show up. One of you ladies is getting zapped tonight. It's you or her."

Wichachpi moaned pitifully and the moan was taken up by the entire Clutch tribe, which was disconnected, divided, spread out across the lawn to subdue Sam's tribe and the newly freed MeanDreams, free no longer. The sound was visceral, tormented. Even being apart for this short amount of time was sapping their souls of life. If they lost Wichachpi . . .

I said we had choices. But I don't have a choice.

Madalynn/Sam was watching her and she did a fist pump. "Yes! I knew it! Look at your face! No way is the Helper gonna let that freako Clutch girl take the fall! Oh, I am *brilliant*."

"No! Sam, no!" Jax was trying to yell through the gag in his mouth, which Sam suddenly recognized as the material

Alyssa had used for Bree's turban. The beige girl whimpered again, turning away from the sight.

"Jax. It's okay." Sam's voice was shaking, but she was settled. "I'm not gonna die or anything. I'm just . . . going back." A sudden image of nearly being decapitated by a chain saw in a half-built tree house flashed through her mind. But she couldn't think about that now. Wouldn't.

"Sam . . ." Jax moaned through his gag, near tears.

"Jax. Let her do what she needs to do." Margie was crazy calm all of a sudden, and it made Sam want to hug her ferociously. "I tried to stop a Helper once, too, remember? It doesn't work."

"Aw, your family is so sweet," crooned Madalynn/Sam. "They're just going to let me parade your bod outta here. Now, that's love."

"Can I say good-bye to my tribe?" It sounded more plaintive than Sam had intended, but darned if she hadn't just fallen in like with all of them in this short time, even crazy Emmy. And Byron . . . *Yeah, that might be a little bit more than like.*

"Well, sure," purred Madalynn/Sam. "I'll let you do that. I'm not a mean girl, after all." There was a moment of silence as every single being on the lawn, Waker and Later, gave Madalynn/Sam a "seriously?" look. She looked around incredulously. "What?"

One by one, the Clutch released Sam's tribe. Dev and Alyssa ran over, and the Juvenold hugged her around the waist while the OCDeed sadly smoothed Sam's pajamas. Noa loped over slowly and put his hand out for a fist bump, whispering, "Godspeedo." Emmy pounded her chest a few times and then spread her arms wide for a hug. As she yanked Sam into her embrace, she whispered in her ear, "Boss Lady. I got an idea."

"No knives, Emmy," Sam whispered back.

"Blade-free, I swear on my bungee cord," Emmy whispered.

Madalynn/Sam called out, "Okay, that's enough! Girls whispering secrets is always a bad idea. I learned that from leading the anti-bullying sessions at school." She chuckled, then looked a bit miffed at the wedged-hairball sound that came out.

Sam pulled back from the hug, and Emmy winked at her, making a series of motions with her hands that obviously was meant to explain her new plan, but looked more like she was one of those workers at the airport with orange lights bringing in a big jet. Sam just shook her head.

"Okay, well, bye-bye, Sleep Sis." Madalynn/Sam grinned. "I'm gonna take a couple of the kooky Clutchers with me so they can speed me along a bit. And listen, sorry that I have to do this, but we're gonna have to give this bod of yours some meds to conk you out, which means you're gonna feel lousy tomorrow, but that's the price I have to pay to keep Dr. X's identity my little secret, right?" Madalynn/Sam reached around and patted herself on the back. "I thought of everything, didn't I?!"

"Not everything!" A voice came from the gloom, punctuated by an indignant bark.

Jaida ran into the center of the circle, panting, carrying Weezy, and dragging at least six Clutch behind her.

"Jeez, you took long enough!" Sam hissed to Jaida.

"*You* try fighting off invisible beings sometime!" Jaida hissed back. "They put a sock in my mouth! A dirty, wet sock!"

The grin had dropped off Madalynn/Sam's face, which was now pooled into a streaming wet mask of rage. She approached Jaida, Sam's body jerking and twitching. Weezy started to growl.

"I should have known," Madalynn/Sam muttered. "I should have known that things could never be even with us, Jaida."

"Maddie, please. It was so long ago . . ." Jaida pleaded.

"You were my best friend!" shrieked Madalynn/Sam. "That's supposed to be forever!"

"I'm sorry." Jaida's voice broke. "I never meant to hurt you. I just wanted us to have other friends, too. You were such a good friend, Maddie, I wanted other people to know that—"

"That's not true! You just decided you were tired of me! You wanted to replace me!"

"No! No. It was just too much. You wanted me all to yourself and I couldn't do it anymore. . . ." Jaida was crying now.

"You left me alone." Madalynn/Sam's voice broke, her face twisting into utter desolation and hopelessness. The sight nearly broken Sam's heart. There was no villain here. *Everybody's got stuff.* "All alone. And now you're gonna pay for that. I don't care what he says; you're all going to pay."

He?

"I don't need any of you! I don't need anybody at all!" Madalynn/Sam's voice rose into an ugly shriek. She whirled around and started off, loping across the lawn with a broken, disfigured gait. She was leaving. She was going to take Sam's body to Dr. X and make her a sleepwalker again— forever. And all Sam could do was watch it happen.

Emmy grabbed Sam, whirled her around. "Boss Lady! Knock her out!"

"What?! I'm not going to hit her—!"

"Noooo!" Emmy howled. "Knock her out of your *body*! Catch her, jump in there, and push her soul out!"

"Yes!" Jax shouted through his gag.

"Totally!" Alyssa shrieked. "Kick out the meanie!"

"I'll hold her down!" Noa hitched up his pajamas, ready to run. "Push out the parasite!"

"I can't!" Sam cried. "If my body doesn't show up tonight, Dr. X will zap Wichachpi!"

"Sam's right." Byron was obviously trying to control himself. "She has to let her go."

"But *why*?!" Emmy wailed.

"Don't you get it?! Because she's a *Helper*!" This time Byron shouted.

Margie started to cry. Alyssa's face crumpled, and Noa hung his head. The Clutch began to wail. Even Bree closed her eyes, and Zac punched her in the arm compassionately.

"Yeah? Well, *I'm* not," Emmy spit out. She turned and took off after Madalynn/Sam.

"Emmy!" Sam shrieked, and gave chase. Weezy jumped from Jaida's arms and barreled after her, barking like a pug possessed. And as she was running, hovering after Emmy, who had traversed the lawn at hyper-cross speed and almost had her hands on Madalynn/Sam, and the Clutch was wailing and the Laters were shouting and her tribe was following and Weezy was howling—

That's when Sam saw it.

Madalynn's silver cord, extending behind Sam's physical

body. It was dim, slight, frayed, so tenuous and fragile, it was almost nonexistent. And she remembered a doctor with raindrops glistening on his green glasses, pacing, mumbling, *"Repeated bodyhopping will fray the lifeline beyond recognition, eventually causing it to snap . . ."*

"Madalynn!" Sam screamed. *"STOP!"*

She must have sounded sincerely desperate, because not only did Madalynn/Sam and Emmy stop, even Weezy did a paw-lock, causing his roly-poly body to tumble, one end over the other. Then they all looked back at her: Madalynn/Sam suspiciously, Emmy quizzically, and Weezy dizzily.

"Your silver cord . . ." Sam almost whispered now, holding up her hands as if in surrender. "Your lifeline . . . it's going to snap. Look at it. Please . . ."

Madalynn/Sam's eyes narrowed. She looked down, slowly, gazing at the glistening wisp that tethered her to herself, connected her soul to another body sleeping peacefully across town, the beautiful physical shell that had fooled so many for so long. Sam held her breath in a prayer.

Madalynn/Sam grinned. "Nice try, loser."

She whirled around and took off, so quickly that Emmy's frantic grasp missed its target.

Sam tried to scream "Stop!" again; it stuck in her throat.

But Madalynn/Sam stopped anyway. Abruptly, sharply, as if she had run into an imperceptible wall. And she started to fall, except it was only Sam's body that fell. Still standing was Madalynn—the essence of Madalynn—separated from the body she'd been hiding in.

All the SleepWakers saw it. Bright and sudden, like it had been ignited, Madalynn's silver cord flared into view. It was broken. Severed, just above where Sam's body lay on the ground.

Madalynn saw it, too, and the comprehension dawned slowly and painfully on her ethereal face.

"Madalynn . . ." Sam whispered. "I'm so sorry. I didn't want this to . . ."

But Madalynn had already begun to fade, to evaporate, to dissolve before them, her bright blue eyes lingering last, giving Sam a final wrathful stare before they, too, ebbed away.

Paralyzed with disbelief, they all stared at the space that a moment ago held the soul of Madalynn and was now empty. Sam was the first to move. She ran to her body and shook it violently, just to make sure.

And just like that, she woke up. In her body, staring up at the Wakers who gathered around her, and beyond, up at the stars, wondering if Madalynn was flying between them, on her way home.

twenty-one

WELL, OF COURSE she'd have a pink coffin. Sam didn't even know such a thing existed, although she had heard of people being buried in piano cases and vintage cars and other odd receptacles.

On a movie-theater-size screen behind the casket (thankfully, closed), an endless loop of videos played: Madalynn doing a high full around at the GottaCheer Classic in Buttzville, Madalynn as Florence Nightingale kick-ball-changing around a prop lamp, Madalynn serving sweet potato pie at the homeless shelter on Thanksgiving wearing an apron inscribed with *#Blessed*, Madalynn being crowned Queen of Everybody and Everything at the eighth-grade dance.

Dr. Fletcher and Joanne were sitting near the front of the jam-packed viewing room when Sam arrived, whispering fervently to each other—not that anything could be heard over the weeping and wailing of the faculty and student body of Wallace Junior High. Eighth-grade girls keened, Mr. Todorov shrieked, "*Cry* for me, Argentina!" over and over, Angry Agnes sobbed, tucking a tiny Tupperware of cafeteria mac 'n' cheese under the mink mortcloth draped over the casket. It was all to be expected; the only thing that caught Sam's attention was Madalynn's über-blond parents fussing with one of the approximately three hundred flower arrangements adorning the room. Partly because they were wearing matching black tuxedos, but mostly because they were completely dry-eyed.

Well, actually, that was not the *only* thing that caught Sam's attention.

Across the room, she spied Byron. He was looking rather uncomfortable, either due to his snugly fitting designer suit, or the snugly clinging gorgeous girl on his arm.

Byron intercepted her gaze, and began the journey over, a pronounced "it sucks that this is how you're finding out" look on his face.

"Hey. Sam, this is Fiona. Fiona, Sam."

"Hi, Fiona, it's nice to meet you," Sam said, with a little pit in her stomach. Really, Fifi just couldn't have been prettier. She was wearing one of those sack dresses that on the average human looked like, well, a sack, but on Fiona was totes haute couture.

"Hello, Sam. Byron told me he met you through his mom?" She said it warmly, but there was a hint of a question, just a wee thread of "I hope that's true."

"Yes." Sam smiled reassuringly, not that it was necessary. How could this potential *Teen Vogue* model think that Sam was any competition? Girls were so weird sometimes.

Byron whispered something in Fiona's ear. She looked mildly annoyed but rearranged her lovely face quickly and said, "I'm going to get us some coffee, would you like some?"

"Oh. Uh . . . no, thanks, I don't drink coffee." *Because I'm thirteen* was what went through Sam's mind, but "Because I'm sensitive to caffeine" was what came out of her mouth.

"Got it." Fiona smiled and walked away. To her credit, she only looked back once.

"So. Helper."

"Yes, Roamer?" Sam wasn't sure why she suddenly felt like either hugging him or crying, but she fought off both impulses.

"You ready for the council tonight?" Byron took a quick glance around before this question. Not that anyone could have figured out what they were talking about, but still.

"I'm ready. We've got one soul from every tribe committed?"

"Yeah. Death has a way of waking people up. Even in the middle of the night." Byron said this ruefully, then with a hint of a smile. "I personally asked Wichachpi. On bended knee. I think she was a little afraid I was proposing at first."

Sam smiled back. *This is good. We're friends.* She could do this. Right?

"Cool. I'm going to tell the tribes it'll be like a neighborhood watch. We check in with each other, we assign block captains, all that stuff. Just . . . spread out across the country. With detached souls." Suddenly it all sounded just too ludicrous, and Sam started to giggle. She put a hand over her mouth. "Help me, I think I'm losing it."

"It's okay, it's a natural tendency to laugh at funerals. A sign of wanting to live." Byron noticed a few mourners giving them dirty looks. "Just keep it kinda chill, 'cause the sadness police are watching."

"Hey, guys." Jaida slipped in next to them as her posse sat down. It was the first time Sam had seen Amy, Gina, and Daisy since the smelly bathroom surveillance; they were giving off a confused, shruggy vibe at seeing Jaida talking to her, which only served to increase Sam's moderate hysteria. She clapped both hands over her mouth, her shoulders shaking. Jaida looked startled. "Are you crying?!"

"It's all good. She's having a . . . let's just call it sort of an emotional release." Byron put his arm around Sam and turned her away from the watchful eyes of the congregation. She allowed herself three seconds of leaning against his chest under the guise of "comfort," then backed away.

"I'm okay now, thanks." She took a deep breath. "I really am okay, Byron." She meant more than just being done with her laughing/crying jag and Byron knew it. He nodded, rather melancholy, but what else could they do? This was real life. The nighttime was the dream.

"So . . ." Jaida suddenly got shy. "I think I have a name for your tribe."

Sam turned to her, intrigued. "Really? What is it?"

"The Grace." She couldn't look at Sam directly. "Because 'grace' means 'kindness that's undeserved.'"

Sam got an immediate lump in her throat. "It's perfect." She would have tackled Jaida in an awkward hug and probably killed the moment, if it hadn't been for Fletch suddenly spying them and waving them over. Sam, Byron, and Jaida walked as somberly and mournfully as possible to his row of chairs and slid in, stepping over Mr. Bain, who was staring at Madalynn's casket with despair. Sam couldn't help thinking of his favorite saying, "Are you in the land of the living?"

Poor dude. He'd probably have to retire that expression now.

They sat next to Fletch, who immediately pulled them into a conspiratorial clump. "There's been a development," he whispered with a clenched jaw.

"What do you mean?" Sam murmured, trying to appear as if they were whispering about the video that was now playing of Madalynn giving a speech at a Junior Daughters of the American Revolution dinner.

Fletch and Joanne exchanged a grim glance.

"There's no body."

Sam heard what he said, heard the individual words, but her stunned brain just couldn't fuse them together into a coherent sentence. She looked over at Byron for help, but he appeared to also be gobsmacked into muteness.

Jaida found her voice first. "What are you talking about, Fletch?!"

He pulled them in farther, creating a little enclave among the wailers, and spoke rapidly. "I went to see the funeral director under the auspices of being Madalynn's physician. He starting sweating profusely, stuttering painfully, and attempted to chase me off with a bottle of formaldehyde. Naturally, this all made me somewhat suspicious. So, I waited until he went off to embalm something or other and I snuck in for a peek." He paused for maximum effect. "That is a very pink, very empty casket."

Is that why her parents weren't crying? Because there's nothing to cry about? Sam wondered. But how could that be? The memory of Madalynn's silver cord, severed, rolled through her reeling mind.

She could hear Byron's tentative question, "Maybe they, uh, cremated her on the sly?" but it sounded far off and faint. Because Sam was now completely focused on the movie screen, where the recently-deceased-or-maybe-not Madalynn was finishing her speech: ". . . and so, in conclusion, let us never forget that life delivers unto us infinite surprises." She smiled then, a huge, gleaming, somehow terrifying smile.

"It always keeps us guessing."

acknowledgments

To my wonderful editor, Kieran Viola, who not only helped shape Sam's journey, but also put up with my endless weepy e-mails, and for everyone at Disney Hyperion, especially Emily Meehan and Mary Mudd. To Nancy Inteli, who was the first to recognize Sam's SleepWaker potential. To Naketha Mattocks, one of my first true supporters. So grateful to Charlie Shahnaian, my "work husband" and best pal, for these 10+ years of laughter. Many thanks to my lawyer, Jon Cantor, and the rock star Mary Pender at UTA. Hugs to Charlotte and Kathleen Keilman for helping me understand what life is like with scary allergies; to Andrea and Madalynn Mathews for letting me steal the spelling of your name for a not-so-savory character; and to Karen Hopkins Harrod, who let me steal her name for a hero. Most of all, thanks to my real husband, Carlito Cabelin, for always believing in me and working a real job so I could write, and my kids, Rosie and Mig, for being so.much.fun. and letting me observe your lives so I could write decent teenaged characters. I love you, crazy fam. And most *most* of all, to my Father and Friend, who continues to teach me the true meaning of Grace.